WINGS OF LIVING FLAME

DAKOTAH GUMM

To everyone searching for a place to belong

CONTENTS

CONTENT NOTES

The mbira featured in this book is a real instrument, but *Wings of Living Flame* is a work of fiction and should not be understood to accurately represent the historical and cultural context of this instrument. The Mutapa were a real empire whose successors are the modern Shona people of southern Africa. Today, the Shona use many varieties of mbira in spiritual and cultural practices, from spirit veneration to entertainment. I have done my best to portray the mbira in a respectful way, but the teams at matepe.org and sympathetic-resonances.org are the experts.

Numerous characters in *Wings of Living Flame* sign. Signed dialogue is formatted the same way as spoken dialogue. Although the syntax and grammar of sign languages are different from spoken English, the signed dialogue in this book should be understood as a translation for more universal readability.

This book contains mentions of

- Sensitive adoption topics, most of which are not best practice

- Racial prejudice

- Long-term sexual assault (off page)

- Hearing loss

- Mentions of attempted genocide

- Mentions of forced sterilization

- Death of parents

- Physical violence

- Kidnapping

- Murder and attempted murder

- Sorcery

- False arrest

- Explicit sex scenes (consensual)

- Execution by beheading

If any of the above topics are disturbing to you, please consider finding a different read. For more specific questions regarding triggering content, email contact@dakotahgumm.com. If you or someone you know are facing a crisis and need someone to talk to, call or text 988 in the US.

ONE OF HIS MOODS

CSILLA

"He's in one of his moods again," Michal said as she walked into the kitchen.

I glanced at the tray she carried. The bowl was filled with congealed porridge, and he hadn't touched the berries and cream she'd set on the side. "Which one?" Kálmán's moods ranged wildly in extremes. If he wasn't eating, he was either excited about a spell or frustrated about a failure. Excitement would be good, leaving him holed up in his workshop for days, weeks, as he worked. Frustration would have him lashing out, most likely at me. He could be benevolent when he wished; he gave me gifts when I pleased him, and he'd educated me in art and literature. Michal and I did our best to keep him happy, but we couldn't manage everything.

"He was muttering about that potion. I don't think he slept."

Frustration, then. "I'll take up his dinner today."

She pursed her lips. "I'll take it. You've got enough to deal with."

"Do you really want the boys to see you coming home with a black eye or broken arm?" Unlike me, Michal lived outside of the tower with her two sons, her brother, and his pregnant wife. If Kálmán hurt her, people would talk, and I doubted the blame for her injury would fall on the sorcerer. They viewed him as a god—if his wrath was aroused against you, it was your own fault.

Her scowl deepened. "At least keep your distance."

"I will, auntie." With the death of my parents, Michal was the closest thing I had to family. She'd taken me under her wing when Kálmán brought me to the tower.

"What's he working on now?" She scraped the uneaten food into a pot for the chickens and dumped the bowl in with the rest of the dirty dishes.

I scooped up the last bite of my own porridge. "I don't know. He hasn't told me much about it." He was always working on something new, whether it was a potion to increase the yield of the nearby farmland or a protection spell for a warlord entering battle. Most of his creations were sold to wealthy people around the globe, though he used a few every year to ensure the loyalty of the townsfolk, cursing someone who had earned his ire or blessing their crops. He wanted them to see him as a god.

I knew he was nothing but human, though. A vicious, capricious human.

I stood, depositing my dishes with the ones Michal was washing. "I'll check on the animals," I told her. "Let me know when dinner is ready."

I picked up the pot of kitchen scraps and walked out into the warm summer air. The smell of wheat in the neighboring field filled my nose. I could hear the call of sheep as they were herded out to graze on the hillside. The sky was clear and blue against the mountain that towered above me. Kálmán had chosen a beautiful spot for his tower, even if his goal had been security, not attraction.

The tower itself was carved directly into the mountain, expanding on the natural cave system. Across the yard from the tower stood the barn, a wooden shelter protected by little more than a picket fence. Not that anyone would be stupid enough to steal from the sorcerer.

The animals greeted me as I opened the door. We had a wide assortment, though only the most mundane creatures were kept in the barn. Chickens and rabbits wouldn't arouse the suspicion of a stray messenger or townsperson who stopped by the tower. The polecats and cobras Kálmán kept in various rooms of the tower would raise questions, ones the sorcerer didn't want to deal with. Better to keep them appeased with the appearance of normalcy and keep his strange magics deep in the tower unless needed.

The chickens gathered around my feet as I pushed the door open wide to let them into the yard. They watched, clucking expectantly, until I scattered the kitchen scraps in the dirt, and then they lunged.

"You only care about me because I feed you, don't you?" I crossed my arms and scowled down at the birds. They ignored me, fighting over berries and carrot greens.

Back in the barn, the rabbits were more hesitant. When I opened the door to their pen, they lifted their twitching noses in the air, but they didn't approach. I filled their long, low trough with hay and waited for them to gather the nerve to come forward.

It didn't take long. They were smarter than the chickens, but not by much. None of them really knew to run from me. I was the harbinger of doom, and still they came to me to fulfill their needs. Not unlike my own relationship with Kálmán, I thought.

As if my thoughts had alerted him, my pocket heated. I pulled out the small bronze tube I carried everywhere and opened it. The scroll inside read, *Two rabbits. One male, one female.*

"Well?" I said, looking down at the creatures that were now happily munching away. "Who shall it be this time?"

They didn't react, oblivious to the fact that I held their fate in my hands. I scooped up a black male and a gray female, ignoring their scrabbling feet as they tried to get away.

"Come on," I said, tightening my grip. "If you survive, I'll get you a slice of apple."

The tower was almost cold after the warmth of the summer morning, and it only seemed to get colder as I ascended the winding stairs up to Kálmán's workshop. The rabbits had quieted, as if they sensed the danger they were in. When I knocked on the door, not even their whiskers twitched, they were so still.

"Enter," Kálmán called.

He sat at a table strewn with papers. His honey-colored hair was tousled as if he'd been clutching it in frustration, and dark bruises circled his eyes. The effect transformed his ethereal beauty feral, like Bacchus at the end of a week-long revel. He watched a glass vial filled with viscous brown liquid bubbled over a small flame.

"Set them down." He jerked his thumb at a small pen on the floor.

I set them down, and they huddled together. I waited for further instructions with my hands linked in front of me.

The sorcerer pulled on a pair of leather gloves and picked up the gray rabbit. With one hand, he took a long string and dipped it into the bubbling potion. After it stopped dripping, he tied it around the rabbit's neck. The creature whimpered, obviously terrified, but he didn't hold her for long. Once the string was secure, he placed her back in the pen.

I watched, barely breathing, as the rabbit got her bearings. Her ears twitched, nose scenting the air. Then she stiffened, let out a loud scream, and fell over on her side.

Another victim of our master's experiments. I watched the tiny body, hoping to spy a sign of life, but there was nothing. She was dead.

"Fuck!" Kálmán grabbed the vial and hurled it into the wall behind me. I tried not to flinch as the glass sailed past me and shattered against the stone. "What am I missing?" He flipped through the pages of the book in front of him.

I remained stock-still, hardly breathing. Any sound could remind him I was still here, and I didn't want him to turn that rage onto me.

After several minutes of muttering to himself and scanning his books, he glared at me. "What are you waiting for, firebird? Clean up the mess and dispose of the specimen."

"Yes, master." I hurried to do as I was told. I wiped up the potion—careful not to touch it, after what I'd seen it do to the doe—then gathered the body in my apron. "Should I leave the male?"

"It's no use without the female," he replied, rubbing his temples as he stared down at the page he was reading. "I'll send for you when I need another pair."

I scooped up the living rabbit and left before he could change his mind.

Down in the kitchen, Michal was chopping onions for dinner. "He called you?" she asked as I grabbed an apple from the bowl on the counter and sliced off a piece for the buck I carried.

"He needed another specimen." I lifted the dead rabbit in explanation. When she looked me over as if assuring herself I was unharmed, I leaned forward to kiss her cheek. "I'm fine. He was too focused on his work to really notice me."

"Hm." She scanned me again, then turned back to her chopping. "Did you get the eggs yet?"

"He needed me before I could. I'll get to it once I deal with this."

We didn't eat the animals killed by Kálmán's experimentation, so once I deposited the buck with the rest of the rabbits, I took the doe's body around the back of the barn to add it to the makeshift graveyard I'd built.

The rabbit was small, but it took me a while to dig her a grave in the rocky soil. By the time I covered the body with dirt and marked the spot with a round black stone, I was drenched with sweat. I wiped my brow and stood.

"Be at peace, little rabbit," I murmured. "You're free."

As I turned to go back into the barn, I noticed a man standing at the gate. His clothes were travel-worn, and he had a long black beard. "Is this the home of Kálmán the sorcerer?" he asked, one hand on the latch.

His accent was Aranite, local, but I hadn't seen him before. A sense of foreboding trickled down my spine. "It is."

"I have a letter for him." He reached into his breast pocket and pulled out a crinkled letter stamped with a golden seal.

"Oh." I almost laughed at my nerves. He was just another messenger, likely bringing a request from some rich nobleman for one of Kálmán's spells. "I can see that he gets it."

"My orders were to deliver it personally."

"He's not accepting visitors at the moment." I knew better than to disturb Kálmán while he was working, unless he summoned me. "I can assure you the message won't be lost."

"He's expecting this. He'll see me."

Then why didn't he tell me you were coming? I bit my tongue, resenting the man for backing me into a metaphorical corner. If Kálmán was expecting him, he'd be angry with me for delaying him; if he wasn't, he'd be angry that he was interrupted. Jerking my head toward the tower, I said, "He's inside."

The messenger let himself through the gate. As we walked inside, he didn't comment on the interior of the tower, the cold darkness and tight staircases. He followed me, a few steps behind, until we reached the workshop.

I hoped I wouldn't regret this. Throat tight, I knocked on the door.

"I said I was not to be disturbed!"

I fought the urge to glare at the messenger over my shoulder. "Beg—"

"*Malum discordiae,*" the messenger interrupted.

The door swung open. Kálmán looked from me to the messenger. "Troy approaches?"

The bearded man dipped his head in affirmation and passed him the letter.

Kálmán tore open the seal and read quickly through what was written. "Yes," he murmured. "This could be it."

It? The solution to his potion problem, or something else entirely? I didn't dare to ask.

Leaving the door open, he strode back to his desk and penned a hasty response. He sealed it with the ring he wore on his right hand and handed the reply to the messenger, who left without another word.

I turned to follow him, but Kálmán stopped me. "I have a job for you, firebird."

Freedom. It was temporary, I knew, but for two or three days, I'd be free. Auntie Michal had packed me a bag full of food, nestled on top of a change of clothes and a bedroll.

"It's almost sunset," Kálmán said, eyes the color of old brass sweeping over me. "You have everything you'll need?"

As if I could forget the time. A shiver knocked my legs together, an indication of my rising body heat. "I'm ready."

"Don't dawdle." He pulled the strings of my kirtle and let it drop to the floor. "Fly there, get the apple, and return home."

"I will," I said as I pulled off the rest of my clothes. I folded them and set them neatly on the chair by the window for my return. Looping the strap of the pack over my neck and shoulder, I looked to my master for any final instructions.

"Turn around." When I faced the window, he swept my loose brown hair to the side and clasped a necklace around my neck. His fingers lingered at the nape. "In case you get lost."

A tracker. I brushed my fingers over the amulet, the chain almost too tight against my skin. "Thank you, Master." He didn't need to track me, but I knew he would tell me it was for my own safety, in case anyone tried to kidnap me. As though he hadn't done that already.

A shiver wracked my body, and I climbed up onto the windowsill.

"Hurry back," he said behind me, his voice as calm and even as a husband sending his wife to the market. I could hear the silent threat underlying his words. *Hurry back, or I'll find you.*

My body erupted in flames, and I dove out the window.

ARANY

TANCRED

The gates to Arany stood open before us, tall and imposing. We were in the land of King Rudolf the Golden, the third king we had visited to petition for refuge. Likely not the last.

I wondered again what had possessed me to leave Laute. Others had remained; why not me? My gaze wandered to the front of the delegation, where the king and queen led us. The king—not the Pied Piper. Though his skin still bore the piebald marks of his former title, no one called him the Pied Piper now. Not since our magic had disappeared.

King Loic the Deaf. King Loic the Wanderer. King Loic the Broken. No one called him by those titles, either. At least not to his face. Even without his magic—*our* magic—the king was a formidable man, more than capable of punishing a disrespectful subject. No one but his wife would mistake him for soft.

Queen Annika walked by her husband's side, her human head held high. Rumor said that her presence had caused the king's downfall, his broken horn, the loss of his hearing, and the end of Piper magic. Anyone who made such claims had never witnessed the queen's devotion to King Loic. She'd killed the witch who kidnapped him, saving his life.

But despite the queen's bravery, the witch had still managed to take our magic, the only thing that kept our tiny valley kingdom from destruction at the hands of the larger countries around us. King Loic had given every citizen of Laute a choice: leave with him in search of a new land, or remain and take our chances at integrating into human society. My mother and I had chosen the former, but more than a year later, we were still searching. Which is what brought us to Arany. Most of our people—the thousand or so left—remained at camp a few miles away, while the king, queen, and council came to the city to meet with King Rudolf.

I rubbed at my beard, wishing I'd been able to shave. All our travel left little time for personal grooming. Like the other men, I wore a hat to hide my pointed ears and curved silver horns, not that it did any good. Wherever we went, our slitted pupils gave us away. We were the villains of the continent, the monsters parents told their children of at night.

This new land was lush with natural resources, richer than most human kingdoms, though not as rich as Laute. I looked around the city as we approached the small castle. People stared at our delegation, though whether they recognized us as Pipers, I didn't know. At least here, our varied skin tones didn't stand out as much as they had in England and France. As we traveled through the countryside, I'd seen Turks, Mongols, and even a group from Africa with skin as dark as my own.

At the castle, I looked with scorn at the simple stone walls. In Laute, everything had been gilded, the castle doors formed from an enormous single slab of wood. Here, it seemed, aesthetic wasn't everything.

The guards opened the bronze-handled doors for us, and we entered the dark halls of the Aranite castle. I saw Queen Annika shiver and take her husband's hand. He used his free hand to sign something to her that I couldn't make out, and her shoulders relaxed slightly.

Even the queen was nervous. That didn't bode well for our chances. But maybe she was just anxious about leaving the princes behind at camp. Prince Falk and his younger half-brother, Prince David, were too young to help on a diplomatic visit, and given how King Henry had responded when King Loic showed up in England with not one but two sons, my king and queen had decided not to take the risk of bringing the princes to meet another royal family. Not yet, at least.

With luck, King Rudolf would see our wealth as an opportunity to enrich his kingdom. Our presence could boost their economy, and with the looming threat of the Turks and the unrest in the nearby kingdom of Hungary, our men could help defend the border. We'd lost our magic, but we could still wield weapons, and we had plenty of knowledge of swordsmanship. Laute had needed all its men trained in warfare in case the countries around us attacked.

Not that our training had helped us at the end of Laute. There had been two attacks. My father, a guard for the Pied Piper, died in the first; in the second, King Loic was abducted, and everyone else in the castle was killed. I'd been on the team that had gone in after the second attack, searching for survivors. We'd found none. My friends and neighbors, loyal servants to the king, all dead where they stood. I'd found the body of my best friend, Josef, the king's sword still in his hand as he lay in a pool of congealed blood.

I pushed the memories behind me, along with the accompanying guilt. The king and queen needed me attentive today. After over a year of wandering, we could finally have found a place to call home.

We filed into the throne room. Tapestries with religious imagery hung on the walls, and a red carpet lined the floor leading to the dais. A stout, pockmarked man sat on a tall throne, his beauty of a wife next to him.

King Rudolf stood, stretching his arms out wide. "Welcome to Arany," he said. "You've come a long way to be here."

Queen Annika interpreted the words into signs for her husband. As she finished, he looked back at King Rudolf. "Thank you for having us, your majesty. I hope this will be the beginning of a long and mutually beneficial friendship."

"We shall see." His gaze roamed over our delegation, eyes pinched tight. "My wife, Queen Sarolt, has prepared a banquet for our guests. My servants can show you where you can clean up before we eat."

Two young men in yellow servants' livery showed us to a small suite of rooms. Once they left us, we gathered in the solar.

King Loic sat in a large armchair and drew his queen onto his knee. "First impressions?" he signed.

"He wants us here," Lord Dominik replied. "They don't need the money, but did you see the way he was sizing us up?"

I leaned against the wall. "I saw that, too." King Rudolf's gaze had made my skin crawl. "We should lean hard on that. Give him a demonstration of our swordsmanship, show him what he'd be gaining if he gave us our own land."

Queen Annika's gaze turned sharp. "What exactly would we be offering? Our sons as mercenaries for a foreign power?"

"It's no different than what they'd be doing if we'd stayed in Laute." The king nudged her chin with a finger. "Defending our borders."

Lady Teta leaned back in her seat. "Falk and David won't be grown for years, Annika. We're not shipping them off to fight the Turks tomorrow." The tawny-skinned noblewoman was more casual with the king and queen than anyone else. She'd known the king since they were children together, and she'd befriended Queen Annika when our queen was nothing more than an unwelcome visitor in the Pied Piper's court.

Queen Annika sighed. "I don't trust him." She had earned her place at King Loic's side, and we were loyal to her. Still, sometimes it was easy to remember she came from a small human village, without the cares and responsibilities of ruling.

"My wife, distrustful of a Catholic ruler?" The king's eyes widened. "I never thought I'd see the day."

I grinned. We'd all been present for her tirade against Henry VIII after a loose-lipped courtier mentioned the English king's mistress. Our staunchly Catholic queen had no patience for hypocritical monarchs.

She swatted King Loic on the arm. "Don't tease me."

"I would never tease the mother of my sons," he signed with one hand, using the other to lift her hand to his lips. "Fairest of all women."

My stomach twisted in a sensation strangely akin to jealousy. I had no particular attraction to Queen Annika, but I envied the king and queen their intimacy. I hadn't been in a rush to settle down, and now that we had left Laute, my odds of finding a wife were limited. I knew all the women who traveled with us; the ones that weren't already taken held no appeal for me. Humans were an unlikely option, as well.

Most were terrified of Pipers after generations of the Catholic Church painting us as demons. I didn't have time to search for a wife, anyway, and I wouldn't settle for anything less than what my parents had.

"Negotiations will take weeks," Lady Teta said, cutting through the awkwardness of watching the king and queen's intimate moment. "We just need to remember that they need us as much as we need them."

That hadn't been the case with England and France, two of the most powerful nations in the world. In Arany, we came as equals.

"We will." The king looked around at each of us. "I'm grateful for the loyalty you've all shown me this past year. I can't promise it's over, but I swear to you, I will find us a home."

I believed he would do everything in his power, but if Arany denied us, where else could we go?

Though not as ornate as the Pied Piper's banquet hall in Laute, King Rudolf's hall was richly furnished, and the food was, I could guess, better than anything I'd eaten in months. Not that I could enjoy it. The tastes and textures were strange, and I found myself wishing for Mother's simpler cooking.

I sat at the high table, Lady Teta on my left and Rudolf's Palatine, his second-in-command, on my right. In the middle of the table sat both kings, their queens next to them. The rest of our delegation filled out the table, while King Rudolf's small court sat at tables before us. The abundance of food in the room rivaled even the French and English courts. Mutton roasted in exotic spices was served with rice, and chicken had been cooked with peppers to form a thick stew. Yogurt sauces with herbs helped to cut down the heat. Fruits like figs and pomegranates were abundant, and wine flowed like water. I managed to find a few bites of rice that hadn't been drenched with the unfamiliar sauces, and I pushed the rest of the food back and forth, trying to make it seem as though I'd eaten while my stomach was growling.

When everyone had eaten their fill, the servants brought in silver trays filled with frozen bowls of yellow cream. The taste was sweet and floral, and tiny green nuts speckled the top of it.

"It's Persian," the Palatine said. "Made with saffron and rose."

"It's good," I lied. I wished I could enjoy it. The summer heat was stifling in the castle, with so many people in close proximity. The iced cream would have cooled me, cutting the tension that was creeping up my spine from the oppressive air, but I couldn't abide the cloying floral taste.

After the cream came cups of a thick, aromatic black drink. "Coffee," King Rudolf explained to the room at large. "A Turkish drink. It's quite bitter, but it can keep one awake all night long." He gave King Loic a conspicuous wink.

I took a tentative sip of mine as the man next to me stirred a liberal amount of sugar into his cup. It was bitter, as Rudolf had said, but I was surprised to find that I liked it.

"Now that we've fattened ourselves up, and our wives are sufficiently lubricated with wine..." King Rudolf belched loudly, then laughed. "Make your proposal, Loic. Let's get the politics out of the way so we can go get our dicks wet, eh?"

King Loic hid his distaste well, but Queen Annika grimaced as she interpreted the words for her husband. Luckily Rudolf didn't seem to care much for the opinions of women; he ignored her as he did his own wife.

"There's no need to rush," King Loic said smoothly. "We're in no hurry."

"Nonsense. You've been landless for over a year. Why wait another night?" He leaned back in his chair and slapped his legs. "Tell me. What can the Pipers offer Arany?"

My king and queen shared a look before King Loic began his well-practiced speech.

"Our magic may be gone, but Laute has long been renowned for our wealth and wisdom. You grant us a small region of land, just enough to house our people, and we in turn provide you with taxes that can enrich your economy."

King Rudolf let out a booming laugh. "Why would we need your gold? We grow our own."

Grow? I didn't let my confusion show on my face, but I glanced at Lady Teta. Her eyes were wide, brow furrowed as the Aranite king clapped his hands.

A young man in servant's livery entered the room immediately, as if he'd been waiting outside the door. He bore an enormous silver tray, which he deposited among the remains of the feast in front of King Rudolf.

"My golden apples," Rudolf said, lifting the lid. His chest swelled as his greedy eyes stared down at the tray.

Apples of pure gold piled high in a pyramid. Small and plump, they caught the light, casting it in rays around the room. Rudolf took his knife in one hand and an apple in the other. Carefully peeling a bit of the skin away, he let it drop to the table. The flesh beneath was blood-red.

"The skin is pure gold," he said. "And the flesh? It has powers you've never heard of."

"They grow in your orchard?" The corners of King Loic's eyes narrowed, unnoticeable to anyone who didn't know him well. He was calculating how this new development could be used to our advantage. We'd heard about the wealth of Arany, but not its source—not its magic.

"I grew the tree myself, with seeds imported from the Far East."

King Loic inclined his head, affecting casual interest. "Impressive. Most countries have to mine their precious metals."

King Rudolf wore a smug, self-satisfied look. "As you can see, we don't need your money."

"All the money in the world can't buy safety," Lord Dominik said.

"Is that a threat?" Storm clouds passed over his face. "I will not be strong-armed into any agreement."

"No threat was intended, Rudolf," King Loic said. "What my advisor was implying was that we know about the dangers your kingdom already faces." He leaned forward. "Why dance around the topic? You need men. We have men. With the Turks on one side and Hungary on the other, Arany is in a precarious position. How will you defend yourselves?"

"My ispans command thousands."

"Five thousand, I believe." Rudolf's eyes flashed at King Loic's words, but he couldn't refute my king's knowledge of the troops commanded by the Aranite noblemen. "A sufficient number for putting down petty rebellions or minor border disputes, I'm sure, but can it stand against the might of the Ottoman Empire, should Selim set his sights on you?"

The corner of Rudolf's mouth twitched. "And your paltry two hundred men can tip the scales against the Turks."

"Two hundred and forty-seven," I corrected. "Your majesty."

He waved his hand. "Practically nothing."

King Loic tilted his head. "A miniscule force, I admit, but our strength lies in more than numbers. We have superior sight and hearing—"

"Yourself excepted," King Rudolf interrupted.

I gritted my teeth together at the man's audacity, but King Loic continued. "—and we've had access to education your ispans can only dream of. We've studied the greatest warriors in history, Roman generals and Mongol khans and men who conquered half the known world."

"Impressive." Rudolf picked up his wine, swirling it around. "How about a demonstration?"

"What do you suggest?"

"I'll hold a tournament here next week. A celebration of our friendship and an opportunity for all our men to display their prowess. Once the tournament is over, we can discuss just how useful your men can be to Arany."

We'd expected something like this. King Loic raised his cup. "I look forward to it."

TOURNAMENT

Csilla

Wind rushed through my wings, making my flames dance. I took in the view as I soared over the land. I'd flown past the capital before, but never directly over it. A large camp had settled a couple miles away, hundreds of tents from some foreign land. I cocked my head. Invaders? They didn't seem to be an army; I didn't see any artillery or warhorses, and the camp was quiet but for a few guards who patrolled the outer limits.

I did a pass around the city, staying high above the walls, no more than a comet shooting past. Watchmen walked the walls, but the streets were silent. Near the castle, tournament grounds were ready for an event, the sand from the lists raked smooth and a sign marking the order of the competition. In the center of the city stood my target, the castle, its tall walls and towers proud, a bastion of safety against thieves and attackers.

I grinned to myself. Unless those thieves had wings.

When the guards weren't looking, I swooped over the walls and into the castle orchard.

The tree Kálmán had sent me for wasn't hard to find. It stood separate from the rest of the trees, a padlocked iron gate forming a wide circle around its trunk. The soft green leaves rustled as I landed on a branch. The apples that hung all around me were golden—not yellow or burnished red, but gold as a coin. The light from my flames gleamed on their skin.

I selected the largest apple and used my beak to pluck it from the tree. Nudging the bag open with my talon, I dropped the apple inside.

Prize secured, I lifted off from the branch. Kálmán would be pleased. As I soared out of the city, I looked toward the horizon. For one more day, one more night, I was free.

Tancred

I walked back toward the camp, sweat coating my skin from the drills I'd put myself through in one last night of practice. The tournament was tomorrow. I would be competing in two events: the archery competition and the joust. Archery, my strength, would be my best, but I was confident in my jousting and melee abilities.

I wasn't anxious, or at least no more so than usual. I'd participated in tournaments before, and I always acquitted myself well. King Edric, Loic's father, had enjoyed watching competitions, and every few years he held one open to the entire valley. I'd grown up watching my father joust—he always carried my mother's favor into the lists—and when I was old enough, I'd competed as well. While we were in England, I'd tilted with some of King Henry's men. This would be no different than any other tournament.

Only the results of this tournament could secure us a home.

Near the outermost tents, I looked up. A million stars stretched over the camp, and in the distance, I could see mountains silhouetted against the sky. It was late, the summer night cool. The surroundings were like home, and yet so different.

Far off, near the horizon, a blaze of orange and yellow streaked across the sky. I squinted at it, trying to make it out. A comet? If I was more superstitious, less educated, I might have assumed it was a harbinger of change or an omen of some kind.

I rubbed the back of my neck. The late hour was getting to me, making me search for order and meaning in the midst of chaos. The comet was nothing more than a celestial body passing over the earth. I needed to get to sleep before I started hearing angelic voices in the wind or finding hidden messages in the stars.

I listened to the clamor of the crowd as Luc, my ten-year-old brother, helped me don my armor. His twin, Theo, was already in the stands with mother, though Theo's nose was probably buried in a book. It was almost time for the joust to begin.

I'd placed third in the archery competition. Not my best, but a man from the Mongolian ambassador's entourage had taken the top spot, succeeded by the son of Rudolf's Palatine. A melee fight followed archery, but I hadn't participated, preferring to save my strength for the joust, the crowning event of the tournament. I was glad I hadn't participated in every event. The air was dry today. Too dry. Dust clung to my skin and clogged my nose and throat, and after fighting in close proximity with the other competitors, armor covering every inch of my body, I would have been in no condition to joust.

As it was, I was already choking on the hot, dusty air. In the stands, I could see Mother holding a handkerchief to her face. She seemed almost as uncomfortable as I was. Theo sat next to her, reading, as I'd expected. No one else seemed bothered by the dust.

"Water," I said, holding my hand down to Luc. He passed it up to me without looking as he scanned the arena.

"You're up against the Aranite captain of the guard first," he said. "Then Lord Dominik, then someone from Mongolia. I can't pronounce his name. I think he's a diplomat or something."

I took a swig of water, hoping it would help clear my senses. It helped, but only marginally. "Did you see them practicing?" I knew

Dominik's skills, but the Mongolian and Aranite were unfamiliar to me.

"The Mongolian is good. Probably better than you." I shot him a sideways glare, and he grinned. "He's fast. He's small, though, and the lance is heavy. By the time you face him, he might be tired."

Or he might not. "And the Aranite captain?"

"Nothing you can't take. He's over-confident."

"Good." It was time. I took my helmet from Luc and fitted it over my head. The horns on it were larger than my own, curved upward in a display of beauty and power. I lifted my lance and waited for my moment.

As the herald called my name, I rode forward, saluting the royals in King Rudolf's box. Rudolf's prince, a young boy still in skirts, sat on his mother's lap sucking his thumb. Falk and David, my own princes, had both been allowed to come with King Loic and Queen Annika. Loic held Prince David, the infant asleep despite the cheering crowd and sweltering heat. Prince Falk grinned at me, clapping with abandon. My queen gave me a small smile of encouragement, her arm around her older son.

Once the kings had acknowledged me with a wave, I turned to greet the crowd. A few bold young women held out their favors, clamoring for me to notice them. Most of them were Pipers, friends of my mother or women I'd known since childhood, but two dark-haired, light-skinned Aranites stood at the bottom of the stadium steps, handkerchiefs waving frantically for my attention.

I'd planned on giving my favor to a Piper, someone I knew and was comfortable with, but King Loic had reminded me this morning about the importance of diplomacy today. "We're here to make inroads with the Aranites," he'd said. "It's not just about showing off our military prowess. We need to make the people love us."

A difficult ask, given our reputation across the continent, but I'd promised to try. I guided my stallion toward the young women—sisters, I assumed, judging by their similar facial features—and lowered my lance in front of the shorter of the two.

Her face was the color of a beet as she tied the handkerchief to the end of my lance. Lifting it up, I removed the favor and pressed it to my lips. I gave her my most dazzling smile and tucked the handkerchief into my armor.

Bernát, Rudolf's captain, was called out next. He took the favor of his queen. Trite, but he didn't have anything to prove today. All he had to do was maintain his status.

We took our places on opposite sides of the tilt and nodded at each other in recognition. I dropped my visor over my face, narrowing my view of the world to a small slit. At the drop of the flag, I nudged my horse into action, and we thundered down the lists toward Bernát.

The dust puffed up in clouds around us. It gritted on my tongue and obscured my vision, but I kept my lance steady, watching the blurred figure of my opponent draw nearer. Almost there now—

We crashed together with the force of a landslide. The blunted point of his lance hit me in the center of my chest, knocking the wind from me as my own lance broke against his shoulder. The blow knocked me backward, but I managed to keep my seat. Cheers from the crowd filled the air at the spectacle of violence. As blood roared in my ears, I rode back toward my side of the list. My groom took my shattered lance.

"Tie," my brother shouted. I lifted my visor and looked down the tilt. Bernát had broken his lance as well, giving us two points each, but there were still two more passes. I could pull ahead.

"Water," I said. Luc passed up the skin, and I guzzled it down. My mouth and nose felt sticky, full of dirt, and the heat of the sun on my armor was beginning to bake me. The cries of the spectators were too loud, echoing within my iron helmet.

Finishing the water, I handed the empty skin back to Luc and took a fresh lance. Across the list, I could see Bernát pandering to the crowd, waving and smiling. I needed to do the same, but everything was so *loud*. I gritted my teeth and hefted the lance. Dropping my visor once more, I took my position and waited for the drop of the flag.

It seemed to take forever, and with every second that ticked past, the air grew thicker, the crowd louder, the sun hotter. Sweat dripped down my back, a slick feeling that made my skin crawl. Even my horse seemed to feel the tension, ears twitching restlessly.

Finally the flag dropped. I charged toward Bernát. A ray of sun found its way through the slit in my visor, temporarily blinding me. I gripped the reins tighter. My horse tossed his head, thrown off guard by the pull.

As we crossed, my lance went wide. The captain's struck my shoulder, splinters flying as the blow shuddered through me.

"It's okay!" Luc shouted as I reached them again. "It's only four to two. You can still make this."

Not unless I unseated him. *Fuck.* It was a stupid mistake. I'd let the circumstances get into my head. The dust, the heat, the noise, none of it mattered. What mattered was keeping my eye on the target. Once this pass was over, I could deal with the itching desire to crawl out of my skin.

Luc passed me a new skin of water as the groom took my lance. I lifted my visor to take a drink, and across the yard, Mother caught my eye. She waved her handkerchief in front of her nose and scrunched up her face. She, at least, would understand why I'd choked. Mother was as sensitive to overwhelming sensations as I was. I waved back at her and took a quick swallow of the water before dropping my visor and accepting the final lance from Luc.

One last run. I could do this. Through the slit in my visor, I could barely see my opponent, but I kept my eyes on him as I took my position. My arm ached from where he'd struck my shoulder. Once more, and I could rest.

Time slowed as the flag fluttered to the ground. The sound of my horse's hooves on the sand was all I could hear, the glint of sunlight on Bernát's armor all I could see. As we neared, my lance lowered, lowered, lowered.

I struck him in the center of his chest. His lance went wide, and he flew backward off his horse, crashing into the ground.

The sound of cheers came into focus once more. I wheeled my horse around, lifting my lance in triumph. The sounds and sensations still grated on me, but I'd finished. As the herald called out the final score of five to four and announced the next competitors, I dismounted. My groom took the horse's reins, and Luc took my helm and broken lance.

"You did it!" Luc was giddy with excitement, jumping up and down. He threw his arms around me, and I sucked in a breath at the clang of the objects he held hitting my armor.

"It's not over yet," I said. "Give the horse a break. I'm going to wait in the tent until the next match."

The tent was empty, all the other competitors waiting for their own matches or watching the joust between two Aranite nobles. I tore off as many pieces of armor as I could reach. Luc would complain about having to help me put it back on, but I needed to be rid of the interminable pressure of everything touching my body, everything invading my senses. Peace. I just needed a bit of peace. My breath came sharp, heart pounding in my ears as loudly as if I was waiting to ride into battle.

I sat down on a stool in the corner, the clank of my armor striking every nerve. Closing my eyes, I called up home in my mind. The scent of snow on the pine trees of our valley. The barely audible crunch of leaves beneath my feet as I stalked my prey on a hunt. I could see it still, the early morning sunlight dappling the ground through the trees. As I let my mind settle in that space, the chaos of the tournament slowly faded.

There wasn't time to remove all my armor and wipe down completely, but I wetted a cloth and cleaned the dust from my face and neck. I took a deep breath, grateful for the temporary relief.

"My melody?" Mother's voice floated through the tent curtains.

"In here."

She stepped inside. When she saw me, she smiled. "Well done."

"Thanks." My armor creaked as I leaned forward to rest my arms on my knees. "I'll be back out in a bit. I just needed a break from the noise."

"And the dust." She kept her voice low and soothing, not condescending, but respectful of my need for quiet. She held out a small jar. "I brought you some cucumber slices."

I took the offering and plucked out a piece. The cool crunch of the fresh green vegetable seemed to wash away the dust that lingered in my mouth.

"Is there anything else you need?" she asked.

I shook my head. "Were you watching the kings?" Rudolf's reaction to my joust would be important to note. Loic would tell me later, I knew, but I was curious how the Aranite king had reacted to me unseating his captain of the guard.

"No. I was watching you." She wiped my cheek with her thumb, removing a spot of dirt. "I'll let you prepare for your next match."

As she left me alone, I closed my eyes and breathed deeply. I'd almost lost it on that last match. I couldn't afford another one like that. Reaching into my armor, I pulled out the handkerchief the young Aranite girl had tied to my lance. It was simple, with a red poppy embroidered in one corner. There were so many Aranite competitors for her to choose from. Why give it to me?

Maybe my skepticism about this alliance was unjustified. I had to trust my king and queen. This tournament could be a turning point for us, an opportunity to build new connections in Arany. This could become our home.

I tucked the favor back into my armor and picked up a few more cucumber slices. The roar of the crowd outside grew, likely marking the end of the match. It was time to go back out—but this time I wouldn't choke. I'd keep my focus and do my king and queen proud.

THIEVES

TANCRED

Despite my meltdown during the first joust, I performed well in the rest. I'd made it to the final match, where King Rudolf's nephew had unseated me on a final pass. I was stiff and sore from head to toe, but I'd done my king and people proud.

Finally alone in the improvised bedroom in my tent, I stripped off my shirt. My bed took up most of the space behind the curtain, and I gave it a longing glance. I needed to bathe, but the call of my pillow was almost too great to resist.

Before I could give in to temptation, Mother called for me through the curtain. "Lady Teta is looking for you, my melody."

I groaned inwardly. We'd only been back at camp a half hour. What could they possibly need now? "I'll be right out." If the king or queen required my presence, a bath and clean clothes would have to wait. Throwing my sweat- and dirt-stained shirt back on, I trudged back out to the main room of the tent.

Lady Teta stood near the entrance, a barely-noticeable tightness around her usually cheerful eyes, but it wasn't the expression on her face that concerned me. It was the man who stood at her side. One of Rudolf's guards, he eyed everything in the tent with thinly veiled distaste. When he caught sight of me, he scowled.

I bowed. "Lady Teta. What can I do for you this evening?"

"King Rudolf requested the honor of our presence again. It seems he wasn't ready for the day's festivities to be over." Her tone was lighthearted, causing the irritation on the guard's face to deepen.

"Will you be gone long?" Mother asked.

"As long as their majesties require us." I pulled her in for a hug, resting my chin between her horns on top of her head. Then I bent down as if to kiss her cheek. "If I haven't sent word by nightfall, go to Silvia," I whispered. "She'll help you get out." If Rudolf turned on us, it wouldn't be safe to stay with the rest of the Pipers. The queen's maid was tasked with getting the princes to safety in case of an attack; she'd be able to do the same for my mother and brothers. I just hoped it wouldn't come to that.

She nodded briskly, turning back to the dough she was kneading as though nothing had happened. "Supper will be ready in an hour. I'll keep it warm for you if you're not back in time."

"Come. The king is waiting." The guard lifted the tent flap.

"What's happened?" I signed to Lady Teta, but she just shrugged and followed him outside. The knot in my chest tightened as I waved a final goodbye to my mother. These summons didn't bode well for us.

"Do you consider yourselves above the laws of God and man?" King Rudolf looked down on us in purple fury. "Or is theft merely second nature to you servants of the devil?"

"How dare you."

My head whipped around at the sound of Queen Annika's voice, quiet but firm. She rarely spoke directly in such audiences, preferring to let her more politically experienced husband take the lead. King Loic put his hand on her arm, but she shook him off and stepped closer to the throne.

"I don't know what you think has been stolen from you, but I can assure you, it was not one of my people who stole it. The Pipers are *good people.* They—*we*—are no demons, and we will not tolerate such slander."

King Rudolf crossed his arms, leaning back in his seat. "Tell your doxy to hold her tongue in a man's presence," he said to Loic.

Lady Teta was interpreting the exchange. As she finished, my king's face turned stormy. A promise of death chilled his voice. "Only a fool rejects wisdom because he doesn't like the source. My *queen's* words have merit, Rudolf. What was stolen, and why do you suspect my people?"

Queen Annika let her husband pull her back to him. Her light skin was red with rage, but she and Lady Teta shared a few silent signs, and some of the rigidness in her posture eased.

"One of my apples is missing." Rudolf scowled at us as Queen Annika resumed interpreting. "I opened my borders to you, granted you safe passage and hospitality, and one of my precious golden apples goes missing while you are in the city. It cannot be a coincidence."

"What would be the purpose of stealing your gold?" Loic asked. "We have plenty of our own. Perhaps you've misplaced the fruit."

Rage twisted Rudolf's features, and he bolted to his feet. "It was plucked from the tree!" he shouted, spittle flying from his lips. "My gardeners are meticulous. Every evening, the apples are counted. Last night, they counted them just before sunset. Tonight, one was missing!"

"Again I ask," King Loic's voice, dark and promising violence, filled the room, "what need have we of your gold?"

"Do not act as if these are mere gold!" Every word was louder and more shrill. "You've stolen it! Stolen it to restore your magic!"

Restore our magic? It wasn't possible. If it was, King Loic would have found a way by now. I glanced sideways at my king. Was this some plot I hadn't been involved in?

Judging by the look of shock Queen Annika wore, it wasn't. The king might keep things from his advisors, but he kept nothing from his wife.

"My people have not stolen from you," Loic said, steady against Rudolf's explosive anger. "I trust all of my people implicitly, and I have no desire to tarnish the goodwill between our two peoples by stealing what is rightfully yours."

"Prove it," Rudolf hissed.

What did he want us to do? King Loic dropped his hands to his side. "We can find them," he signed to us silently. "The thief and the apple."

I stepped within his field of vision and nodded my head slightly in agreement. Dominik did the same.

"Well?" King Rudolf prompted. "What proof will you offer me?"

King Loic straightened his shoulders, meeting his fellow monarch's gaze. "We will find your thief."

"And how do you propose to do that? Will you search every man and woman in my kingdom? I have no intention of letting you barbarians run roughshod over my people, accusing them of theft."

And yet he had no problem accusing us, the hypocrite.

"Greed is an insatiable monster. Once it has been fed, it demands more. Your thief will be back, and I suspect it won't be long." Loic indicated me and Dominik. I bit my tongue, keeping my face blank beneath Rudolf's menacing glare. "Let my men guard your orchard until the thief returns."

"And give you access so you can steal more? Not a chance."

"You can search them every time they leave the orchard. Send your own men to guard alongside them. You'll be conducting your own investigation into the theft; allow us to assist."

"And what makes you think your councilors can catch a thief my own guards couldn't stop?"

I bristled internally at that. Even without our magic, we were worth a dozen of his men. Their rounded human ears weren't as sensitive as ours, and they could see nothing in the dark. I'd been hunting in the woods for years before my magic manifested, and Dominik had been training to join the king's guard. We could hunt down this thief in half the time it would take the human guards.

"Tancred and Dominik are my greatest hunters. If they can't find your thief, there isn't one to find. At night, they'll join your men in guarding the orchard, and during the day, they'll question the gardeners and anyone who had access to the castle yesterday and today. Under your supervision, of course."

"My men are capable of investigating without your assistance."

King Loic shrugged, feigning nonchalance. "You wished for proof that my people were not at fault. Wouldn't finding the true thief be the best proof we could give you?"

The silence in the room was thicker than water. I kept my posture casual, but I watched King Rudolf's face for any indication of danger. We'd come here to his kingdom, his castle, without our weapons. We were surrounded on all sides, accused of being thieves. In an instant, he could demand that his guards come and drag us to his dungeons, and who would help us then? No one. Pipers had neither friends nor allies.

It couldn't be allowed to happen. I would fight my way back to my mother and brothers with my bare hands if I had to. There were four guards, all armed. If I took one by surprise, I'd have a good chance of disarming him. Next to me, I could sense King Loic and Lord Dominik doing the same, calculating our chances of escape. Queen Annika would be the king's priority. For all her strengths, our queen couldn't fight. Lady Teta could, though. The four of us against the four guards and the king—we could win, but only if we were fast. Reinforcements were only a shout away, and we would be outnumbered in moments.

"Allow us to do this for you," my king urged. "You said you wanted our friendship. Let us prove our commitment to this alliance."

Finally, Rudolf inclined his head. "Very well. I will allow your men to guard the tree. They will be searched every time they enter and leave the orchard, and my own men will be with them at all times."

"And the investigation?"

Rudolf scanned us. "Do your men not sleep, Loic?"

"Not while our people are in danger."

A tight-lipped pause from Rudolf, then he nodded. "I'll allow it. Only Lords Tancred and Dominik. Again, they will be closely observed."

"Thank you, King Rudolf. We look forward to proving our innocence." King Loic took a step back toward the door, hand on his wife's arm, but Rudolf stopped him.

"If I learn one of your people is at fault for this," he said, eyes narrowing, "I will wipe you from the map."

A shiver of hatred crawled up my neck. How far our people had fallen, that we were reduced to accepting threats from this prat.

INVESTIGATION

TANCRED

King Loic had never steered us wrong before, but there was a first time for everything. Working with Rudolf's men was not going well.

Bernát, captain of Rudolf's guard, had been assigned to *manage* us. As if Lord Dominik and I were unruly children and not rich nobles. As soon as we were alone, he turned to us with a glare. "Stay out of my way."

"Likewise," I said. No matter how the sour-faced guard felt about the Pipers, he wasn't going to stop me from clearing my king's name. "Where are we starting?"

"The orchard." His words were clipped, and he turned on his heel to stalk out of the room. We followed after him.

Scowling eyes tracked us as we walked through the castle. I was used to the suspicion, and so was Dominik. Even in places where dark skin like mine was common, our horns and pointed ears drew attention. Rome's campaign of hatred against the Pipers had been thorough; their depictions of horned demons made people the world over hate us without ever laying eyes on us. There were few places we could go without being looked on with fear and suspicion.

I glanced over at Dominik, who, like me, was ignoring our onlookers. His skin was lighter than mine, almost white, but his chestnut horns were tall enough to make hats almost impossible. It hadn't been a problem in Laute. No one wore hats in our home kingdom. Our horns were a source of pride, and we styled our hair to draw attention to them. But now our horns attracted notice, and notice was dangerous.

The orchard was less crowded than the castle, only a few gardeners pruning trees and bushes. They mostly paid us no attention, though I noticed one or two tracking our movements when they thought we weren't looking.

Bernát didn't say a word as he headed for a tree in the middle of the orchard. A wrought iron gate separated it from the rest of the trees. The leaves were the color of emeralds, swaying slightly in the summer breeze. And nestled among the branches were nearly a hundred golden apples of varying sizes and shades. The smaller apples were a dull, brassy yellow, not yet ripe, but the largest ones glittered like the jewelry of a corrupt priest.

I reached toward one of the branches that draped over the fence.

"Hands off," Bernát snarled.

I glowered at him. "How are we supposed to investigate the tree if we can't touch it?"

"And plant evidence, no doubt." He rested his hand on the hilt of his sword, waiting for me to make another move so he could draw it. "Hands off, or I'll go straight back to the king and tell him I caught you in the act of trying to steal another."

A new strategy, then. I started to sign a question to Dominik, but the guard stepped between us. "And you speak aloud or not at all."

Dominik and I shared a tight-lipped look of annoyance. Neither of us were as fluent as the king and queen or Lady Teta, but signing had become a convenient way to communicate with other Pipers, especially in unfriendly settings.

"You there!" Dominik pointed to a nearby gardener, who nearly fell off the stool he was using to prune a dead branch from a pear tree. "Come here."

He looked to Bernát for confirmation. The guard gave a terse nod, though his face was pinched as if he'd swallowed a sour prune.

The gardener clutched his shears with white knuckles and approached, narrowed eyes raking over Dominik. "Milord?"

"You tend to King Rudolf's orchard?"

Again the questioning look at Bernát before he answered. "Yes."

"Did you notice anything suspicious the day of the tournament?"

"No."

As they spoke, I circled the tree, looking for broken twigs or other signs of disturbance. There was nothing, not a leaf out of place. Even the birds and insects seemed to avoid it. A barely noticeable buzz emanated from the tree, the distant hum of an angry hive. It was too faint for human ears, but obviously it drove away any creatures that might disturb the tree. "Has anyone touched the tree since the theft?" I asked.

"It's been left alone," Bernát answered through gritted teeth.

"With what guards?"

"There's no need for it to be guarded. The gardeners are here all day."

And who watched the gardeners? From the look on Dominik's face, I knew he was thinking the same thing. One of them could easily have stolen the apple. One fruit would be worth more than their combined salaries.

Bernát jerked his head at the gardener. "Get back to work."

As he walked away, I told the other two men, "We should question everyone who works in the orchard. Someone must have seen something."

"Everyone who works for King Rudolf is above reproach." Bernát's expression said what he couldn't—that the Pipers were to blame for this. His mind was made up as to our guilt, and nothing we could say or do would change his mind.

I shared a look with Dominik. The captain clearly intended to block us at every turn. "Even so," I said, "we'll question them. Unless you intend to disobey your king and deny us the right to investigate?"

His nostrils flared, but he couldn't argue. "I'll get you a list of everyone who works in the orchard."

TEMPORARY FREEDOM

CSILLA

"It's not enough." The cold disappointment in Kálmán's voice frightened me more than the roar of a wounded bear. He was unpredictable when displeased. I dared a glance at the bits of fruit on the table, the shavings of gold skin and morsels of desiccated red flesh. Another rabbit lay on the floor, its ears still twitching with its death throes.

"You should have had her bring back more." Izsák, the newest hired brute, snorted, missing the flicker of disgust in Kálmán's eyes. He wouldn't last long working for the sorcerer. He was too brash, too willing to offer his opinion unsolicited. Kálmán had no patience for a talkative servant. He'd be dead within a fortnight.

"No matter," Kálmán said, straightening and turning to me. I kept my hands clasped in front of me and my head tilted down, in the position of submissiveness he preferred. "She can make the journey again. It wasn't difficult, was it, my firebird?"

"No, Master." The answer he wanted wasn't a lie. The flight had been long, and I'd been reduced to sleeping beneath a bush several miles from the city before I could return home, but for that one, glorious day, I'd been free—as free as I could be. I would gladly return to the orchard if it meant I could have another taste of that brief freedom. Opportunities to get out of the tower were rare.

He nudged the dead rabbit—no longer moving—with his foot. "Dispose of this, boy," he said. Izsák was in his late thirties, far from a boy, but Kálmán didn't concern himself with such trivialities. He was far older than he looked. He hadn't aged a day since he took me thirteen years ago. If I had to guess, based on little comments he'd made throughout our time together, I would say he was at least eighty. Compared to him, Izsák practically *was* a boy.

Izsák shot me a glare as he skirted around me to gather the rabbit. I doubted he'd do anything with the body besides toss it on the garbage heap. I made a mental note to give the poor thing a proper burial if I had time later.

A small silver clock stood on the back of Kálmán's work table. "Two hours to sunset," he said. "Pack a bag. You can leave tonight. Bring back three this time; too many more, and someone might notice they're going missing."

It was hard to imagine that anyone who owned something so precious as a magic apple tree would overlook the absence of even a single apple, but I'd long since learned not to question the sorcerer. He understood the world of wealth and magic better than I did.

"Yes, Master." I hurried out before he could think of another task for me.

Downstairs, I stopped in the kitchen to let Michal know I needed a bag. "Csilla!" Ádám, Michal's oldest son, ran across the room and threw his arms around me.

I hugged him back. "Done with your chores already?" I asked. His brother, Álmos, sat next to Michal, helping her chop apples for supper. It wasn't unusual for the boys to join Michal in the kitchen when they were done with their work, as long as their aunt and uncle didn't need them at home.

"Yes, auntie." A smudge of flour dusted Ádám's sun-darkened cheek. He couldn't have been here more than ten minutes. How did he get so dirty? I brushed the flour off with my thumb, and he shrugged off my touch.

"Where are you going?" Álmos, the younger boy, frowned at me. He didn't miss anything.

I took a seat across from him. "Kálmán needs another apple."

Michal pursed her lips in disapproval, but she didn't say anything. She knew where I'd gotten the first apple from, and though it was unlikely that anyone would be expecting a firebird to steal from the orchard, she worried about the danger I was in. If the king's guard caught me, I'd be in a worse situation than imprisonment by Kálmán.

Ádám grabbed a small red apple from the bowl next to his brother and tossed it to me. "I've got an apple for him right here. Why go halfway across the kingdom?"

I caught it and took a bite, grinning at him. "I don't think this kind works for potions."

"Why send you?" Álmos asked as he pushed the now-full bowl of chopped apples back. "Get Izsák to go, the lazy lout." He dodged the swat his mother aimed for his head.

"Mind your tongue," she scolded. "Remember where we are."

I glanced at the doorway, but we were still alone. Not that Izsák could do much about anything the boys said. Michal had served the sorcerer faithfully since before I came to be here. Kálmán—at least when he was in a good mood—treated her well. He wouldn't side with the grasping, indolent Izsák if it came to a disagreement between his two servants.

"I don't mind," I told them. "It gives me a day or two of freedom. Besides, if Izsák goes, he won't bring it back." Whereas I had no choice but to return.

Michal and I shared a look over the table. She knew the words I didn't say. She reached over to pat my hand. "I'll pack you plenty to eat. Is there anything specific you want?"

"Whatever I can carry." The transformation was exhausting and always left me famished. I'd need as much food as I could get in the morning.

She grinned, dark eyes twinkling. "I'll find something. I think I have some halva left over from breakfast."

The two boys whipped their heads around in unison, mouths wide. "You promised we could have that tomorrow!" Álmos cried.

I laughed and ruffled his hair. "I wouldn't want to take your food."

Michal clicked her tongue. "You'll take it. They can help me make more."

They groaned as Michal started filling a sack with plums, a link of hard salami, and some smoked cheese. I finished my apple and tossed the core into the bowl of kitchen scraps. "I should go pack the rest of my things," I said. Not that there was much for me to take. A change of clothes and a bedroll for the next day was all I would need. Kálmán wouldn't even send money with me, for fear that I might use it to flee from him.

"I'll bring this up to the workshop when I'm finished," Michal said.

I threw an arm around Ádám and squeezed his shoulders. "I'll see you boys later, okay? Maybe I'll find something I can bring back for you." Without money, I couldn't purchase anything on my travels, but I often found an interesting flower or unique rock to show them.

"We're too old to collect feathers." Ádám hugged me back. "You don't have to bring us anything."

A lump formed in my throat. I'd known Ádám for most of his life, and Álmos had been born after I came to work for Kálmán. Ádám had just celebrated his bar mitzvah a month earlier. Álmos's wouldn't be for another year, but it seemed like both of them had outgrown the childish presents I used to give them when I went away.

"Okay. No feathers," I promised, ruffling his hair. I waved at Álmos and Michal. "I'll see you soon."

"Be careful," Michal told me as I walked out.

I was halfway down the hall before Álmos caught me. He threw his arms around me. Surprised, I folded him in a hug. He'd gotten tall this summer; the top of his head was up to my chin.

"I don't mind if you bring me something, auntie," he whispered.

My heart melted, and I kissed his hair. "I'll bring every feather, shiny rock, and spiky leaf I find," I told him.

He let go. "Be careful," he said, echoing his mother's words. Then he took off down the hall.

I watched him go, tears pricking my eyes. Michal and her boys were the closest thing I had to a family. I was glad that at least one of them wasn't in a hurry to grow up.

The tube in my pocket heated, reminding me that Kálmán was waiting. I sighed and turned back to the task of preparing for my upcoming journey.

THE TREE

TANCRED

Of all the jobs I'd done in my life, this was the most tedious.

It was my third night guarding the apples, a week into the investigation. Dominik and I traded nights guarding. There had been no sign of the thief. Two of King Rudolf's guards dozed nearby, Bernát and another man whose name I couldn't remember. If someone stole another apple, they could just blame it on me. They didn't care that this thief threatened my life and the lives of everyone I loved.

I hoped Dominik was getting some rest tonight, too. One of us should. I'd barely slept since we arrived in Arany. My mind was too tangled up in knots over our predicament. With no indication of who had stolen from Rudolf, I didn't dare to think what would happen. The Aranite king's patience wouldn't last forever.

Whoever this thief was, I would find him. He couldn't be allowed to threaten my people. He would pay for what he'd done. I'd been given leave to shoot any intruders on sight, much to Bernát's dismay, and I intended to do so. I ran a callused hand along the curve of my bow, unable to stop moving. The touch of the soft wood provided a slight comfort as I listened to the noises around me. Near the magical tree, there was no familiar song of crickets, but the hum of the tree itself was almost deafening. It set my teeth on edge, and I rubbed the wood of my bow harder, faster, trying to ease the noise in my mind. Far off, an owl hooted.

A soft crackle rose above the sound of the tree, like the whisper of flames. A torch, maybe? I stopped moving, pressing my back to the trunk of the nearest pear tree. Looking around, I kept the golden apples in the corner of my eye.

The crackling drew nearer, but I saw no one. I pulled an arrow from my quiver, the hairs on the back of my neck prickling with warning. The sound was close now. A warm yellow light illuminated the orchard. I looked up, and my heart dropped into my stomach.

A flame perched on a branch of the apple tree. A brilliant orange flame with wings and a tail.

A bird. A fucking bird made of fire.

I held my breath, not daring to make a sound as I stepped back to get a better look.

It had the body of a swan with a long, lush tail. Its flames shimmered red, orange, and yellow, and its beak and talons were black and red smoldering embers. In its talons it carried a leather satchel. The crackling sound I heard was coming from the bird itself, the low hiss and pop of a flickering fire.

Despite the creature's burning body, the tree didn't ignite, even as the long flames of its tail brushed the branches beneath.

It took no note of my presence, shifting on its feet and looking at the surrounding fruit as if deciding which to take.

If I told King Rudolf his thief was a bird made of fire, he'd have me beheaded for a liar. I nocked my arrow and took aim. Magical creature or not, I wasn't going to let it escape. I fired just as it stretched out its long neck to snatch one of the apples.

A sudden gust of wind blew the arrow off course, and I missed by a matter of inches. The bird startled, released the apple with an ear-piercing shriek, and took flight.

Fuck.

It wasn't getting away so easily. I watched as it flew low above the trees, heading south. A shower of sparks trailed behind it.

The bird's cry roused King Rudolf's men, as well as our horses, which were tied loosely to a nearby post. Ignoring the groggy guards, I untied my horse and vaulted onto its back, aiming him southward at a gallop. I'd drag the burning thief back and lay it at the feet of the kings, dead or alive.

Csilla

Stupid! A stupid mistake. I should have been more cautious, should have looked for guards before swooping down to claim my target. Kálmán would be furious that I'd failed to take the apples. He wouldn't care that I'd nearly been shot.

A shudder ran through me as I flew, and my flames guttered. The arrow had barely missed me. What would have happened if it had pierced my heart? Could a firebird be injured? Killed? Could someone kill a bird made of fire? In all the years since Kálmán cursed me, I'd never once been injured. Not in this form, at least.

The sorcerer's curse had been specific, perhaps too specific. My flames could burn flesh, but nothing else, whether wood or grass or iron. Otherwise the arrow would have been no threat—it would have turned to ash as it struck me.

It wasn't my fault for leaving the apples. If I'd been sent to gather a whole bag the first time, I wouldn't have been in the orchard tonight. Kálmán's arrogance, his pride in assuming he only needed one apple, was responsible for this.

He wouldn't care, though. He'd beat me senseless for failing him. What was worse? Kálmán's wrath, or the arrows waiting for me in the orchard?

Undoubtedly, Kálmán's wrath was the greater threat.

Up ahead, I saw a clearing with a small pond. I let out a smoky sigh of relief. The sky was turning pink in the east. In just a few minutes, my wings would disappear. I needed to land. To think.

I dropped my satchel onto the shore and alighted on the water, which hissed at the touch of my flames. As I reached the long grass on the edge of the pond, the fiery rays of the sun peeked over the horizon. My blood cooled, my body lengthening and solidifying back into that of a woman. I stepped, naked and shivering, out of the water and onto dry ground.

Grabbing my pack from where it had landed, I pulled out two fat plums. I bit into one, and the sweet juice burst onto my tongue as I pondered what to do next.

Now that I'd been spotted trying to steal from the tree, the guards would be on high alert. If I tried to go back, they'd shoot me for sure. I could go during the day, though. The castle guards wouldn't be looking for a firebird. They wouldn't pay any attention to an inconspicuous woman. I could probably just walk into the castle.

And what if someone sees you, Csilla? I berated myself. *Duck your head and say, "Oh, pardon me, I was just popping in for a few of your magical golden apples?"*

Even though I was less conspicuous during the day, I wasn't invisible. Kálmán hadn't trained me to be a burglar; he'd trained me to be his bed-servant. Flying into the orchard in the middle of the night and stealing an apple had been easy enough the first time, but now they were looking for a thief. And if I went back to Kálmán empty-handed, I might not be the only one he punished.

Tancred

The firebird didn't travel far before descending behind a treeline. I urged the horse after it. Up ahead through the trees, barely visible in the pre-dawn light, was a small crystalline pond. I stopped the horse and dismounted, looping the reins loosely around a low-hanging branch as the firebird landed in the middle of the water.

The pond hissed its protest at the unwelcome heat, but the bird's flames weren't extinguished. I crept to the edge of the treeline and watched the bird swim gracefully toward the shore.

The sun's rays peeked up over the trees as the bird reached the reeds on the edge of the pond. It began to change shape, stretching and growing. I watched, awestruck, as the flames died down, winking out into nothing, and the body of a woman took shape in the light of the sunrise.

She was naked but for a tiny necklace that hung on her collar. Her full brown hair flowed down to her waist. Her body was lush and curved, the early sunlight silhouetting her form. She faced away from me, stretching her arms toward the sky as though just waking.

She picked up a brown leather bag at her feet and drew out a couple plums. A wrinkle formed on her forehead, her eyes going distant while she ate one of the fruits.

This was King Rudolf's thief? A beautiful woman who could transform into a bird made of fire. Why did she need the apples? She obviously had magic of her own. Unless the apples were necessary for her transformation. If she'd stolen the first one—which seemed a reasonable assumption—then maybe she needed more to continue transforming herself, or to work the same spell on her co-conspirators.

She was built like a goddess, with proud features, an arched nose, and light, olive-toned skin, but I knew better than to trust that beauty. I had no kind feelings for witches, not since a witch stole my people's magic.

The witch-thief finished her plums and tossed the pits into the pond. As she took a dress from her satchel and slipped it over her head, I stepped from the shadows.

CAGED

CSILLA

Hunger pangs eased, I tossed the pits of my plums into the pond and took my dress from the bag. The soft fabric warmed my chilled skin as I pulled it over my head, and I turned toward the pond for a drink of cool water.

Strong arms wrapped around me from behind, pulling me against a firm body, and a large hand covered my mouth before I could scream. Izsák? He knew better than to touch me. Kálmán had killed men for less. But Kálmán wouldn't know of my failure yet. He couldn't have sent someone already.

"Don't scream," my captor whispered.

My heart was pounding out of my chest, but I nodded. He took his hand from my mouth, still keeping a tight grip on my body.

"What do you want?" Had one of the guards followed me from the orchard? If this man had seen my transformation, Kálmán would slaughter him for it. The only question was how much damage my captor could do before my absence was noticed.

"What do I want?" His breath brushed my ear, and I shivered, skin tingling at his nearness. It had been years since any man but Kálmán had dared to touch me. "I want a lot of things, little thief. Most importantly, my people's survival. Your actions threaten that, so I'll be taking you to answer for your crimes."

"Thief?" I choked out. If I could convince him he'd seen something else, that I wasn't the firebird—

He chuckled, the sound low and dark. "Yes, thief. You stole from the king."

He was the one who'd shot at me in the orchard. I couldn't think over the blood coursing through my head. "I haven't stolen anything from your king."

"Not from *my* king." He spun me around in his grasp, so our faces were inches apart. Coiled black curls and pointed ears peeked out beneath his blue velvet hat, which stood up in an odd fashion. A scowl pinched his dark, bearded face, and burnt umber eyes with slitted pupils glared at me, not quite looking into mine. He wasn't human, and that fact should have terrified me, but I'd spent almost half my life living with death. This beautiful man didn't frighten me. "Don't deny it, firebird. I saw everything."

I wetted my lips. "What are you going to do with me?"

"I'm taking you back to King Rudolf, obviously." Gathering both my wrists in one of his hands, he used the other to pull off his belt and tie my wrists together. "I'm sure he'll have some punishment planned for you. Unless you'd like to return the apple?"

He paused, waiting for my answer, but the apple was gone. I couldn't return it, even if it was mine to return.

What punishment awaited me with this strange man's king? It couldn't be worse than anything Kálmán would dream up for me, could it? Kálmán scared me more than any king. Better to take my chances with my new captor than to return to the sorcerer a failure.

My hands now bound, the stranger pulled me toward the treeline. "Wait!" I tugged against the belt.

He continued walking. "I've been waiting a week for you. I'm not waiting until whoever you're expecting arrives. We leave now."

"No, that's not what I—" I planted my feet. "I need my bag."

He rolled his eyes. "Do you think you'll need it in Rudolf's dungeon?"

A fair point, but I owned precious little in the world. I didn't want to leave the satchel behind. And silly as it was, I'd been looking forward to eating the halva Michal sent with me. He didn't strike me as a complete monster; surely he would let me take the bag with me. I looked into his cold face, unflinching. "Please?"

His gaze traveled up and down my body, and he sighed before picking the bag up and searching it. Besides the food and my bedroll, I had nothing in there but a small knife for eating. The bronze tube Kálmán used to send me messages was in the pocket of my dress.

The man pocketed the knife and handed me the bag. "Anything else you'd like to request?"

I straightened my shoulders. I didn't have my freedom, but that was nothing new. I still had my dignity. "I'd like to know my captor's name, at least."

He went still. For a moment, I thought he would refuse to tell me. Then he said, "Tancred."

A warmth went through me at the sound, like his name was the answer to a question 'd been asking my whole life. "I'm Csilla. Novakné Csilla."

"Csilla," he repeated. It was soft and melodic on his tongue. *Chill-ah.* "We need to go. You'll come quietly?"

"I will." To demonstrate my compliance, I stepped toward the treeline. Hidden in the shadows ahead, I could see a sturdy chestnut stallion tied to a low branch. "But it won't matter. Even if you kill me, Kálmán will still come for the apples."

He went preternaturally still. His eyes held the calm before a summer storm. "Who?"

"Kálmán. My master." The words tumbled out of me. "He's the most powerful sorcerer in the world. He sent me first, but if I don't come back with the apples he wants, he'll send someone else. I'm not the only thief he has at his disposal." Just the fastest. The most convenient. "And if they don't bring me back, he'll come for me. Then he'll burn your whole city down and take everything in it for himself. No one can stand against him." I didn't know why I was telling him all this. It didn't matter to me if Kálmán destroyed his city. My fate wouldn't change.

Tancred searched my face, the storm clouds in his eyes gathering intensity as he tried to judge my sincerity. My heart pounded in my throat.

After several long, tense moments, he looked away. "Fuck," he muttered. *"Fuck."*

I shifted on the balls of my feet, unsure how to respond.

"All right," he said. "Fine. I can't take you directly to Rudolf, not now. I need to talk to my king first."

His king? If he didn't serve the Aranite king, who was he? He wouldn't get far taking me out of the kingdom. With Kálmán tracking me, we'd be overtaken in a matter of days.

I didn't let myself feel disappointed. It was too much to hope that he'd let me go. Even if we reached his king before Kálmán caught us, I'd sit in a dungeon and rot until my master could arrive and burn the castle down around me. Then he'd drag me back to my cage, and I'd never get out again.

Tancred

I led the firebird woman—*Csilla*—back to my horse. Coming to this kingdom was a mistake. Rudolf was bad enough, but now a sorcerer was involved. I couldn't handle this myself. I needed to talk to King Loic and Queen Annika.

The one bright spot was that Csilla didn't seem interested in trying to escape. She didn't fight me as I set her on the horse's saddle and took the reins. Our weight combined would be too much for him, but camp wasn't far. We just had to make it back before Rudolf's men found us.

"Put this on." I pulled the cloak I was wearing off my shoulders and wrapped it around her, tucking the hood over her face. If someone saw us, at least they wouldn't wonder what a human woman was doing with a Piper. I stood out enough already.

As I guided the horse out of the trees, she craned her neck at the city rising up beyond the hills to the south. "Where are we going?"

"I don't answer to Rudolf," I said. "I'm taking you to my king. Loic, king of the Pipers."

"Is it far?"

"No."

I could almost hear the questions burning on her tongue, but she didn't ask more. She settled back into the saddle, and we continued on in silence.

I kept my eyes peeled for signs of Rudolf's men. My knuckles rubbed a steady path against my leg as we walked, the repetitive motion keeping my thoughts from spilling out everywhere. When we passed the first tents of camp, some of the tension in my shoulders eased. The danger wasn't gone yet, but I was among my people. We could figure this out.

It was early enough in the day that I didn't attract attention bringing a strange hooded woman into camp. My tent was on the opposite side; Mother would be awake by now, but I wouldn't have to stop and explain myself to her. I didn't have time to answer all her well-meaning questions right now.

Lady Teta sat on a stool outside of her tent next to the king's, signing a conversation with Prince Falk. When she saw me, her eyebrows rose almost into her perfectly braided hair.

"You found our quarry?" she asked aloud, peering closely at Csilla's shrouded form before turning her piercing brown eyes on me.

"Not exactly," I signed. "I need to see the king and queen. Are they awake?"

She turned back to Prince Falk. "Get your parents," she signed. He nodded, jumping up and running inside on gangly legs. A moment later, he peeked back out the tent flap. "Mama says to come in, Lord Tancred."

A sturdy wooden table with six chairs stood in the middle of the room. King Loic sat at the head, holding Prince David. Queen Annika sat next to him. They were both dressed for the day, though the queen still had her hair tied up in a scarf—something the king usually divested her of at the first opportunity. I bowed, pushing Csilla into a bow as well.

"You found the thief?" King Loic's face was stern, emotionless, the way it always wawa in front of strangers. He spoke aloud, eyeing Csilla, who was still wrapped in my black cloak.

"I did." I pulled the hood off to reveal her face. I didn't bother signing my words—it was too difficult to sign and speak at the same time, and the queen was already interpreting for me. "Your majesties, this is Csilla, Rudolf's thief. Csilla, you're in the presence of King Loic and Queen Annika of the Pipers."

"You're certain it was her?" Queen Annika asked.

"I caught her in the act. She's not human, your majesty, no matter how harmless she might look."

Csilla's chin jutted upward in defiance. "I am human." Then, as if realizing her position, she ducked her head. "Your majesty."

I frowned at her. "I've never seen a human who can turn into a bird made of fire."

King Loic watched his wife's interpretation. "A firebird?"

"I was cursed," she said. "By a sorcerer who's held me prisoner for over a decade. But I am human."

"And a thief," I reminded her.

"It sounds like there's a lot to discuss," Queen Annika said. "Falk, can you take your brother back to Silvia? And have someone fetch Lord Dominik. Tancred, Csilla, please sit down."

As Falk took David from the king's arms and scampered out of the tent—"Walk!" the queen called after him—I set Csilla in a chair, pulling my cloak off and draping it around the back of the seat. I sat next to her.

"So." The queen leaned back into King Loic's arm. "Tell us your story, Csilla."

PIPERS

CSILLA

The strange people around the table watched me, waiting in silence for me to speak. They weren't human; I could tell by their pointed ears and cat-like eyes. The king and the woman with braided hair both had horns on top of their heads. The queen wore a scarf over her hair, so I couldn't tell if she had a small set of horns, but her eyes looked human. Even the baby, who'd been carried out by his older brother, had two tiny buds peeking out from the top of his bald head, like little buttons. The older prince and perhaps the queen were the only humans.

Who were these people? They were travelers, obviously, or they wouldn't be living in tents outside of the city. But if they were foreigners, what would they think of the fact that I'd stolen from the Aranite king? And what was one of them doing working for him?

I had few options here, so I settled on telling them the truth.

"When I was seventeen, the sorcerer Kálmán came through my town." I could almost smell the warm air of that summer, see the sun rippling on the cobalt waves. He'd ridden into town on his white horse, as regal as any king. "He was looking for a mythical sea monster, a serpent whose venom, he said, could be used to control the weather. He asked for hospitality while he waited for a ship to carry him, and my father invited him into our home."

I'd been enthralled by the golden-haired man. His eyes held a wild, exotic danger, promises of worlds I've never dreamed of. "During dinner, I caught his eye. He offered to take me with him, even told my parents he would pay them for the privilege of having me as a traveling companion. They refused."

My throat grew tight at the memory. I'd begged my parents to let me go with him. The amount of money he promised would have been enough for them to live comfortably for the rest of their lives, but apart from the impropriety of a single young woman traveling alone with a man she wasn't related to, my mother had a bad feeling about the sorcerer. She'd been right. "When it became clear that my parents wouldn't change their mind, he pulled something from his pocket and blew it in their direction, and as he spoke his incantation, I watched my parents dissolve into ashes."

"How awful." The queen had been making signs with her hands as I spoke, and the look on her face made it clear that she'd suffered loss as well. Great loss. "And then he took you with him?"

I nodded, tears forming a lump in my throat. "I tried to fight him, and he punished me by—by casting a spell on me. He turned me into a firebird." That first transformation had been the most painful. I'd thought I was dying as my bones snapped and my body erupted into flames. "Every night since then, from sunset to sunrise, I've been trapped in that form."

The king watched his queen's hands fly in rapid movements, then his disconcerting flicked to mine. "He uses you to do his bidding?"

"Sometimes." I looked down at my hands, the rope that still bound them together. "Usually he keeps me in the tower, but if he needs someone to travel a long distance, I'm the fastest servant he has at his command."

"Why not leave?" Tancred's voice held bitterness, a vitriol I didn't understand. Did he think it was my fault I'd been cursed?

"And go where?" I looked at him with equal venom in my gaze, but he was staring at the table. "I turn into a bird made of living fire every night. I'm not exactly inconspicuous. He'd find me." My hand went to the tracker around my throat. I could take it off, even destroy it, but rumors of the firebird would follow me wherever I flew. It wouldn't take long for Kálmán to catch up, no matter how far I went. "He's tracking me now."

At that, all eyes went to me, even Tancred's. "Tracking you how?" the braided lady asked.

"My necklace. It tells him where I am. I don't know how accurate it is." He'd used it in the past, but I'd never dared to go off course before today.

The king stood, coming toward me like a predator stalking his prey. "Can he see us?"

"I don't think so." I fought to keep my chin high beneath the daunting stare of the king. "He knows where I am, but he doesn't know who I'm with or what I'm doing." If he did, he would already know about my failure, and I would have heard from him by now.

"Loic, you're scaring her." The queen put her hand on her husband's arm. He held my gaze for a moment longer, then resumed his seat.

The king and queen made signs at each other, her face expressive, his void of all emotion. The lady across from me joined in, but tancred just watched the interaction.

He caught me looking at him, and his scowl deepened. I frowned back. Why did he hold such hatred for me? I'd stolen from King Rudolf, not him. Not even from his people.

The arrival of a newcomer interrupted the silent conversation. He took a seat at the table, signing what I assumed was a greeting.

"Good morning, Lord Dominik," the queen said. "I'm sorry we had to summon you so early this morning."

"I'm at your majesties' disposal," he answered, inclining his head. He gave me a curious look before Tancred drew his attention with a series of signs.

The queen spoke. "Csilla, do you want to be free?"

Freedom. It was an impossible dream. Only Kálmán's death could free me, and even that was no guarantee. What if, after he died, his curse remained, or even worsened? I could be trapped in the form he'd forced on me for all eternity. But if I could... "I would do anything, your majesty."

She nodded at her husband. The king leaned back and considered me again, eyes searching mine with an expression I couldn't read. Then he stood.

"Dominik, Tancred, let me speak with you in private."

My sullen-faced captor stood, casting a wary look at me. What did he think I was going to do, attack the queen? I was outnumbered and still bound, and I had no intention of hurting anyone.

The three men walked out of the tent. Almost immediately they were replaced by a young woman, her arms full of food. My mouth watered at the sight, but I turned my face to the table, not wishing to seem rude.

"Thank you, Silvia," the queen said. "Are you hungry, Csilla?"

I opened my mouth to respond as my stomach gave a loud rumble. My cheeks burned with humiliation. None of the women were tactless enough to comment, though. The servant set a plate in front of me and filled it with sausage, bread, fresh mulberries, and soft goat cheese.

"Cut her bonds, please." Queen Annika passed a knife to the servant, Silvia, who hesitated.

"Loic won't like it," Lady Teta said.

"Let me worry about that." The queen nodded at Silvia. "She's not going to harm us. Are you, Csilla?"

"No." They hadn't turned me over to King Rudolf, and that gesture in itself was enough to earn my gratitude. As the rope around my wrists was cut loose, I rubbed the chafed skin. "Thank you, your majesty."

As the servant left, the queen made a crossing sign over her breast and bowed her head. Lady Teta did the same. In unison, they intoned, "Bless us, O Lord, and these, Thy gifts, which we are about to receive from Thy bounty. Through Jesus Christ, our Lord. Amen."

Kálmán didn't pray—I was fairly certain the only god he recognized was himself—but I was used to the Hebrew prayers Michal and her family said at mealtime. "Amen," I muttered.

The queen and Lady Teta dug into their food. Part of me knew I should be wary of them. They were being too kind to me. Strangers didn't harbor fugitives without consideration of the risk. What did they want? But I couldn't bring myself to care. After the overnight journey, near-death experience, and subsequent kidnapping, I was exhausted and famished. I used the bread to scoop up a bit of cheese and brought it to my mouth. Delicious.

"How long have you been with the sorcerer, Csilla?" Lady Teta asked.

I wiped my mouth. "For thirteen years." Thirteen years since he'd killed my parents and forced me to serve him. My thirtieth birthday had come and gone, unobserved even by me. Not that I ever celebrated the day, but it was strange to think that such a milestone had been overlooked.

The queen reached over and took my hand. "We're going to help you." Her eyes met mine, full of compassion. "I promise."

Tancred

Silvia, the queen's handmaiden, had just reached the tent as we stepped out. I held the flap open for her and tried not to stare at the tray she carried, full of sausage, bread, cheese, and fruit. It had been a long night, and I was hungry. But other priorities took precedence over my stomach.

"Rudolf isn't going to like this," the king signed with one hand, running the fingers of the other over the jagged end of his broken horn. He'd developed the habit after the loss of our magic, and it was one of the few signs of anxiety he ever showed. "Whether we turn the firebird in or not, he's still going to hold us responsible."

"She could be lying," I said. "There may not even be a sorcerer."

The king tilted his head in consideration. "She could, but I don't think she is. This isn't the first I've heard of a sorcerer in the region. She might be in league with him, though."

Dominik shook his head. "I don't think she's lying. I barely saw her, and even I could see she was terrified."

"She's a prisoner," I signed. "Of course she's afraid."

"Either way," the king said, "we can't just turn her in and expect Rudolf to forgive our imagined debt. He's looking for an excuse to move against me. If we want to prove we weren't responsible for the theft, we need evidence. Undeniable evidence."

"Like the apple." It was a good plan, if we could find it. But her sorcerer had sent her for more. I doubted the first one she'd stolen still existed. He'd probably used it for some spell or potion.

"The apple and the thief together. If we return what was stolen, bring him a perpetrator to punish, and provide a witness, he'll have to admit that the pipers weren't responsible."

"And if it can't be retrieved?" Dominik asked, voicing what I'd been thinking.

"We'll have to hope the sorcerer and his servant are enough on their own to convince him to let us go."

"Let us go?" The plan had been to convince him to grant us land. We'd exhausted most of the possibilities for refuge on the continent. Where else could we go?

"I've been in contact with a boyar in the land beyond Muscovy. His people are swan shifters. They're at war with another clan of shifters, but if we agree to support them in the war, he's offered his people's assistance in settling the land nearby. It's sparsely populated, mostly nomadic peoples. Our biggest threat will be the land itself."

A better option than any of the monarchies we'd petitioned so far. Especially Arany. Rudolf wanted our men, but he didn't want to share their loyalty. He would look for any reason to depose King Loic and keep our people under his power. My king knew that. We had to provide undeniable proof if we planned to make it out of Arany without further trouble.

"I've written back to the boyar and accepted his offer. All we need is a way out of Arany." the king pulled over a nearby stool and sat. "I'd send you both, but I can't afford to leave us vulnerable. The council is too small as it is."

Of the two of us, Dominik was the diplomat. I was a hunter, only ennobled out of necessity and as thanks for my father's sacrifice in protecting King Loic's father, the previous Pied Piper. "I'll do it," I said. "This requires stealth. If he's as powerful as the firebird says, the only way to defeat him will be with the element of surprise. I can travel faster alone."

The corner of the king's mouth turned upward. "Not alone. You'll have to take her with you."

Fuck. I hadn't thought of that. "Wouldn't it be better to get her to identify his location on a map?" She'd slow me down, and she could flee on the road. Here at camp, she could be locked up until I returned with the sorcerer.

"It's not worth the risk. You need someone who knows him to get you close. As long as she agrees, you'll leave in the morning. We'll send her tracker in the opposite direction, so whatever servant he sends after her can't ambush you on the road."

"And if she doesn't agree to work with us?" Dominik asked.

"She will. She won't want to be executed for her master's sins."

I couldn't argue with my king's command. "If things go wrong—"

King Loic cut me off with a wave of his hand. "They won't."

I pressed on. "Send my mother and brothers to Bavaria, please." Pipers were no safer there than anywhere else in the world, but my grandparents had settled there, near the valley we'd once called home. There was a small community of Pipers they could live with. Konrad Bach, the leader of that population, would make sure they were safe if King Loic couldn't protect them anymore.

"If the Pipers fall, we'll see that your family makes it back to Bavaria," the king signed. "But don't let us fall."

A near-impossible task, but I bowed. "Yes, your majesty."

THE CAMP

CSILLA

Freedom from Kálmán. Was it possible? They'd promised me nothing but a chance, but it was more than I'd had in years. The closest I got to freedom was when Kálmán let me attend Purim celebrations with Michal's family, a few hours of stolen peace every year. He didn't like to share me.

If this foolhardy plan worked, I could do what I wished. Go where I wished. I'd be a free woman at night as well as during the day. As long as Kálmán's death ended the curse.

And if we failed, what would happen to me? Kálmán would be furious with me for leading the would-be assassin to his tower. He could turn me into the firebird permanently or keep me locked in a cage for the rest of my life.

My neck was already in the noose. Why not take the chance?

Breakfast was a quiet affair once we'd established that Tancred and I would leave in the morning. As we finished eating, the queen turned to me. "You must be tired after being up all night, Csilla." She made signs with her hands as she spoke, almost as if it was second nature to her. "I had Silvia prepare an extra bed for you in my tent. You're welcome to sleep there as long as you like."

"Thank you, your majesty." Under normal circumstances, I'd be exhausted, but in the past two hours, I'd been kidnapped, threatened, and promised freedom from my curse. I wouldn't be able to sleep if I tried.

"Unless you'd prefer to stay awake. I could give you a tour of the camp."

Tancred looked up sharply at that, and the king frowned, signing silently at her. She responded in kind, a hidden smile lurking on her face. "I planned on walking through camp this morning," she went on out loud. "I'd be happy to introduce you to my people."

"If you're sure it's all right, your majesty," I said slowly. "A walk would be nice." Should I add another *your majesty?* How many times was I expected to use her title in conversation? My experience with royalty was nonexistent, and I knew nothing about the proper etiquette.

The queen didn't seem bothered by my rudimentary manners. She smiled brightly at me. "Absolutely."

The king stood, his imposing figure seeming to take up the whole tent. "I'm going to find Falk," he said. "I promised I'd spar with him this morning."

The young prince was going to spar with King Loic? I felt sorry for the boy, having to face off against his intimidating father.

"Tancred, Dominik, join me." The king leaned down to kiss his wife, far less chaste than was appropriate for the setting. When he pulled back, the queen's whole face was red, and he had her head scarf in his hand. I tried not to stare as my own cheeks heated, but the others in the tent didn't react.

As the men left, the queen turned back to me, skin still pink. "I like to walk around after breakfast," she said, as if nothing had interrupted us. "It helps me keep track of how everyone is doing. Life on the road hasn't been easy."

"Oh?" I wasn't sure what I was expected to say.

"We lost our land a year ago," Lady Teta explained. "Political problems. It was a mess. We've been looking for a place to settle since then."

A queen without a country. I sized her up inconspicuously. Was that the reason for her lack of formality? But the king, he was exactly what I pictured a king to be like.

Queen Annika stood. "You've eaten enough?" When I nodded, she smiled again. "Then let's go."

The camp was bustling with activity. We stopped by the queen's tent first, where the baby, Prince David, was playing with a rattle under the watchful eye of the queen's maid, Silvia. Queen Annika scooped him up and pressed a kiss between his button-like horns. He was our escort, it seemed; she carried him out of the tent, babbling and cooing to him.

As we wove through the tents, the two women carried on light conversation about the weather, the tournament from earlier that week, and other trivial topics. Everywhere I looked, someone was waving to the queen or nodding a greeting at Lady Teta. They didn't look twice at me, which was a refreshing change. In Kálmán's village, everyone knew who I was—and whose I was. No one was going to mess with Kálmán's property. I wasn't excluded here, though. The other women made sure to ask my thoughts on whatever topic came up.

"Good morning, your majesty." A dark-skinned boy, a year or two younger than Álmos, dropped a clumsy bow before Queen Annika. "Is Falk around?"

"Good morning, Luc. I think he and the king were sparring this morning."

"Oh." His face fell.

"Csilla, this is Luc Schwarz, Lord Tancred's brother. Luc, meet Csilla—" She paused, glancing at me. "I'm sorry, Csilla. I don't know your surname."

"Novakné."

"Csilla Novakné," she went on. "She and your brother are going to be working together for the next few days."

She'd said my name backward. I'd learned from Kálmán that in certain cultures, the given name came before the family name, but here in Arany—as well as the surrounding nations—our surname came first. Was it rude to correct a queen? It probably was. I kept my mouth closed, not wishing to offend her.

"A pleasure, miss." Luc bowed, but I saw gears whirring behind his eyes as he processed the queen's words. Lord Tancred's brother. I could see the resemblance, the strong brow, the full lips.

Lady Teta signed something to the queen, who covered her mouth as if hiding a smile. "I'm sure the king won't mind if you join in sparring," she told the boy. "If he says no, tell him I said you could."

Luc screwed up his face as if trying to determine whether she was joking. Lady Teta laughed. "Don't you know the king does everything Queen Annika asks?"

A blush stole across the queen's cheeks, but she didn't deny it. Given the deference I'd seen the king give her, I could believe it was true, strange though it seemed. Why would the terrifying, stone-faced man feel any obligation to such a normal woman?

"I'll go find them," Luc said. He bowed again and ran off.

Queen Annika shifted the baby on her hip as he tugged on her ear. "He doesn't do *everything* I ask, Teta."

"Close enough. When was the last time he told you no?"

"When I told him to take that terrifying stallion back and find me a nice, sturdy mule to ride on instead."

Lady Teta threw her head back in laughter. "Point taken." She leaned toward me and said in a much-too-loud whisper, "You should have seen them when they met. Loic pretended he was her master, but even then he wouldn't do anything without her approval." She glanced sideways at the queen. "Well, maybe one or two things."

"Teta!" The queen swatted her arm. "You'll make her think we have no decorum."

"I never claimed to."

Queen Annika pursed her lips at the noblewoman. "You'll have to excuse us, Csilla. It seems even being raised with royalty isn't enough to teach some people proper etiquette."

As we walked, they continued to bicker, and I looked around the camp. There was a sense of peace here. They were refugees, but they were happy. They trusted one another. They trusted their rulers. What would that feel like, to serve someone I trusted, who cared for me? Maybe, if I succeeded, I would have a chance to find out.

The queen waved at a woman up ahead who was taking down her laundry. Her clothing was simpler than the queen's and Lady Teta's, but still fine. She had short, black-and-silver horns and cool brown skin, and her hair was pulled into chunky, box-shaped braids.

"Your majesty. Lady Teta." As we approached, the woman pulled the last item from the line and set it in the basket. "Good morning. Are we hosting visitors?"

"Good morning, Mrs. Schwarz," the queen said. "This is Csilla Novakné."

"Novakné Csilla," I corrected, giving the woman a bow. Even if it was rude to contradict a queen, names had power. I didn't want the misuse of mine to become a habit.

The queen's face turned red to the roots of her hair. "I'm so sorry. Novakné Csilla, this is Cordula Schwarz, Lord Tancred's mother. Mrs. Schwarz, Csilla is going to be assisting us with a matter of diplomacy."

"It's a pleasure to meet you, milady," Mrs. Schwarz said, bowing back to me. "Are you from the capital?"

As I opened my mouth to answer, a drop of water landed directly on the tip of my nose. Rain. I glanced up at the cloudy sky as another drop landed on the top of my head. "No," I said distractedly. "No, my village is a few days away from here."

"Why don't you come inside out of the rain?" she offered. "Unless you have somewhere else to be, your majesty."

The queen brushed a raindrop from the baby's head. "No, we can come in."

Inside, the tent was cozy. Curtains had been hung, dividing it into rooms. The main room was quite large. Woven straw mats covered the ground, keeping the dirt from the living space. A small table sat in one corner with four stools, and a chest in the opposite corner had been topped with cushions for additional seating. Several oil lamps decorated various surfaces; Mrs. Schwarz lit two, adding to the wan light coming from the tied-back entrance flap.

"Please, sit!" our host urged us. "Can I get you anything to drink?"

We all demurred, but she brought out a pitcher of watered wine and set it on the table, along with a tray of sliced bread. "In case anyone changes their mind," she said.

Lady Teta had settled onto a stool at the table. "How have the boys been, Cordula?"

"They're well!" Her face beamed as she took a seat on the chest. "Theo is somewhere around here reading, and I think Luc went to find Prince Falk."

"We saw him earlier this morning," the queen said, sitting next to Lady Teta. "He was going to join Falk and Loic for their training."

"He'll be glad of the opportunity, I'm sure." She turned to me, where I sat opposite the queen trying not to fidget. "The queen said you're helping us with a matter of diplomacy. Do you work for King Rudolf?"

Diplomacy was a generous way to describe the service I would be providing these people. I looked to the queen for assistance. I was no diplomat, but I doubted she wanted word of their difficulty with King Rudolf to be made public.

"She's helping with Lord Tancred and Lord Dominik's work," the queen answered for me. "Csilla has some information that may help us uncover who's behind the theft."

So the news had already spread. "I see." Mrs. Schwarz considered me with a look that seemed to see too much, like the ones my mother would give me when I was a child or Michal often gave me now. A mother's look. "We're grateful for your assistance. The sooner this nasty business is over, the better."

"I'm sure it will all be resolved soon," the queen said delicately.

"Mother?" A young boy peeked out from one of the curtained rooms. "Oh, sorry. I didn't realize you had visitors."

Mrs. Schwarz waved him over. "Theo, this is Novakné Csilla, a friend of the king and queen. She's working with your brother this week. Csilla, my son Theo."

He dipped a bow and mumbled a cursory greeting. He was shorter than his brother Luc but obviously close in age. His nose was shaped like a button, and he had a green cloth-bound book under his arm.

"What are you reading today?" the queen asked him.

He held it up for her to inspect. "A collection of Arthurian legends."

She smiled. "Oh, Falk loves stories about King Arthur. Which story is your favorite?"

He shrugged. "*Yvain* is good, I guess. There's a lion."

"I read that one to the children when I was teaching in Laute," she said. "It's a good story."

"Did you need something, my melody?" Mrs. Schwarz asked him.

"Oh. Umm." He shook his head. "Nothing."

"Luc went out to train with Falk," Lady Teta said. "I'm sure they're still out there, if you want to join them."

He wrinkled his nose. "No, thanks. I'll just go back to my book."

As he went back to his room, the queen laughed quietly. "I wish Falk read half as much as Theo. He'd much rather be out watching the knights than reading about them. I can hardly get him to sit still long enough to make it through our daily lessons, let alone read for enjoyment." She glanced at me. "Do you enjoy reading, Csilla?"

"I don't have much occasion to," I said honestly. Kálmán had plenty of books, but they were mostly spellbooks. "I can read and write, but we don't have many books."

"I didn't, either, until I came to Laute." She twisted her mouth in a wry expression. "When Teta let me borrow *Le Morte d'Arthur*, I almost cried. I'd never even held a real book before then."

Lady Teta waved it off. "You needed something to entertain you."

How had she gone from someone who had never owned a book to the queen of an entire people? I had a feeling it would be impolite to ask.

Lord Tancred walked into the tent at that moment. He shook rainwater from his head, but he stopped, eyes narrowing when he caught sight of me.

"Good morning, my melody." Mrs. Schwarz kissed her son's cheek, and he wrapped an arm around her. "Queen Annika and Lady Teta introduced me to your new companion. How was the night?"

"Long," he said, tight-lipped. "She should go."

"Tancred!" She swatted his arm. "Be polite."

"I'm sorry." He didn't look apologetic in the least.

"No, he's right." The queen stood. "I'm sure you and Csilla both want to get some rest."

Tancred

They brought that woman around my mother? I clenched my jaw, watching the firebird rise from her seat at the table. It was bad enough letting her walk around the camp. The king should have given her an armed escort. Even if Lady Teta carried a large dagger and was capable of defending her queen, I didn't want the thief in my tent.

As she, the queen, and Lady Teta moved to leave, Luc burst into the tent. "Tancred brought a giiiiiiirl home!" he sang out. When he caught sight of the *girl* in question, his mouth went wide with embarrassment.

"We already know." Theo, who had poked his head out of his bedroom, stuck his tongue out.

Luc picked up a cushion from the chest and chucked it at him. "No one asked you."

I cast an eye around for an escape, but there was no one to help me. Lady Teta was openly snickering, and even the queen was hiding a smile as she pretended to be busy focusing on Prince David. Csilla's face was bright red.

"Boys!" Mother stepped between them. "That's no way to behave."

"Thank you for having us, Cordula," the queen said, inching toward the exit. "Lord Tancred, you'll be ready at dawn?"

I inclined my head in agreement. Then the three women were gone, and it was just me, Mother, and the boys in the tent.

Mother clapped her hands together. "Well."

I sank onto a stool. "I'm going to be gone for a few days."

"With the *girl?*" Luc's sly voice matched his grin.

"Luc, Theo, go fetch some water," Mother said.

Theo snapped his book shut as Luc groaned. "But I'm reading!"

"Not anymore, you're not." She pointed toward the tent entrance. "Go. I need to get the stew started."

They both scowled at me as they trudged outside. I ignored them, too tired to care. When they were gone, Mother reached for her apron. "Tell me everything."

"Someone came to the orchard last night."

"Csilla. The woman with the queen." Her sharp eyes missed nothing. "She's the thief?"

I rubbed my face, still damp from the rain outside. "Yes. But she claims she was forced to do it."

"You don't believe her?" Mother pursed her lips. "You never used to be this skeptical. Has she given you a reason to think she's lying?"

"I never used to be responsible for so many people. Just because there's no reason to think she's lying doesn't mean she's telling the truth."

"I worry for you, my melody."

"You shouldn't. You've got enough to worry about with the boys." Father's death had left Luc and Theo without the firm hand they needed. They were good boys, and I did what I could to help, but Mother was raising them alone. She didn't need to be concerned for me on top of that.

"It's my job to worry about you. You don't think parents stop caring just because their children are grown, do you?"

Trying to convince Mother to stop worrying was like trying to make the sun stop shining. I sighed. "Anyway, the king and queen want me to take her and find the man she's working for. I may be gone a week or two."

"I see." She didn't seem pleased about it, but Mother knew I wouldn't disobey the king.

I stood and stretched. "I'm going to try to get some sleep before I start packing."

She walked over to me and took my face in her hands. "Be careful, my melody. I know the past year has been hard on you, but don't let your new duties break you." She pulled my head down and kissed my brow.

Still fretting incessantly. "I won't," I told her.

"Sleep well."

SETTING OUT

TANCRED

As the sun slowly climbed up the horizon, I stood in the entrance to the queen's tent, eyes locked on the sleeping firebird. She kept a wing over her face, as if to block out the light, though I couldn't imagine it helped. The queen, as usual, had slept in the king's tent; although tradition dictated that each royal had their own sleeping quarters, King Loic never let his wife sleep alone.

In the space of a few seconds, the flames died down to nothing, and the human woman lay where the bird had been. She sat up, blinking at her surroundings.

"Get dressed," I told her. "We leave in ten minutes."

She grabbed the blanket to her bare chest. "Am I not allowed some privacy?"

"No." But I did avert my eyes as she dressed.

A soft cough behind me alerted me to the queen's presence. "Good morning, Lord Tancred."

I stepped aside and bowed, letting her into the tent. "Good morning, your majesty. I didn't expect to see you this early."

She was already dressed for the day, her head scarf still in place. "I wanted to see our guest off. Good morning, Csilla. How did you sleep?"

"Well, thank you." The firebird woman bobbed her head in an imitation of a bow, too busy braiding her hair to show my queen the respect she deserved.

"I know you have to leave, but I had breakfast prepared for you." She handed me a bundle, its contents still warm. "King Loic and I wish to express our gratitude to you both for this. If there's anything else you need, let us know. We'll do everything in our power to ensure you succeed."

"Just time, your majesty," I said.

She nodded. "We're already making plans. Loic thinks he can give you two weeks, at most, before Rudolf starts to get suspicious."

"It won't take that long," Csilla chimed in. She'd finished braiding her hair and moved to stand next to me. "It shouldn't be more than a three day journey there. We'll be back within a week."

Back or dead. I didn't say the words. We all knew it was true.

"Leave your tracker," the queen told her. "You're going north, right? We'll send it south with a rider. If the sorcerer sends someone to bring you back, they won't find you. He won't be expecting you to return."

Hopefully the element of surprise would give us an edge to defeat him. Csilla raised her hands to the necklace hanging high on her neck. She seemed to hesitate, but after a moment, she pulled it off and placed it in the queen's outstretched hand.

"I won't delay you." The queen tucked the necklace into her pocket, then took Csilla's hands and squeezed them. "God go with you both." She let go of Csilla and placed a hand on my shoulder. "Return soon and safely."

I didn't let Csilla out of my sight the entire morning, though the first leg of our journey passed without incident. We rode side by side on the horses King Loic had lent us, and we kept a steady pace, stopping as rarely as possible. Both of us would be as exhausted as the horses when we stopped for the night.

Daylight would be easy, but what would happen when night fell? Now that we were alone, I didn't know how I was supposed to keep her from flying off as soon as she grew wings. Tying her up would do nothing but ensure she refused to cooperate, but I didn't trust her. I had to hope that the long day of riding would leave her too tired to try to escape.

We spoke only out of necessity as the day lengthened. Stormy clouds gathered on the horizon, a sure sign of impending trouble.

"Is there shelter up ahead?" I asked her as thunder rumbled in the distance. It had rained several times this week already, and the ground was wet and muddy. Too much more rain would make travel impossible for the horses, whose legs were already speckled with mud.

She peered ahead. "We're almost to the river. There's a village just past the ridge."

"With an inn?" If we could get a private room, we'd be able to stay there tonight, but I didn't want to risk revealing what Csilla was to anyone around us. Not with both Rudolf and the sorcerer looking for us. An inn would have the added benefit of locked doors, keeping her inside as long as she had wings.

She shrugged. "I wouldn't know. I've only flown over it."

She was useless. If there wasn't an inn, though, maybe we could pay to sleep in someone's barn. We had a small tent, but with the soft ground and approaching rain, I preferred to have a solid roof over my head.

When we reached the river, all my hopes of a warm shelter vanished.

"Fuck." The word slipped out under my breath as I looked at the bridge. Or rather, where the bridge used to be. The river, swollen from days of rain, had washed it away. I could see the wooden posts on either side that marked its position. On the other side of the river, a few small shacks—hardly enough to be called a village—stood on the bank.

I picked up a stick and tossed it into the middle of the water. The current swept it under immediately.

"We can't swim," I said. It might have been a reasonably sized river at one point, even shallow enough to walk across, but with the flooding, it would be impossible. "We'll have to take a different route."

Csilla scanned the horizon. "The only other path takes us through the mountains. It'll add another week to our journey, at least."

Fuck! Even though the queen had said they could stall Rudolf for a couple weeks, we hadn't been prepared for such a length of time. We'd need to get more provisions, find shelter along the path—places where a firebird wouldn't be noticed in the middle of the night. Places she couldn't fly out of while I slept. And the horses wouldn't be able to manage the mountains. They'd have to be sold or traded at the first town we came to. "There's no other way across?"

"Not unless you want me to carry you."

I stopped and turned to her, brows raised. Carry me? She couldn't carry me across the river.

"After sunset," she clarified.

"You can carry another person as the firebird?" She'd carried a pack in the orchard, but that was a far cry from carrying a fully grown man. I wasn't small, either.

"For short distances." She shrugged. "As long as there's something for me to hold. I can't actually touch you without burning you."

We had rope that could be fashioned into a harness. It wouldn't be hard to create. If we journeyed downriver, far enough that local residents wouldn't catch sight of us, it might be possible.

Considering the river again, I shook my head. If she wanted me dead, she could wait until we were halfway over the water and drop me in. The fall or the current would kill me. And it would require leaving the horses behind, anyway. "No. We take the long way."

She propped a hand on her hip. "You trust me that little?"

"I don't want to run the risk of being seen," I said. Close to the truth. "Let's go. I want some distance behind us before the rain starts."

An hour later, a light drizzle began. I pulled my hood up. "Where can we stop?"

"I wouldn't know," she replied. "I've never had to take this path."

"If we can't find a place to stay soon, we'll find a copse of trees or an overhanging rock." The muddy ground would make for a wet, uncomfortable night, and the horses would be miserable, but at least our tent would be more protected from the rain.

Before long, it was coming down in sheets, and we hadn't passed anything resembling shelter.

"We should have stopped at the bridge!" Csilla shouted over the rain.

Much as I hated to admit it, she was right. We were soaked to the bone, and sunset was inching closer by the second. "I think I see some trees up ahead," I shouted back, pointing to a patch of shadows in the distance. We angled the horses toward it, heads down and hoods up.

It wasn't a patch of trees, but a rocky hill covered in brush. I swung down off the horse and felt my way along the edge of it, hoping for a depression in the rock. This region was known for its caves; I prayed we'd stumbled upon one by accident.

Whatever deity there might have been was looking out for us. A narrow entrance, just wide enough for the horses to pass through, led into a cool, large chamber. I turned back to Csilla.

"There's a cave!" I called. "You'll have to get off your horse."

She dismounted, and I led first my horse and then hers out of the rain. Csilla followed us inside. The space was tight, with just enough room that we would be able to lie down without being kicked in the head or stepped on by one of the horses.

We stood inches apart, but I could feel the heat radiating from Csilla's skin despite the frigid water that dripped from both our bodies. The noise of the rain was dampened by the rock around us. In the darkness, everything was gray, though Csilla, I knew, would be able to see nothing with her limited human eyes. I could hear her teeth chattering, and she wrapped her arms around her torso.

"Get undressed," I told her. "Once you get your wet clothes off, you'll feel better."

"Not likely. It's almost sunset."

The transformation wasn't a pleasant process, then. I filed the information away for later. Should I express some sympathy? Comfort her? That was the appropriate thing to do when someone was in pain, wasn't it?

She was the reason we were in this mess, I reminded myself. No matter what she was suffering, I didn't owe her social niceties.

"Still, you'll need to get those off so they can dry before morning," I said. Her flames would heat the space for the night, hopefully enough to dry our soaked belongings. Which was good, because I was certain that any wood nearby was too wet to make a fire.

I turned toward the entrance of the cave, stripping off my shirt. The air inside was cool, but warmer than it was out in the rain. Once I had changed into drier clothes, I began removing the saddles and blankets from the horses.

Behind me, Csilla's teeth continued to chatter. "Are you still cold?" I asked. If she fell sick after being out in the rain, this trip would take even longer.

"No more than usual."

I set the horses' tack to the side of the cave, as out of the way as possible in the small space. The bags we'd taken were well-sealed against water, so our belongings were still dry. I dug into one of them and pulled out a loaf of hard brown bread, which I split in half. "Here. Eat. I'd build a fire, but…" I turned to pass her portion of bread to her, but I froze when I caught sight of her. She'd stripped off her wet clothes, and she hadn't bothered to put on anything else. The image wasn't as clear as it had been in the sunrise of the previous day, but I could still see the hardened point of her nipples, the patch of hair between her legs, the soft curve of her belly. Did she think I couldn't see her in the dark? The tips of my ears burned, and I thrust the bread toward her as I trained my gaze on the ground. "Here."

"A fire wouldn't help." She reached out to take the food from me. When her hand brushed my bare arm, I flinched.

"You're burning up." Her skin was feverish and sweaty.

"Every night," she said.

I dropped my hand. "Is the transformation always like this?" I wasn't concerned for her, but for the success of our mission. A fever could slow us down for days. Longer.

"Always. It starts like a fever. I get hotter and hotter until I finally burst into flames."

"Is there nothing that helps?"

"Not really."

It wasn't a pleasant fact, but at least it wouldn't slow us down further. "So it is real flame, then. You didn't burn the tree when you landed in it."

"It's real enough." She turned her face toward the wall. "Part of the curse. I can feel it, and anyone who touches me would be burned. But like I said before, it only affects flesh. A safeguard against anyone who would try to steal me away, I suppose. Kálmán is a creative sadist."

That much was clear. I took out a pouch of salted pork and split it between us. Csilla groaned.

"You should eat," I said. "Sit down."

She obeyed. I pushed her portion of the meat toward her, still keeping my gaze lowered. The sounds of the storm outside were the only accompaniment to our meal.

She let out a sudden gasp, and my hand shot out toward her of its own accord. "What's wrong?"

"Stay back," she panted. "It's starting."

The horses were growing restless. I went to them, stroking their necks and whispering assurances to them. A horrible cracking sound filled the cave, and Csilla shrieked like the cry of a wounded hawk. The food turned in my stomach, threatening to reappear as the cracking sound continued. "It's okay," I murmured, and I wasn't sure if I was speaking to her, the horses, or myself.

She groaned, low and pained, and a bright light erupted in the cave.

When I could see again, the firebird sat opposite me. She rested her head against the wall, breast heaving.

"Are you okay?"

She bobbed her head in confirmation, but I didn't believe her. Was it always that horrific? And she'd been suffering through that every night for years.

The sorcerer was a monster. My king and queen were right—he had to be ended. I just hoped Csilla realized that as well and didn't plan to betray me.

"You should sleep," I said. "We'll leave at dawn."

In the light emanating from her body. I took my bedroll and laid it out between Csilla and the horses, who were closest to the cave entrance. If she tried to escape tonight, it wouldn't be easy for her. She'd have to make sure not to wake us.

Her flames heated the cave like a campfire, and when I laid down, I was warm, almost cozy. I glanced over and saw she'd tucked her head beneath her wing.

As much as I hated to admit it, we weren't so different, she and I. We'd both lost our homes, our loved ones, and the ability to control our own bodies. In another world, another lifetime, we might have been friends.

The only problem was that her actions in this world and this lifetime could get my people killed.

I reached into my pocket and pulled out my mbira. I hadn't played it in months; the wooden box and polished metal keys of the small instrument only served to remind me of what I'd lost. What I was working to save. I ran my thumb over the keys, wishing to feel the rush of magic through my fingers once more.

As with every night for over a year now, it didn't come. Letting out a long breath, I tucked the precious item back into my bag and rolled over to get some rest.

A MESSAGE

CSILLA

As my flames disappeared with the sunrise and my body knit back together, I reached for my now-dry cloak. The air was cool, chilled by the rainstorm, and after the sweltering heat of my firebird form, I was cold.

Tancred was still asleep, his breathing even as the dappled sunlight that came through the cave entrance played over his face. He looked peaceful this way. His brow, knit in a perpetual frown, was smooth and free from worries.

He was handsome. Not quite as ethereally beautiful as Kálmán, but Kálmán's beauty was a facade, a mask that made him look soft and sweet. Tancred's appearance was far from soft; his hands were callused, his body bulky and muscled, and his expression exuded anger at the world. But I could tell that when he smiled, the room would light up around him.

The horses were nuzzling the cave floor in search of food. They'd need to eat before we could start our journey. I dressed, then grabbed a pack and led them outside to graze.

Fog drifted over the ground in soft tendrils. Birds twittered, leaves rustled in the breeze, and water dripped into a puddle somewhere nearby. The sky was cloudless, and in the distance, the mountains—mountains we would now have to cross—formed a stern silhouette of gray against the blue. As the horses found a patch of grass and began gorging themselves, I leaned against the rocky wall outside the cave and pulled a water skin and some dried berries from my pack.

A sudden scrambling sound inside the cave told me Tancred had awoken. A moment later, he burst into the sunlight, looking around wildly. He wore a long pair of pants but no shirt, and my cheeks flushed as I looked at the broad expanse of his chest, covered in a smattering of black curls.

"Did you lose something?" I asked.

He stopped, staring at me. "You're still here."

"Obviously." I popped a berry into my mouth and swallowed it down with a swig of water, washing away the smoky taste that lingered in my mouth from the night. "Where would I have gone?"

He didn't answer me. "I should have been up an hour ago. We're losing daylight. Are you ready?"

"Yes." His impatience was his own fault. If we'd crossed the river yesterday as planned, we would have been only a day or two away from the tower. Instead, he'd decided we would take the long way around, trudging through the mountains for the next week. I didn't know what he intended to do with the horses, but they wouldn't be able to travel the narrow mountain path. They'd throw a shoe or break a leg on a loose rock, and it would make the trip even longer. "I think there's a town we can stop in before we enter the mountains. If we make good time, we should reach it by midday."

"Good. Give me a minute to get the rest of our things, and we can go."

As he disappeared back into the dark cave, I reached into my pack for some bread, and my hand brushed something hot.

My hands shook as I pulled out the message tube and opened it. The message that dropped into my hand made my heart stop.

You've removed your tracker, firebird. I know you're not foolish enough to run from me. Izsák is coming for you. Fly home before he finds you, and your punishment will be less severe. Disobey me, and you won't like the results.

I felt the blood drain from my face. He knew I'd removed the tracker. He knew I'd turned against him.

A shadow fell across the paper. Tancred was back. He crossed his arms, scowling down at me. "What's wrong?"

"He knows." Trembling, I held out the paper to him. "He knows I disobeyed." Would Kálmán punish me alone, or would he harm the people I cared about once he realized the extent of my betrayal?

Tancred scanned the paper, the wrinkle between his eyebrows growing deeper by the second. "You're communicating with him."

"No, it—it only goes one way. I can receive messages, but I can't respond to them." Why was he worried about that? Couldn't he see the danger I was in? We both were in? "He's going to kill me. He's going to lock me in that cage and burn me alive." My breath sawed raggedly in and out of me, and I stared at the paper he held like Kálmán could materialize out of it.

"Csilla." Tancred dropped to one knee and grabbed me by the shoulders, his expression stern. "He's not here. He can't touch you."

"He can. He will. He'll find me, and if I don't come home, if Izsák finds me and brings me back to him, he'll *kill* me. And then he'll kill Michal and Ádám and my— He'll kill everyone I care about." I clutched at my throat, the tiny bits of air I was gasping in not enough to sustain me. I'd made a mistake, a horrible mistake. I should never have plotted against him. How many times did I have to learn this lesson?

Tancred shook me so hard my teeth rattled together. *"Listen to me, Csilla."* I sucked in a deep breath and forced myself to focus on his face. "He's not going to get you. I'm going to kill him. I'll kill this Izsák, I'll kill your sorcerer, and then you can do whatever you want to do. But only if you work with me. Do you understand that?"

Did I understand it? Yes. But what if he couldn't? What if we failed and I got all of us killed in the process? Not just me and Tancred, but Michal's family and the Pipers, too.

"If you go back to him now, he'll punish you. You know what he's capable of. You can't go back to that." His voice was less stern now, almost sympathetic. "Your only chance is to stay with me and fight."

"But what if you're wrong?" I breathed.

"I'm not."

He sounded so certain, I had to believe him. I nodded slowly. "You're right. It's the only option."

He released me, still watching me as if I might bolt at any moment. "How did he contact you?"

I picked up the tube that I'd dropped in my panic. "He sends me messages through this. It heats up when there's one waiting. He must have sent it yesterday, but I didn't notice it in my bag until this morning."

"It's not a secondary tracker, is it? Just a one-way system to send notes?"

I thought back through the years since Kálmán had given it to me. I'd never heard him say anything that implied that he knew what I was doing or where I was when I was out of his sight. "No. I think the tracker was a recent creation."

"Good. We should get going."

Tancred

I kept a close eye on Csilla as we saddled the horses and prepared to leave. I didn't think she'd been lying to me, but I wasn't the best judge of character. Father used to tell me I was too trusting of people. *It's all in the eyes,* he would say. *Their mouths can lie, but their eyes never can.* I'd never figured out what he saw in their eyes that I didn't. Whether Csilla was planning to fly back to her master or not, my plans remained the same. I would find and kill the sorcerer and take his head back to King Rudolf.

It was later than I'd planned when we finally got on the road. The ground grew rockier and more uneven the further we rode. I didn't let Csilla out of my sight for a moment. Did her posture seem stiffer than yesterday? Her expression more uncomfortable? But maybe she wasn't used to so much riding.

As the sun reached its peak, she finally spoke. "Tell me something about yourself."

I looked sideways at her. Was she fishing for information to take back to her master? "Why?"

"Why not?" She shifted in the saddle, wincing at the movement. "Do you have something to hide?"

Definitely fishing for information. "I'm not hiding anything," I told her. "I'm just not in the habit of conversing with my prisoners."

She snorted. "I'm not your prisoner."

"Aren't you?" If she tried to escape, she'd learn quickly how wrong she was.

"Prisoners are bound and forced to go wherever their captors wish. I've been a prisoner before. Right now, I'm free."

"Are you implying that I should tie you up?" I had the rope, and it would give me peace of mind.

Spots of color bloomed on her cheeks. "That's not what I meant, and you know it."

I grunted. I'd let her remain free for now. If I bound her, she wouldn't be willing to cooperate anymore.

"Fine," she said. "If you don't want to talk, don't."

I didn't respond.

"I haven't spent much time in this part of the country. It's beautiful, isn't it?" She looked around at the flowers along the side of the road. "I bet there aren't wildflowers like this in Bavaria, where you're from."

The flowers around us included cornflower and yarrow, both plentiful in my homeland. "I'm from Laute. Not Bavaria." She would know that if she'd paid any attention.

"Oh, right," she said. "What's it like?"

"Green." I missed the colors of the valley, brilliant emerald speckled with yellows and blues in summer, and earthy green dusted with snow in winter. I could find endless peace and solitude among those trees. Whether I was hunting or simply strolling through the trees, the sights, sounds, and smells of the forest were my greatest comfort.

"It sounds like where I grew up," Csilla continued, her chatter disrupting my memories. "My village was right on the coast, and it was green for months and months. And of course there were the flowers. All colors. Red, blue, orange—"

"Enough!" The word came out louder than I planned it to, and my horse tossed his head. I patted his neck, soothing him. "You don't have to spend the whole journey rambling incessantly," I told her.

From the way her face fell, I knew my words had been chosen poorly. "I'm sorry," she said. "I just—I couldn't handle the quiet anymore. I need something to focus on besides..." She waved a hand around as her words trailed off.

Mother often did the same, filling the air with conversation so she didn't have to think about her worries. I bit my tongue. On one hand, listening to Csilla's constant chatter for the next week would take me to the edge of my sanity, but on the other, if talking was the only way to soothe her nerves so she didn't run away back to the sorcerer, why wouldn't I be willing to pay the low price of my mental state?

"I'm sorry," I gritted out at last. "That was rude of me."

She pulled her horse to a stop, staring at me with her mouth slack.

"What?" I asked, stopping as well with a wary glance around us.

"I didn't expect you to apologize."

I jerked my chin toward the mountains. "We should keep going. I'd like to reach the mountains before nightfall."

NOT ALL BAD

CSILLA

A small town lay in the shadow of the mountains. As we walked through it, Csilla clung to my side, eyeing everyone we passed as though she expected someone to attack her at any second. I kept a wary eye out for anyone out of place, but I doubted the sorcerer would send someone here. Not yet, at least. A reasonable man would assume his runaway servant was getting as far from him as possible, not traveling toward his tower.

We found a farmer willing to take both horses in exchange for several coins and a pack of travel provisions. The horses were worth more, but I'd never been good at negotiating. It didn't matter, anyway.

We needed supplies, not money. From what he told us, there weren't many places to restock along the way. The occasional hunting shack and a single village made up the entirety of the population our path would take us past.

"It'll be a hard trip," the man said as he counted out the money. "With all that rain, the trail will be slick. Sure you don't want to wait a couple days?"

"My wife is anxious to make it home," I said, falling back on the lie we'd agreed to use. My appearance drew enough notice already; telling people I was an Ottoman who'd defected when I met Csilla would arouse interest, but so long as no one looked too closely at my eyes and I kept my hat on and my hood up, we could avoid word getting back to anyone who might be looking for us. "But we appreciate the advice."

We made camp on the edge of the trail that evening, mountains towering all around us. While Csilla built up a fire, I butchered and spatchcocked the chicken we'd gotten in town. Two forked branches and a long stick formed the spit to roast our dinner, and then there was nothing to do but wait for it to cook.

As we listened to the pop and sizzle of juices, I pulled the length of rope from my bag and began absently tying and untying knots in it. Rarely could I sit still without something to occupy my hands. In the past, music had been my first choice, but I didn't play in front of people. Not anymore.

"You're good with that," Csilla said, nodding at the rope.

I made a noncommittal grunting sound. "Tell me about your sorcerer." I was a skilled soldier. I'd studied philosophy and war, weapons and strategy. None of that had prepared me to fight magic. Not without magic of my own.

Words from the ancient Zhou general drifted through my mind. *If you know your enemy and know yourself, you need not fear the result of a hundred battles.* I didn't know if I knew myself anymore, but at least I could know my enemy.

Her body stilled, and she stared at the fire. "What about him?"

"What are his powers? What can he do?" It was as good of a place to start as any.

"What *can't* he do?" she replied.

I ran the rope through my fingers, focusing on the friction to still my mind. Panicking would do me no good.

"He…" She raised her hand, looking at her palm. "He'll speak an incantation, and sparks or ribbons will shoot from his hands to do his bidding. I've seen him make a potion that can turn a man into a goat, or a goat into a man." She shuddered and dropped her hand. "With enough time, he can do anything he wishes. The more difficult spells, like the ones that involve transforming people, take longer. He has to sacrifice an animal, or burn something, or combine certain ingredients before speaking his incantation. But given enough time and resources, he's all-powerful."

The knot behind my breastbone tightened, and I rubbed at it with my knuckle. I should have taken her to Rudolf, rather than going on this fool's errand to capture an omnipotent sorcerer.

I couldn't have done that to her. She was his slave, not his partner. Condemning her would be condemning an innocent woman to death.

"He has to speak the spells?" An inkling of a plan began to form in my mind. If we could keep him from speaking—kill him in his sleep, maybe—he wouldn't be able to ensorcell us.

"Every spell I've ever seen, he had to speak the words."

Good. That was something in our favor. A weakness, small though it was. "Does he ward his tower?"

"I don't think so." She screwed up her face, thinking. "He leaves his window open on warm nights, and I can fly in and out of the tower freely."

That was something. If he truly had no spells to keep intruders out, I could climb in through the window and slice his neck before he woke.

Csilla

He was thinking about how to kill Kálmán. I could see a vicious glint in his eyes, lust for the blood of the man who'd endangered his people. This was what I'd agreed to do. To murder the man who'd dictated every moment of my life for the past thirteen years.

Why did that thought twist something deep in my chest? The sorcerer had killed my parents, held me captive, tortured me, taken everything I loved. I should hate him. But he'd also taught me about the world, given me opportunities I never would have had in my small coastal village. When he was in a good mood, he was a good man. Could I kill that man, the one who was witty and charming and generous, just to destroy the one who hurt me?

"He's not all bad."

Tancred gave me an incredulous look.

"He treats me well as long as I obey him. He doesn't—" My skin heated. "He doesn't hurt me when he's taking his pleasure. He gives me gifts. I know he's done some awful things, but—"

He crossed his arms, the action making his broad chest and shoulders seem even larger. "But nothing. You think he's worth saving just because he gave you a few trinkets?"

"I didn't ask you to spare him." Even if I asked, I knew he wouldn't do it. Not when the death of the sorcerer could ensure his people's safety. "Nevermind. Forget it." I shouldn't have said anything. Tancred already didn't trust me. Admitting that I had conflicting feelings for the sorcerer would do nothing but add to that impression.

He pinned me with his dark eyes. "He has to die. You understand that, right?"

Of course I understood. If I wanted my freedom, the only way to get it was for Kálmán to die. That didn't mean that I deserved freedom, though. Not if it came at the cost of a life.

"When this is over, someone will be dead. Him or us. There's no other way it can end."

"I know." I had to come to terms with that. It wasn't just about me. It was about the people whose lives would be better without Kálmán in them. His best moments didn't erase his worst, no matter how much I wished they did.

I wished a lot of things. That my parents were still alive. That Kálmán was a better man. That we didn't have to kill him. That I could hate him.

But wishing didn't make things true. My parents were dead. Kálmán was a vicious, cruel man whose good traits only masked the evil within. He had to die.

And no matter how much I wanted to, I didn't hate Kálmán. Not in the way that I should. Maybe it was my heart's way of protecting itself. If his every touch repulsed me, I would have killed myself long ago to escape. I had too much to live for. My friends, my family, the possibility of a future.

There was another element to my feelings, too. Part of me refused to give him the satisfaction of breaking me. If I could find happiness with Kálmán, see the good even in him, I would still be master of my own fate. He controlled my body, but only I controlled my heart.

None of that changed what had to happen, though. Tancred was right. The sorcerer had to die, and I had to help him make that happen.

I pointed toward the fire. "That should be done cooking by now."

The look Tancred gave me said he didn't think our conversation was at an end, but I was done talking. I had chosen my path. There was no changing it now.

HEIGHTS

TANCRED

We saw no one our first two days walking through the mountains. I kept a wary eye out for the man Csilla's sorcerer had sent to hunt her down. He wasn't the only one I had to be cautious of. At any moment, the firebird could stop cooperating. *He's not all bad.* Stupid woman. Did she honestly believe that? After everything he'd done to her? Unless she'd been lying about what he'd done to her. Maybe he hadn't killed her parents. Maybe she was working with him and had been all along. But that wouldn't explain her fear at the message he'd sent. She was an enigma, a puzzle I couldn't figure out. I hated puzzles.

The path led us higher and further into the mountains. It was narrower here, barren of plant life. On one side, it hugged the mountain; on the other side was a steep drop of several feet. Wind whistled an eerie tune through the peaks, and in the distance, a hawk shrieked. Csilla walked in front of me, picking each footstep carefully.

Her shoulders were tense as we walked, and she kept glancing down over the edge of the trail, walking as close to the mountainside as she could. A thin sheen of sweat covered her face, although it was nowhere near sunset.

She was acting strange, and for once it didn't seem that her fear had anything to do with the sorcerer we were hunting. "Are you afraid of heights?" I asked as she looked down again.

She shot me a glare over her shoulder. "I don't have wings at the moment, in case you hadn't noticed."

I couldn't quite keep the bark of laughter from my voice as I said, "I'd have thought flying would rid you of that fear."

She remained silent, either too focused on her steps or too annoyed with me to answer. I took another step, opening my mouth to speak, and the ground crumbled beneath my feet.

I grabbed for purchase, but there was nothing to hold on to. Csilla's scream pierced the air as I fell. Rocks bit into my skin on the way down, and my right leg slammed into the mountain just before I landed on my back.

"Ow. Fuck." I sat up slowly, assessing my bruised and aching body for any injuries. Apart from a shooting pain in my right ankle and a number of what were sure to become nasty bruises, nothing seemed to be damaged.

"Are you okay?" Csilla asked. She was about twenty feet above me, peering over the edge.

"I may have broken my ankle." I didn't want to risk taking off my boot to check. Not until we were somewhere more secure.

"Should I go find help?"

"No!" The word came out sharp. "Don't go anywhere. I have that rope in my bag. I'll toss it up to you. Tie it off so I can pull myself up." It would hurt like hell, but there wasn't any other choice. I wasn't waiting for her to go find help—if she left my sight, she might decide she was better off running back to her master and leaving me to die. Not that a broken ankle would kill me, but exposure or wild animals could.

Csilla fidgeted above me as I rooted through my pack for the long coil of rope. I hadn't expected it to get much use, but I'd packed it in case I needed to set a snare or—if the firebird turned against me—use it on her.

I tied one end of the rope around a rock and threw it up toward her. It thudded onto the path.

"Got it!" She tugged on the end.

"Good. Now find a sturdy branch or boulder to tie it to." Shit. Did she know how to tie a decent knot? If she didn't, it wouldn't matter how solid the anchor she found was. "Can you tie a knot?"

"My father was a fisherman. There aren't many I can't tie."

I filed that bit of information away for later. "Make sure it's secure."

As I finished securing the rope to my waist, Csilla called down, "It's ready."

I pulled on the rope, testing its strength. If she wanted to kill me, now would be her chance. But why go to the trouble? She could abandon me here without going through the pretense of trying to save me. It wasn't as though I'd be able to chase her now.

I'd have to rely on her, whether I trusted her or not. Gritting my teeth, I dragged myself to my feet. Though I put as little weight on my injured leg as possible, the pain that shot through me was enough to make stars wink in the corner of my vision.

Every inch was torture, but I pulled myself up bit by bit, ignoring the pain in my leg. Csilla pulled the rope and tied off my slack as I climbed. When I neared the top, she knelt and reached over the edge.

"Give me your hand," she said. "I'll pull you up."

"I'm fine," I gritted out, clinging to the rope. She wouldn't have the strength to move me, and I didn't have the energy to waste arguing with her.

"You're not. Let me help you."

My arms shook with the pain and the weight of my body. Did I trust her?

"You're going to fall." She extended her hand further.

She was right. I didn't have a choice. Closing my eyes, I took her hand. My heart thundered in my ears as she pulled me up. At the top, I found enough purchase to scramble over the edge and onto solid ground, and we both leaned against the cliffside, breathing hard.

When I'd caught my breath, I looked over at Csilla. Her olive-toned cheeks were flushed with exertion, and she was staring at the broken edge of the path where I'd fallen.

"Thank you," I said. "For helping me." Saving me, more like. Without her help, I wouldn't have made it back up.

Then again, without her, I wouldn't be in this mess in the first place.

"I wasn't going to leave you behind."

"Well." I cleared my throat. "We should keep going."

"Can you walk?"

If the throbbing in my ankle was any indication, not well, but I didn't have a choice. "I'll be fine." I grabbed a cleft in the rock wall and pulled myself to my feet, putting as little pressure on my injured leg as possible.

It only took two steps for my ankle to give out beneath me.

Csilla's voice was a mix of exasperation and concern. "It won't do us any good to have you falling all over the place. I think there's a house up ahead. I'll go and—"

"No!" The word snapped out of me. I wasn't letting her out of my sight until we found her master. Even if she had saved me. "We stay together."

Her jaw clenched. "At least let me help you walk. Just until we find a stick you can use to prop yourself up with."

"Fine." I let her wrap my arm around her shoulder. Her slender frame pressed against my body, giving me support. She was tall for a woman, and wiry muscles hid beneath her dress. Despite myself, I was grateful for her help.

We kept close to the mountainside to avoid another fall. Our progress was slow. Neither of us were inclined to conversation, and the afternoon dragged on with only the sounds of our labored breathing—mine from pain, hers from the effort of supporting me—and the wind through the mountains.

When the trail widened, we finally stopped for a break. Csilla sank to the ground, pulling out her leather water skin and drinking deep. I didn't dare to sit down, for fear that I wouldn't be able to get back up, but I took a few much-needed gulps from my own bottle.

"If I'm right, the house should be just around the next bend," she said, peering down the path.

"Good." It was a risk, staying with people for the night, but one we'd have to take. We wouldn't be able to go on much longer like this. "We'll have to set up the tent before sunset. Hopefully the fabric will block enough of the light that whoever lives there won't be suspicious."

She shrugged. "It won't matter if they see me. If there's someone living up here, they're isolated. I doubt they have much contact with society."

"Word travels fast, even in places like this. If they see you transform, they're bound to talk about it the next time they travel to the nearest village. The news will beat us back to your sorcerer."

"And what choice do we have? We'll have to risk it. You can't keep walking. It'll be days before your ankle is healed enough to walk long distances, even with a crutch."

She was right, and I hated it. We were only a couple days into our journey, and we'd already faced too many delays. It would take a miracle to pull this off, and I didn't believe in miracles. "If they see you transform, I'll have to kill them." My words came out without inflection, and Csilla blanched.

I wouldn't apologize for it. When it came to a choice between my people's safety and that of strangers, it was no contest. These people couldn't be allowed to threaten my mission. I'd do whatever it took to keep my family and all the Pipers safe. That was the reason King Loic had chosen me to be part of his council, one of his noblemen. Like him, there was no line I wouldn't cross for the people I cared about.

"Come on." I swung my pack back over my shoulder. "This might be our only shelter for the next few nights."

As it turned out, the house she'd remembered seeing on a previous flight over the mountains wasn't occupied. The dilapidated shack we saw as we rounded the curve in the trail was long since abandoned. The thatching on the roof was wearing off, leaving holes that opened the house to the elements, and several birds had made the chimney their home.

"It's not hospitality," I said, "but at least we'll be out of the weather." A wide stream passed by the shack, deep enough for fishing. The water bubbled as it tripped over the rocks. We'd have the chance to refill our depleted water stores, and if the stream was as cold as it looked, it would help bring down the swelling of my ankle. If we were lucky, we might even catch some dinner.

We stopped by the side of the stream. Csilla knelt, opening her water skin and dunking it. I sat on a large boulder to pull off my boot and examine my injury. The ankle was swollen, and a black bruise was beginning to form on my skin. I gingerly pressed the spot, searching for breaks in the bone, but I couldn't make anything out.

I plunged my foot into the stream, hissing at the icy chill of the water. It numbed the pain, even as it sent daggers of cold into my skin.

"Is it broken?" Csilla asked, watching me.

"Too swollen to tell." Hopefully rest and water would lower the swelling.

She rose to her feet. "I'll see what's left in the house."

Some instinct urged me to call after her, warning her against bears or wildcats that might have made their shelter in the abandoned house, but I bit my tongue. She was capable of caring for herself. It wasn't as though I cared what happened to her. She'd done little but slow me down so far.

You've slowed yourself down, a nagging voice in my head said. *You were the one who chose to go through the mountains, and she helped you when you fell.*

I ignored that voice, as well.

Csilla

The door creaked as I pushed it open. Wan light from outside dotted the floor through holes in the roof, illuminating the filthy room. Animal droppings littered the corners, and the stench of mildew tickled my nose. Some creature had used the bed in the corner for a nest; I didn't look too closely at the stains on the bedding.

Next to the fireplace was a single cupboard. When I opened it, something brown and hairy skittered across the floor. I shrieked, jumping backward.

"What's wrong?" Tancred called.

"Nothing," I hollered back. "Just a mouse." I pressed a hand to my chest to soothe my racing heart.

Any food I might have found in the cupboard was long gone, rotted or eaten by the wildlife, but I found a few fishing supplies still in good condition, as well as a broom that I used to sweep up the worst of the dirt from the floor. It wouldn't be the most comfortable place to sleep for the night, but at least we'd have shelter.

The chimney was blocked, and lacking a means to clean it, I didn't want to risk setting a fire in the hearth. Leaving the door open to let out any lingering miasma, I rejoined Tancred by the stream.

"If you want a fire, we'll need to build it out here," I said, searching for a place to sit upstream from him. He watched in silence as I prepared the fishing rod. A bit of cheese from my pack served as bait, and I let out the line.

Trout were biting, and before long I had a line full of them.

Tancred watched as I pulled them out of the water and set to cleaning them. "Who taught you to fish?"

"I told you my father was a fisherman." I used the blunt end of my knife to scale the fish, then rinsed it off in the stream and began fileting it. "I was an only child, so he taught me everything he knew." Not that I had the opportunity to use those skills much, unless Kálmán gave me a day off to spend with Michal and the boys. I could count on a single hand the number of times that had happened.

"I was never one for fishing."

I looked up at him, surprised. He spoke so rarely, I'd resigned myself to carrying all of the conversation for the rest of our journey. "No?"

"I prefer hunting."

If he was willing to talk, I'd encourage it. "Who taught you to hunt?"

"My father."

I hadn't seen his father when I met his mother and brothers. "He must be proud of you, being on the king's council and all that."

"He's dead."

My gaze snapped upward at the matter-of-fact statement. I should have guessed. He wouldn't be a lord if his father was living. "Oh, I'm sorry. Was it recent?"

He watched the silver stream of water make its way down the gentle slope of the mountain. "Last year."

Around the same time that his people had been forced to leave their homeland. It was no wonder he didn't speak much. How much pain was he in, to have lost his home and his father in such close succession?

He cleared his throat. "Did you see anything that could serve as a walking stick? If I can get up and around, I'll get a fire started. You'll want to eat before sunset."

I took it that our discussion—brief as it had been—was at an end. "I'll go find you something to use."

MUSIC

TANCRED

I lay awake that night, my ankle throbbing. Csilla was already asleep. Outside the little house, our fire was banked, while inside, her body filled the room with light and heat. With the cold stream water, the swelling of my ankle had gone down enough that I could tell it wasn't broken, but the sprain would keep me from traveling for several more days, at least. I cursed myself for the delay. If I'd been more careful, or even trusted Csilla to carry me over the river, we wouldn't be in this situation.

Not that I trusted her fully, but our goals were aligned. For the moment, at least. We'd have to rely on one another.

We had to rely on one another, but that didn't mean I had to tell her everything about my past. What had I been thinking this afternoon? She didn't need to know about my father. She didn't need to know anything about me.

I pulled out my mbira and stroked the keys, soft enough not to make a sound. It was a gift from my father, but since his death it felt empty. Magic didn't echo through me with every move of my thumbs.

Thinking about him left an ache in my chest. I plucked out an old tune, one I'd learned before my powers manifested. Father played a pan flute, not a mbira, but he always played this song. When the twins were first born, he'd stayed up for hours, playing our melody to soothe them to sleep.

It wasn't the same as before, with my magic, but the familiar song helped to calm me. I lost myself in it, and gradually the pain in both my ankle and my chest faded to a dull, background pulse.

I miss you, Father. I sent the thought out to him, wherever he was, as I tucked the mbira back into my pack and laid down to sleep

Csilla

"What was that music you played last night?"

Tancred looked up sharply, eyes narrowing at the question.

"I wasn't eavesdropping," I said. "I wasn't quite asleep when you started playing." The music had been beautiful, almost magical, like the laughter of a springtime brook. It reminded me of a flower I'd collected once for Kálmán, a bloom that tinkled with music whenever the wind blew over it. The sounds were night and day, but there was a natural feel to them both, like they were an inherent part of creation.

He turned back to the knife he was sharpening. "Just an old song my father taught me."

There was a depth of sadness in him that I recognized. The pain of loss. But I didn't want to push him away, so I didn't mention it. Instead I asked, "May I see the instrument?"

He hesitated momentarily, then reached into his bag and pulled out a small box-shaped instrument. "It's called a mbira."

"I've never seen one before." I trailed my fingers over the keys, making a soft ringing sound I could barely hear. "Are they common among your people?"

"Hardly." He huffed a laugh. "We all specialize in our own instruments. Flutes are the most common. Drums are popular, too. As far as I'm aware, I'm the only Piper to ever play a mbira."

I looked up at him, wide-eyed. "Really? How did you learn, then?"

"A delegation was visiting the Pied Piper—our king—when I was a child. I went to the castle to see my father, a guard, and the delegation was performing for the king. I wanted to learn to play." He shrugged, like he was trying to be nonchalant, but I could sense an excitement in him. He was eager to talk about this. "My father paid them to teach me."

"It's beautiful." I handed the precious instrument back to him. "Who were they?"

"The people?" He set his knife aside and held the mbira in both hands, staring at it with shining, reverent eyes. The expression softened his usually hard face, and he rocked slightly, as if filled with too much energy to contain. "They're called the Mutapa. They're an African empire ruled by a conquering warrior called the Mwene Mutapa. They rule the coast, trading all over the Eastern Ocean."

His enthusiasm was palpable, infectious. I leaned in closer. "And they traveled all the way to Laute?"

He nodded, setting the mbira aside and rubbing his hands up and down his legs. "The Pied Piper heard about their conquest and invited a delegation to establish trade. Unlike the other kingdoms in Europe, they weren't afraid of us."

Why would other kingdoms be afraid of them? As far as I'd seen, the Pipers were a tiny, powerless people.

Tancred went on, oblivious to my confusion. "They came with salt and gold and ivory, instruments we'd never seen, languages we'd never heard. They were rich—not rich like the Pipers, but they had goods and money and knowledge. And they were interested in our magic. They didn't think it was a sign of evil, but a blessing from the Creator."

"Magic?"

His body stilled, and his eyes focused on me. "You didn't know we had magic?"

"You do?" If the Pipers had magic, why were we doing this? They could defeat Kálmán without my help.

"I assumed someone had told you about the demons of Europe," he said. "About the magic we had."

"You have magic?" I couldn't move past that revelation. They could stop him, end my curse without risking our lives.

A shadow fell over him, drooping his shoulders. "We used to. When we lost it, we lost everything."

Used to. The brief flicker of hope I'd felt for a simple resolution to our problem winked out. How did one lose magic? Spells were something one did, not something that could be lost. "What happened?"

He stared at the mbira, a wistful look in his eyes. "Magic has always been a part of the Pipers. Our king, the Pied Piper, was the source. Last year, a human, a witch, kidnapped him. She made a potion that took his hearing and our magic. Now the music—"

"—isn't the same," I finished for him.

He nodded. "It used to feel real. Powerful. Now when I play, it's just a song."

What must it be like to lose an ability that had been part of you for so long? It would be like never flying again.

Which would be reality for me, if we succeeded in killing Kálmán. Or if we failed, and Kálmán was angry enough to lock me up for the rest of my life. I loathed the transformation, but at night, with my wings spread wide over the countryside, I was free.

"Do you miss it?" I asked. As I would miss my wings, no matter the pain I had to go through to get them.

For a moment, I thought he wouldn't answer. Then, so quiet that I almost missed it, he said, "Yes."

The rest of the day, I searched the area around the shack for mushrooms and berries, anything that could serve for food during the rest of our time in the mountains. Our food stores weren't running low yet, and Tancred seemed to be healing quickly, but we didn't know when we'd next see civilization. It was better to be prepared.

As I searched, Tancred's revelation buzzed at the back of my mind. What had he been like with his magic? I could only imagine the power he'd wielded. The ability to enchant objects with nothing more than a song...

But his magic was more than power. It was a part of him. The pain of losing it would be immeasurable.

I thought again about the flowers Kálmán had sent me to collect a few years ago. They held magical properties, a fact evident not only by the sorcerer wanting them but also by the blooms themselves. The sound had rustled through me like the wind, filling me with a serenity that had to be magic. The flower patch wasn't far from here. It wouldn't heal Tancred's wounds, but maybe the reminder that magic and music coexisted somewhere in this world would bring him comfort.

FLOWERS

TANCRED

W hen I opened my eyes the next morning, a flower lay by my head. Long and trumpet-shaped with red and black petals, it stared back at me.

I sat up, looking around for Csilla. Was this a message? The idea that she was trying to poison me flashed into my head and was dismissed just as quickly. An apology, perhaps? Though for what, I wasn't sure. Maybe it was some expression of sympathy. I hated the thought that she was looking at me with pity, but after the miserable expression of emotion I'd shown yesterday, it was to be expected. I was usually better at keeping my emotions in check until I was alone, but her line of questioning took me by surprise.

She wasn't in the shack, but I found her outside, building the fire back up from embers so she could cook a few small eggs she'd found in her foraging adventure the previous afternoon. I held up the flower. "What is this?"

She started at the sound of my voice and dropped the stick in her hand. "I didn't realize you were awake."

I waved the flower back and forth. "This was next to me when I woke up. What is it?"

"It's a flower."

"I can see that." I knew my words would be misinterpreted as rudeness, but that wasn't my intention. I just wanted a simple answer. Why had she given me a flower? "Where did it come from?"

Her cheeks tinged pink. "On top of the mountain. I thought you'd like it."

She thought I'd like a flower. "Why?"

"It's not just a flower. She wasn't even trying to meet my eyes, which was uncharacteristic. Was she embarrassed? "It's easier if I show you."

She took it from my hand and put the petals to her lips. As she blew into it, a melody erupted, sweet as any I'd ever played. A sense of peace washed over me, a wholeness I hadn't felt in months. No, longer. Since my father died. Since that cursed pain had torn through my head and ripped out the one thing that gave my life meaning. It was magic; not Piper magic, but magic nonetheless. Magic in melody.

"Where did you get this from?" Tears stung my eyes, but I blinked them back.

"Kálmán sent me here once. The flowers contain some property he needed for an enchantment. They're rare—they only grow at the top of the mountain here."

I looked up at the rock face above us. "You flew there."

"It's only reachable by flight. Even Kálmán can't access it, unless he grows wings."

What if this was it? What if this was the key to restoring our magic? Getting to the top of the mountain would be difficult, but once this was over and we'd resolved the conflict with King Rudolf, we could figure it out. And once our magic was restored, we could take back Laute. We could go *home.*

The ache in my chest was almost enough to bring me to my knees.

"Draw me—" No, I had to be tactful about this. Diplomacy wasn't my strength, but this was too important. "Can you draw me a map to the flowers?"

"Why?"

Careful, I told myself. She didn't need to know my reasons. "They're beautiful. I'd like to see them myself."

"You won't be able to climb there." She looked up at a nearby peak. "But I could fly you there, if you want."

Why was she so anxious to get me in the air? First when the bridge was out, and now in the mountains. She didn't want me dead, obviously, but maybe she was luring me into a false sense of security. If she got me in her talons, she could carry me off to the sorcerer. I couldn't take the risk. I was too much at her mercy already.

"I appreciate the offer, but I'll keep my feet on the ground."

Her mouth pinched together. "I thought we'd moved past this mistrust."

Lie, lie, lie. I don't know what you mean."

"One day you bare your heart to me, and then the next you look at me like I'm going to turn on you any instant. Haven't I earned a modicum of trust?"

"If I didn't trust you, I wouldn't turn my back on you."

"You may trust me not to kill you in your sleep, but that doesn't mean you trust me. You won't even look into my eyes."

"I look at you all the time. I'm looking at you right now."

"At my eyes."

"Why?" I did as she asked, looking directly into her eyes. They were dark brown, I'd noticed before, but I hadn't seen the striations going through them like lightning over a storm-darkened sea at sunset. My skin prickled, electrified by the sustained eye contact.

"Why not?"

What did she want from me? I held her gaze, noting everything about her eyes, the long lashes, the soft lines in the corners, the freckle on top of her left eyelid. Finally, she looked away, letting out a long breath.

"Are you satisfied?" I asked.

"Nevermind."

"No, tell me. What am I doing wrong?" She was impossible to read. What did she want from me? "You're obviously upset with me, but I don't know how to change it."

"You don't believe I'm on your side in this, do you?"

I believe you want to get away from your sorcerer." How far was she willing to go for that, though? She'd proven that she didn't want me dead, but would she risk her life to see this through?

She threw up her hands. "I'm here, aren't I? I could have been back with Kálmán in a single night, but instead I've been out here, schlepping around the countryside with you for days. When you fell, I could have left you behind. You wouldn't have made it back up that slope without me. I pulled you back up. And yet at every turn you treat me like I'm going to betray you. Why would I do that? I would do *anything* to get away from Kálmán. Don't you understand that? Do you not understand what he's done to me?"

I shook my head, but she didn't wait for my response before continuing. "He killed my parents in front of me and took me away from everyone I've ever loved. He took my—he took my freedom. I want him dead, and I have tried *everything* to make that happen. I can't stop him."

"What do you mean?" Cold fear pulsed through me. She'd tried to escape before, to kill him?

"I—" Her voice broke, and she started over, quieter. "A few months after he first took me, I managed to get a hold of some cyanide. I put it in his dinner, and he ate the whole thing. I was sure he wouldn't survive. But he did. He didn't even get sick."

She was almost whispering now. "He knew that I'd done it, of course. He knows everything. He built a golden cage, just large enough to fit my body. My human body. He locked me in it for a week." Her eyes were fixed on some distant image of the past. "It was hell. Every day, I longed for sunset, because at least at night, I could stretch my wings."

Her eyes locked on mine, and her voice grew stronger. "So yes, Tancred, I want to get away from him. And I will do whatever it takes. I'm with you through this to the end. You're my last chance to get away, to have a normal life. One where my body isn't snapped to bits every night for his sick amusement. I want him dead, and you're the only way to make it happen. And if it kills me, at least I'll be free."

I watched the fire in her eyes, the determination in the set of her mouth. Tears brimmed but didn't fall. I was no good at comfort, but I took a step closer, my hand moving of its own accord to cup her cheek.

"Take me there," I said.

Csilla

What had possessed me to tell him all that? As I fashioned the rope into a harness late that afternoon, my cheeks burned with shame. I was usually more cautious about my anger and grief. Michal was the only one who got to see my tears. Kálmán had taught me the dangers of showing weakness in front of men.

I hadn't realized how far I was willing to go until I'd seen the distrust on Tancred's face. I still felt guilty, would probably always carry some guilt over it, but killing Kálmán was the only way for me to be free. I didn't *want* freedom, I *needed* it. No matter how kind he was on good days.

A feverish shiver wracked my body. Was it so near sunset already?

"I can finish that," Tancred said. When I looked up at him in question, he gestured at the harness. "You're shaking. I can help."

"It's almost done." I tied off the last knot and held it up. "But thank you." I'd learned to work through my pain. Kálmán often left me working until the sun dropped below the horizon. "You can check it if you like." I wouldn't give him more reason to distrust me. If he wanted to inspect everything I did, he could.

He took the harness from my hands, but he didn't examine the knots. He glanced at it briefly before looking back at me. "You're different than I expected."

"Different?"

"After everything you've been through, you're still..." He waved his hand about. "Positive. Cheerful."

"Spite fuels me." I gave him a sideways grin. "When Kálmán took me, I realized I had a choice. I could either break beneath him, or I could thrive despite him. I didn't want to give him the satisfaction of letting him break me. Since I couldn't kill him, surviving him was the next best thing."

He nodded slowly, his expression ponderous. After a moment, he cleared his throat. "How does this work?"

"You need to put your legs through the hoops." I took the harness and held it open, kneeling in front of him.

He slipped the left one on, but when he lifted his injured leg, he winced.

"Here. Let me." I picked up his booted foot, careful not to jostle his ankle, and slipped it through the loop. "When you stand, you can pull it up around your waist." The ends of the rope remained in my hands. "I'll hold on to these."

Worry pinched his features. "And you're sure they won't burn up?"

I turned my head to hide my smile. "As long as it's not a living being, my flames can't harm it," I reminded him. "You might get a little warm, but don't try to touch me, and you'll be fine."

"I understand."

Our eyes met, and I was suddenly hyper-aware of my position on my knees before him. My mouth went dry.

I cast around for a distraction. "Thank you. For trusting me to do this."

His voice was low when he answered. "Don't drop me, and we'll call it even."

The laugh that slipped out of my lips was barely more than a breath. Our faces were closer together now, and I didn't know which of us had moved—or was it both of us?

How long had it been since I kissed someone out of desire? Not since Kálmán took me. And I wanted to kiss Tancred. Wanted to feel those lips on mine. His hands were gentler than I'd expected; I'd felt them on my cheek earlier as I fought back tears. I wanted to feel them elsewhere.

It didn't have to mean anything. Kálmán was probably going to kill us both in a few days. Shouldn't we enjoy ourselves until he did? If I was going to be punished for my offenses, I could at least make them worth the punishment.

Tancred's eyes darkened with desire that matched my own. I closed my eyes and leaned closer.

A tremor went through me at that moment, another reminder of my impending transformation. It broke the silent spell between us. Tancred straightened, eyes looking anywhere but at me.

"I should go get ready," I said, standing up. Before he could say anything to stop me, I hurried into the hut to undress before sunset.

TOP OF THE WORLD

TANCRED

As Csilla lifted me into the air, my stomach plummeted. I was an idiot for agreeing to this. I should tell her to stop, to put me down.

Then we were above the trees, and it was too late. The wind rushed around me, growing thinner every second. My eyes stung. I didn't dare look down. I wasn't afraid of heights, but the sensation of flying through the air, nothing holding me up but a length of rope, was nauseating.

We circled around the mountaintop she'd pointed out. Csilla carried me past a ridge, half-shrouded by fog—or was it a cloud?—and I caught sight of the patch of flowers, their dark petals briefly visible in the moonlight. The wind rippled through them, and the melody filled my ears, drowned out an instant later by the sound of the wind in my ears.

She banked around, and I clung to the rope as I swayed. This time, she slowed as we neared the ridge, giving me time to get my feet under me before she stopped. My injured foot hit harder than I would have liked, but I sucked in a breath and pushed through the pain.

I sank to the ground in the middle of the flowers as Csilla dropped the rope. The enchanting music rolled over me. Up here, I could see the whole of the mountain range. A sweet, woodsy scent tickled my nose, along with the sharpness of cold night wind and mist.

Csilla alighted behind me, the crackling of her body and the warmth at my back announcing her arrival. I turned to see her coal-black eyes fixed on me.

"Thank you," I said, my voice hoarse from unexpressed emotions. Surrounded by these flowers, magic flowing over my skin, I could almost pretend I was whole again.

I scooted to the edge of the ridge and let my legs dangle over. Csilla followed me, close enough to lend me her warmth without burning me. We sat there listening to the music, relishing the beauty of the moment.

After a few moments, I laid down amid the petals. "It's like losing an arm."

From the corner of my eye, I saw Csilla cock her head.

"My magic. Even when I was young and hadn't learned to channel it, it was still there. After everything that happened last year, losing my magic was the worst. I lost a part of myself."

She made a soft coo, wordless encouragement to go on.

"King Loic had it worse. He lost a second sense—not just his magic, but his hearing, too. And with my father's death, caring for my mother and brothers..." I sighed, rubbing a petal between my fingers. "I feel guilty for mourning my magic. I have other things to worry about. It shouldn't take up so much of my energy.

"But that was our defense. Most humans hate us. The Catholic Church labeled us demons decades ago. Kings were threatened by our power. Religious leaders, rulers—they'd see us wiped out in an instant. When we had magic, we were protected. Now that it's gone, we have nothing to defend ourselves with."

She bobbed her head in understanding.

"I guess you know what I mean, don't you? We're both powerless." That's what enraged me so much. Rudolf, this imbecilic king who would have been no match for the Pied Piper a few years ago, held all the power now. He could kill us all and suffer no consequences. And if I failed, he would.

"I admire you, you know." I looked over at her. "Your tenacity. I wish I could be more like you, but I have so many people relying on me. The king made me a lord. My mother and brothers need a man to protect them. If I let myself relax, even for a moment, I could lose everything." I'd come so close to losing everything already. I couldn't give up the little that I had left.

She ducked her head in a gesture of sympathy.

"I can manage it," I said. I had no other choice. "Sorry. The music made me melancholy. I shouldn't bother you with this."

Csilla

My heart broke for him. He'd had everything, and he'd lost it all. How could I judge him for not trusting easily? I wanted to say something, to comfort him, but I couldn't speak. I couldn't even touch him. A tear formed in my eye, turning to steam before it could fall.

I stretched out next to him, as close as I could get without making him uncomfortable. *We'll stay as long as you need,* I tried to silently convey to him. Here, above the rest of the world, where kings and sorcerers couldn't touch us, we could steal a moment of peace.

BRANDY

TANCRED

There must have been some healing property in the music of the flowers, because by the next morning, my ankle was healed enough for me to start walking without the crutch. While Csilla slept the morning away, I searched the mountains near our campsite for food. I was in luck; not far from the shack, a blueberry bush hid in the thicket, far enough back that the birds hadn't yet picked it over. Gathering as many berries as I could, I returned to the shack, where Csilla had woken and was fishing for breakfast.

"Afternoon" I said, wary. I'd bared my soul to her last night. I hadn't planned to, but the magic and darkness had loosened my tongue. How would she react? Would she mock me for my extreme emotions? Use what I'd revealed against me?

She looked up from her line. "Where were you?" The question didn't sound accusatory, just curious. "I thought you'd be out by the stream."

I held up the sack of berries. "Foraging. Stretching my legs." After the walk, my ankle was starting to twinge a bit. I'd still need the crutch for walking long distances. "I'd say I'll be ready to leave tomorrow."

"Oh." She turned back to her fishing.

"Something wrong?"

"No!" she said quickly. "No, I just..." She stared into the stream, gathering her thoughts. "I know we need to leave. There are people depending on us. But it's been years since I've had so much time to myself, to do whatever I wanted." She bit her lip. "I was glad to have this week."

A possessive need to protect her filled me, surprising me with its vehemence. She deserved days like this. "In another week, you can do whatever you want for the rest of your life. Your sorcerer will be dead."

"Or we will be." She whispered the words, low enough that a human couldn't have heard it.

"I'll kill him for you," I promised. For her, for my people, and for everyone else who'd suffered for his actions.

She gave me a brief, sad smile. "I hope so."

"What—" I hesitated, then forged ahead. "What would you do with your freedom? If there were no obstacles."

She watched the stream, but the sparkle in her eyes didn't come from the light on the water. "I've always wanted to travel. It's what got me mixed up with Kálmán in the first place. I want to see oceans and deserts, meet people from far-off lands. Like the Mutapa people you told me about. Not just to read about them in books, but to see them with my own eyes." She shrugged as if it didn't really matter. "If I survive, that's what I want to do with the rest of my life."

In the past year, I'd seen more of the world than I'd ever expected to in my entire life, but the way Csilla's face lit up in that moment... It made me want to see it, too.

I cast around for a distraction and saw a glass bottle filled with amber liquid on the ground next to her. "What's that?"

"I don't know. A drink? I found it under the bed this morning. I was going to clean the bottle to use it for water."

I picked it up and sniffed the contents. It was strong, alcoholic. Brandy, maybe? A tentative sip confirmed my thoughts. "Oh, that's good. Try it."

She took the bottle from me and swallowed a drink. She coughed, wrinkling her nose. "What *is* that?"

"Brandy." I laughed. "Haven't you ever had liquor before?"

"Kálmán doesn't share his drinks." She took another sip. "It's warm."

She'd been cut off from the world for so long, she didn't even know what she'd been missing. "You've at least had wine, right?"

"Of course I've had wine. Kálmán let me go to Purim dinner with Michal a couple times. We had wine there."

"Who's Michal?" She'd mentioned him before. A friend, perhaps, or a lover? I pushed down the irrational twinge of jealousy. She didn't owe me anything.

"My auntie. Well—she works for Kálmán. She sort of took me in after he brought me back to the tower."

Not a lover, then. I ignored the sense of relief, too, not wanting to examine it too deeply. "You mentioned Purim. Are you Jewish?"

She laughed. "No. I like their beliefs, though. The stories... They give me peace. Hope that things can get better. And Michal is. She's been sort of like a surrogate mother to me."

"I see."

We passed the bottle back and forth in silence as Csilla fished. She didn't catch anything, and before long she'd abandoned the line on the shore, kicked off her shoes, and dipped her toes in the water.

"It feels good, doesn't it?" I nodded to the water. I'd taken my boots off, as well, letting the water soothe my ankle.

"It's cold." She kicked her legs and giggled. "I don't get to be cold much."

I raised my brows at her. "The drink is getting to you."

"Maybe the drink is getting to *you*." She bumped her leg against mine.

"I think you've had enough," I said, trying to take the bottle from her.

She stood, moving out of reach. "Why? We're not going anywhere." She spun around, arms out wide. "I deserve a little oblivion."

Oblivion. It sounded divine. Just for one day, I wanted to forget all my troubles. With the help of the brandy, I was feeling more relaxed than I had in months. And with relaxation came instant guilt. I should be *doing* something.

She splashed me. The cold water landed on my cheek, distracting me from my thoughts. I huffed at her, and she laughed again.

"Relax a little, Tancred. We're in the middle of nowhere. We've got one more night here. What's it going to hurt if you let go?"

"Fine." I scowled at her. "Keep drinking. But if you fall over and drown, I'm not going to save you."

"Yes, you would." She took another drink, then held the bottle out to me. "But I'm not going to drown. I was swimming in the ocean before I could walk." She stepped deeper into the water. Her skirt clung to her legs, revealing every line of them. She reached into the water and picked up a handful of rocks, dropping them back into the water one by one.

My mouth was suddenly dry. I took another swig, closing my eyes to keep from staring at her.

"Look at this one!" she said. I opened my eyes to see her holding a pebble up to the sky, squinting at it. "It looks like it's got flames inside it."

She was going to feel every bit of the alcohol when she woke up in the morning. I raised a brow at her. "Are you collecting rocks now?"

"Not for me. Michal's boys, they like me to bring them something from my travels. A blue feather or a dried daisy. Or a rock that looks like it's on fire when you hold it up to the light. I just need to find one m—"

Her words cut off with a splash, and water doused me. Once I'd wiped the drips from my eyes, I saw Csilla sitting in the middle of the stream, water up to her shoulders.

"That's it. Get out." I held out a hand to help her up.

"No." She grinned and splashed at me.

"Get out of the water, firebird."

Her expression turned dark. "Don't call me that."

I opened my mouth to say it again, but something in her eyes told me not to press it. "Get out. I don't want to have to come in after you."

She stuck out her tongue. "Make me."

Impossible woman. Groaning, I rolled up my pants and stepped into the stream. When I reached down to lift her up by the arms, she leaned backward, and we both tumbled under the water.

I came back up, sputtering and cold. "You little—"

Her laughter chimed through the air, echoing against the mountains around us. "You look like a wet dog!"

"You're one to talk." Completely drenched, her hair was plastered to her face, and her dress was transparent. I tried not to stare at the honed muscles, the breasts that were the perfect size to fit in my hands. "Come on. We'll be sick if we stay in here." I stood, but my weak ankle caught on a slippery rock, and I fell toward the edge of the stream.

"Tancred!" Csilla grabbed my arm. We landed nose to nose, her body on top of mine. "Sorry," she whispered, unable to stop the giggle.

I'd had too much to drink. It was the only reason I couldn't look away from her. The corners of her eyes crinkled with amusement, and her breath fanned against my lips.

"I don't remember the last time I wanted to kiss someone," she said, the words barely audible over the sound of the water. "Not since my parents died."

It hadn't been quite so long for me. Only since we left Laute. There had been a woman at home—I couldn't think of her right now. Not with Csilla's body on mine. My breath came short. "And now?"

"Now I do." She swallowed audibly. "Do you?"

Much as my mind was screaming that we shouldn't... "Yes."

She ducked her head, and our lips met.

She tasted of summertime and smoke and brandy. I let my instincts take over, and my arms wrapped around her as the water lapped against us. She fit perfectly against me, her body yielding to mine in all the right spots. I slid my hand down her ass and squeezed, and she moaned into my mouth.

I could lose myself in her, I realized. I'd had women before, had sex before, but not like this. It wasn't the long dry spell that left me so hard I ached, either. It was her. She was a living flame, a light that could illuminate my life, and—

That terrified me.

I tore my mouth from hers. "This was a bad idea." I wanted her. Wanted to hear the sounds she might make if I got her under me. To see the way her skin would look flushed with pleasure. And I couldn't take that risk. I'd let down too many walls this week already. I needed to be focused on defeating her sorcerer, making it back to my king so my people would be safe. Attachments, even purely physical ones, would do nothing but slow me down.

Embarrassment or arousal colored her cheeks, and she rolled off of me. The bottle had fallen next to us; she picked it up as she climbed out of the stream. "I'll build a fire. You can go get changed."

I watched her go, hating myself for the disappointment that dragged her shoulders down. If we killed the sorcerer, I promised myself. If we killed him, we could have one night. It wouldn't mean anything but physical release, a celebration of our victory before we took his head back to my king.

Water dripped from my body as I stood. A few more days, and I could indulge myself. For one night only.

THE VALLEY

CSILLA

Everything hurt, and I was dying.

I groaned, throwing a hand over my head.

"Good morning." Tancred's voice was a hammer to my temples. Why was he so pleasant today?"

"You sound cheerful." I peeked at him and hissed as the morning light bored into my eyes.

"And you look like hell. I told you to stop drinking."

It had been worth it. For the first time in years, the pain of transformation had been numbed. Not eliminated entirely, but dulled by alcohol to the point where it was almost bearable.

"Get dressed." Tancred chucked my clothes at me. "We leave in twenty minutes."

We packed up our things and left the mountainside shack behind. Our pace was slow that day, checked by my aching head and Tancred's injured leg. Late that afternoon, we came across the first signs of civilization we'd seen in almost a week.

"Should we turn around?" I murmured, eyeing the smoke that rose from the houses below us in the valley. "Or see if we can find a private shelter down there tonight?"

Tancred shook his head. "It's not worth the risk of someone seeing you."

A stick cracked behind us. He whirled around, bow in his hand and arrow nocked before I even saw him draw it. "Who goes there?"

A young man stepped through the trees, a brace of rabbits slung over his shoulder and a dagger in his hand. "I could ask you the same question. You're not from around here."

Tncred started to respond, but I put a hand on his arm. Tact, not battlefield negotiations, was the order of the day, and I'd learned that tact wasn't his strength.

"My husband and I are traveling to a village on the other side of the mountains," I said. "We were taking the King's Road, but the river flooded and sent us through the mountains instead. We're still going the right way, aren't we?"

The stranger eyed Tancred's bow warily. "Yes."

"You'll have to forgive my husband," I said, trying to push Tancred's arm down. "Understandably, he's concerned about bandits."

Tancred tilted the point of his arrow toward the ground but kept it nocked. "Sorry," he grunted. "Can't be too careful."

"What are you, a Turk?" the man asked, taking in Tancred's dark skin. I silently thanked HaShem that he'd worn his hat today, covering his ears and silver horns.

"Yes, he defected from the Ottoman army after we met." I looped my arm through Tancred's, begging him with my eyes not to turn this into a fight. "We're going home to tell my parents we got married." Putting on a giddy grin, I leaned my head on Tancred's shoulder. "When they sent me to stay with my aunt for the summer, they didn't expect I'd come home with a husband!"

The man's expression shifted from wariness to welcome. "Congratulations," he said, tucking the dagger back into his belt. "You won't want to be out after dark. Come into town with me. We don't have an inn, but we'll find a place for you."

"We don't wish to impose," I said hastily.

"You won't be. I'm Ákos, by the way."

"I'm Csilla. And my husband is Mehmed." It was the first Turkish name I could think of. Tancred didn't look like a Mehmed, but then again, he didn't really look like a Turk, either.

"Nice to meet you, Csilla, Mehmed. Come on. I'll introduce you to my family." He turned, heading down the trail toward the village. "Careful up here. The path can be tricky."

Tancred sheathed his arrow and slung his bow back over his shoulder. He picked up the walking stick he'd dropped, and we followed Ákos down the path into the valley. I still held Tancred's arm, lending him support as he picked his way over roots and stones. He was alert, watching for signs of danger from the woods around us as well as the man leading us into the tiny village below.

Tancred

I considered our options as we descended into the valley. I couldn't kill Ákos—it would be impractical not only for the difficulty of hiding the body, but someone would be sure to come looking for him. We wouldn't be a safe distance away before sunset. On the other hand, if Csilla's transformation was witnessed in the middle of this village full of strangers, we'd be in an even bigger mess.

"It's still early," Csilla whispered. "We'll come up with something before sunset."

I doubted it. If they realized what I was, they'd burn me for a demon and Csilla for a witch. Though I wondered, briefly and with detachment, if flame could even harm her.

As we neared the village, people took notice. Eyes followed us, and by the time our guide stopped at a house, we had collected a following. Most of the adults were trying to be inconspicuous, carrying on a conversation with their neighbor while watching us out of the corner of their eyes, or patching a spot on their roof, or busying themselves harvesting vegetables from their garden. The children were less subtle as they stared openly at the strangers that had come into their village.

No one was hostile yet, but I knew how quickly that could change.

"Don't mind them," Ákos muttered as he put his hand to the latch of the door. "We don't get many visitors around here. Especially not Turks." He pushed the door open and called inside. "Mama, I'm home! I've brought guests."

The rich smell of stew filled the air as a middle-aged woman with spectacles and gray streaks in her reddish hair glided into view. "Guests?" She saw us, and her confusion turned into a warm, welcoming smile. "Oh, hello. Are you traveling through?"

Csilla, still holding my arm, bobbed her head in greeting. "Yes, your son was kind enough to invite us in. I hope we're ot imposing."

"Not at all!" She ushered us to a seat as Ákos closed the door on the prying eyes outside. "I'm Katalin. What brings you to our valley?"

I let Csilla take the lead in the conversation as I scanned our surroundings. Through the single open window, I could still see the neighbors milling about, pretending that their business required them to be nearby, although everyone could clearly see they were searching for gossip. The house had a front and a back door—the back was propped open to catch a cross-breeze—and two small bedrooms. The entire town had maybe a dozen houses, and we were in the center. If we had a head start, we might be able to escape if sentiment turned against us, but then word would get back to the sorcerer. He would be expecting us when we finally reached the tower.

A knock on the door interrupted the story Csilla was telling about our whirlwind love affair—or rather, the fictional love affair between Mehmed the Turk and Csilla the normal human woman.

"Please, excuse me." Katalin went to the door, mouthing over her shoulder, "nosy neighbors." She opened the door, pasting on a smile. "Good afternoon, Evelin."

The woman on the step looked like an older version of Katalin, her hair graying around the temples and lines softening the corners of her mouth, which she held open in an 'o' of feigned surprise. "I didn't realize you had guests, Kati! I would have come at a better time."

"What brings you by?"

The older woman held out a basket. "I've been meaning to return this for ages. I was just heading out to see Mama when it caught my eye."

Katalin took the basket and hung it on a hook by the door. "Yes, thank you. Give your—"

"I'm Evelin, by the way." She took Csilla's hand, and the hairs on my neck raised. Was this an ambush, or nothing more than idle curiosity? "What brings you to our valley, dear?"

Csilla smiled warmly at her. "Just passing through. Ákos met us on the trail and invited us in for the night, which was kind of him. I wasn't sure I could handle another night in a tent in my condition." She dropped her free hand to her stomach.

The two older women made a high-pitched squealing sound in unison. "Are you expecting?" Katalin asked. "So soon!"

"And on the road, too." Evelin clicked her tongue. "You must be exhausted, poor thing."

What was Csilla's goal? The women would want to hover for hours, talking about babies and childbirth and all manner of womanly topics. Until sunset, when Csilla's transformation in front of them would cause them to turn on us.

"I wouldn't dare to complain," Csilla said, sidling closer to me. "I'm so happy, of course, but it hasn't been easy. Evenings are the worst. I get so ill..."

Katalin nodded her head in sympathy. "Oh, I had nausea with Ákos. Mornings were awful. What you need is a nice, hot mint tisane and an early bed. I'll put on a pot—"

"I've got some mint in my garden," Evelin interrupted. "I'll just pop over and get some while Kati puts the water on to boil."

"And you can settle down for the night with some stew and a drink." Katalin thrust a pot into Ákos's hands, where he was standing in the corner watching all the commotion with mild amusement. "Head down to the stream and fill this, please. You can take Mehmed with you."

It took me a moment to realize she was speaking of me. I hesitated. What if this was some trick to separate us?

"Don't worry about me, my love." Csilla grabbed my hand and kissed the palm. "I'll be right here when you get back."

The words did little to soothe my fears, but I had no choice. Making sure my hat was still firmly settled on my horns, I followed the younger man out the back door.

He waited until we were almost to the stream to speak. "Congratulations. How long have you known?"

"Not long." About as long as him, in fact. What Csilla had been thinking with the ridiculous lie, I wasn't sure. It was one thing to pretend to be married, but this was something different. I'd seen how women acted when babies were mentioned. When Mother was expecting the twins, we'd been inundated with guests at all hours of day and night. Add that to the curiosity brought on by the visit of foreigners, and the story of a young woman married to a Turk and bearing his child would have all the women in the village bearing down on us at once.

"You worried about how her parents will react?" he asked as he knelt down by the stream and filled the pot with cool, clean water. "I bet it'll come as a shock when she brings home a—" He coughed. "Well, a stranger."

"I'm sure they'll accept her feelings on the matter." It wouldn't be long before I completely lost track of the threads of the lie she had woven and gave something away. Anxious fear churned in my chest, worse than any tournament or hunt I'd been in. I rubbed my fingers back and forth against each other, wishing we'd flown over the river rather than going through the mountains. There were too many variables, too much that could go wrong. And some of it already had.

"I hope it's not rude to ask..." Ákos nodded at my head. "Your hat. It's an unusual shape. Is it part of your religion?"

I touched my hand to the tips of my horns, hidden beneath the fabric. "Oh. Um, yes." The Bavarian-style hat I wore bore no resemblance to the Ottoman turbans. Which, if I remembered correctly, were a sign of status, not a religious garment, but if the lie stopped him from questioning why I didn't remove my hat, much the better.

"I've never met a Turk. Is it true they—you—I mean—" He stopped and started again. "Is your sultan really planning to invade Arany?"

I shrugged. "I wasn't privy to Sultan Selim's war councils."

"No, of course not." As we headed back toward the house, he appeared deep in thought. "But King Rudolf will need men to fight if it does. Will you fight for Arany?"

"I'll fight for my family," I said, and it wasn't a lie. Whether we remained in Arany—doubtful—or were driven out—more likely—I would fight for my mother and brothers against any enemy, be they Turk, Aranite, or anyone else.

"You've been in battle before?"

"I have." Nothing like the Ottomans had fought, but I'd seen combat twice. The first had been a year and a half ago, when Bavaria had sent mercenaries to attack Laute. We still had our magic then, but it had been ineffective, blocked by some witchcraft cast by the woman who later took my king's magic. My father had been killed in that battle, one of the last defenders of King Loic's father, the former Pied Piper. I hadn't been one of the castle guards, but I'd gone to defend my king and country. We'd pushed the invaders back, but it hadn't stopped them permanently. Only a few weeks later, they'd come again, killing everyone in the castle and kidnapping King Loic. When he returned, deaf and bereft of his magic, we had been forced to leave our home.

The second battle I'd fought was shortly after King Francis of France had denied our petition for safety. While leaving the country, we'd been set upon by a small unit of French soldiers. They hadn't been sent by Francis—if they had, we would have been wiped out by the entire might of France. Most likely it had been a noble, hoping to curry favor with his king by destroying what he assumed were France's enemies. The battle had been nearly bloodless; we'd beaten them back just long enough to escape.

Ákos let out a long breath. "I hope it doesn't come to battle, but if it does, I'll be glad to have you on our side."

I glanced over at the young man. He couldn't have been much older than twenty, and obviously isolated here in his valley home. War would come for him, I was certain of it. The Ottomans were an unstoppable machine, in the process of taking over the entire continent. A larger power might stop them, France or Aragon and Castile, but a tiny kingdom like Arany was unlikely to stand against the empire, no matter how rich they might be.

"I hope it doesn't come to that, too," I said.

When we returned to the house, Katalin and Evelin had bundled Csilla up in a blanket near the fire, despite the warmth of the air. She was finishing a small bowl of stew as the older women fussed over her.

"Oh, good," Katalin said, taking the pot from Ákos and dumping a handful of green mint leaves into it. She hung it on the hook over the fire. "I wondered what was taking you so long."

Sunset was drawing near. The valley was darkening, and Csilla's face had grown pale.

"I hope you aren't getting ill." Evelin took the now-empty bowl from Csilla. "You look a bit peaky, dear."

Csilla gave her a weak smile. "I'm just tired. It's been a long day."

Evelin clucked. "And here we are keeping you up. Go on to bed, dear."

"Yes, you can take my room." Katalin pointed toward the door on the left. "I'm sure you'll be anxious to be on your way tomorrow. Get some rest, and you can start fresh in the morning."

"I don't wish to put you out," Csilla said, biting her lip.

What was she doing? They'd given her a way out. Was she hoping we'd be caught? If she waited too much longer, she'd transform in the middle of the house, in front of Katalin, Evelin, Ákos, and whatever neighbors were still spying to catch a glimpse of us through the window. I glared at her, silently urging her to hurry.

"Nonsense." Katalin pushed the door open. "I can sleep just as well elsewhere."

I stretched, feigning a yawn. "Yes, let's get some sleep, wife. I'm tired as well."

Laughter seemed to spark in Csilla's eyes, but she stood. "If you're sure we're not inconveniencing you."

"Not at all." She practically shoved us toward the bedroom. "Mehmed, are you hungry? There's plenty of stew."

"No, thank you." I picked up our bags and tossed them into the bedroom, then grabbed Csilla's arm. Through the fabric, she was hot to the touch.

"Let me know if there's anything you need. Extra blankets, something to eat. I'll bring that tisane in as soon as it's done."

"I don't think I'll need it." Csilla stood in the way of me closing the door. "I'm sure I'll be asleep before it's ready."

"Well, then, I'll make sure to put it in the coldbox for you to have with breakfast," Katalin said.

Evelin waved at us. "It was nice to meet you!"

"Thank you again," Csilla called as I closed the door and leaned against it with a sigh.

I scowled at her. "Cutting it a little close, don't you think?"

She giggled. "We're fine." She was still pressed up against me, the tiny tremors that wracked her palpable in her touch although they were imperceptible to sight.

"As long as no one else comes in until dawn." The room was small, with a wooden chest at the foot of the bed. No windows, so we didn't have to worry about someone peeking in. A fireplace took up most of the wall, so if anyone saw firelight through the cracks in the door, they would have no reason to be suspicious.

"I'm sorry for the story I had to give them," she said, moving to the bed. Irrationally, I missed the warmth.

I shrugged. "It worked." We'd already been pretending to be a married couple, so I wasn't likely to quibble with any embellishments she added to the story. Especially if it got us out of this valley with no trouble. "But how did you know it would work?"

"When—" She paused, shook her head, and started over. "When Michal was pregnant with her youngest, especially at the beginning, she was tired and nauseous every evening. I figured Katalin would be more sympathetic if I told her I needed rest because I was pregnant."

"I see."

She stared at her hands, her mouth twisted in a wry expression. "Anyway, it's as close as I'll ever come to pregnancy."

"Why?" Once her sorcerer was dead, she could do whatever she wanted. Marry, raise a family, see the world. "You don't want children?"

"Not particularly. I like children, I just don't want to raise them. But even if I did, I can't. Kálmán made sure of it."

Horror spread through me as her words sank in. "He sterilized you?"

"A potion." She shivered, and I couldn't tell if it was from the swiftly approaching sunset or the memory of his actions. "He didn't want to have to worry about getting me pregnant."

I clenched my fists, jaw tightening. If I hadn't been determined to kill him already, this would have settled it for me. Was there any hint of autonomy he hadn't taken from her?

"What about you?" she asked.

"Me?"

"Do you want children? A family?"

She was conversational tonight. Usually the impending transformation made her withdrawn, quiet. Was it nerves?

"It's not something that's likely to happen for me."

"Really?" She cocked her head, wrapping her arms around her middle. "I'd have thought you had a whole swarm of women desperate for your attention."

I chuckled dryly. "No. What would I offer them?"

"Yourself. Isn't that enough?"

I wished it could be. "Even if it was, there aren't many women in my life. Most of the Pipers are already married, or they're too old or too young for me."

"What about Lady Teta?"

I laughed, too loud for our quiet discussion, and I heard the conversation in the other room die down for a moment. "No," I told her once I heard Katalin and Evelin start speaking again. "I'm not interested in Lady Teta, and I'm sure the feeling is mutual."

"But if you could find someone?"

I wouldn't. "My parents—their love was like the kind you read about in ancient stories. Mother was Father's whole world. It's childish, but I want a love like that. I'm not willing to settle for anything less."

"I understand." She shivered again, more violent this time. "At least you can sleep on a real bed tonight."

"I'll sleep on the floor."

She gave me a bewildered look. "What? Why?"

"Someone has to make sure no one comes in during the night, and you're in no condition to keep watch. Besides, it's not like we can both sleep in the bed. I have objections to being immolated in my sleep."

Her cheeks turned red. "I'll be just as comfortable on the floor. And why not move the chest in front of the door?"

I considered it. There was no lock, but she was right. If I moved the chest over, no one would be able to enter the room without waking me. "Ah. That might work."

Csilla stood. "Help me move it."

"What sort of husband would I be if I let my pregnant wife move furniture?" I deadpanned.

She flushed again. "Do it yourself, then." Crossing her arms, she watched me block the door.

"You should undress," I said, straightening and nodding at her shaking body. "The sun will set any minute now."

"I should." She stared at me, and I stared back, skin prickling. In the main room, I could hear Katalin and Evelin still chattering, their conversation occasionally punctuated by Ákos's lower timbre.

"Tancred?" she said after a moment.

"Hm?"

"I need to get undressed."

"Oh. Right." My ears heated, and I turned toward the wall. "Sorry."

Fabric rustled and landed on the floor. I closed my eyes tight, trying not to picture the woman standing—now naked—behind me.

"You can turn around."

When I looked, she had a quilt wrapped around her body. Her teeth chattered together, and she looked so miserable, I wanted to take her in my arms and assure her it would be over soon. But it wouldn't. Not until we killed her sorcerer.

She let out a whimper.

"Shh," I said, half-soothing, half-concerned. The last thing we needed was for someone to come asking questions.

"I'm trying," Csilla groaned.

"I know." I reached out a hand, then thought better of it. "A few more nights. That's all." If luck was on our side.

She nodded. Her lips were white, and she leaned back against the wall. "Will you play for me?"

"Play?"

"Your mbira." She closed her eyes.

I hesitated. I didn't play anymore, had only done it once in the long year without magic. But if the distraction would help her through the pain of transformation...

I pulled the instrument from my bag and sat down cross-legged on the bed to play. Despite her discomfort, a small smile formed on

Csilla's face. A few moments later, it was over. The quilt fell to the floor as her body reformed.

She cooed softly, just loud enough for me to hear, and I stopped. "Are you okay?"

She bobbed her head.

"You should get some sleep." I laid out the bedrolls, one on top of the other, in front of the fireplace. She settled down on them.

I stripped off my shirt and laid down on the bed, on top of the covers. Tonight had been too close to discovery. We couldn't take any more risks like this. If Csilla's estimation was right, we were only two, maybe three days from the sorcerer. We could push our pace during the day and travel into the night. She wouldn't leave me behind; I knew that now.

And once this was over... I didn't let myself think that far ahead. Didn't think about what Csilla might want to do with her newfound freedom. Didn't think about why I might care what she did after my people were safe. We had enough worries for the time being.

My thoughts drifted to the previous day, to our tumble in the water. I'd felt her skin flushed beneath mine, warm despite the cold water. She'd wanted me, and I wanted her, too. I'd seen her naked body on more than one occasion, kissed her, held her up against me, but it wasn't enough. I needed to possess her.

Why did I do this to myself? I groaned as the image of us tangled up together flashed behind my eyes. Soon, I promised myself.

Csilla sat up, cocking her head in silent question.

"Nothing," I whispered. "Go to sleep."

The coal-black eyes that regarded me seemed to hold a twinkle of doubt, but she tucked her head back under her wing. I leaned back against the pillows and closed my eyes. The images continued to fill my imagination, sending blood straight to my cock. I squeezed my eyes tighter, wishing for release, for distraction, anything. Nothing helped, so I rolled over, settling in for a restless night listening to Csilla's flames crackle.

IZSÁK

CSILLA

It was more than an hour past dawn when we finally got on the road. It seemed like everyone in the village had come up with a reason to stop by Katalin and Ákos's house. Finally, we'd managed to escape the villagers and their probing questions.

Before we left, Tancred had offered to pay Katalin for her hospitality, but she'd refused, so he left a coin under the pillow on her bed. It was an extravagant sum, probably more money than the entire village earned in a month, but he'd said he could afford it.

"Thank you for last night," I said later that morning, looking up at the sky. It was a bright, sunny day, the clouds no more than wisps above us. "For playing. And for offering to guard the door."

He grunted a wordless reply.

After two hours of walking, his silence was beginning to grate on me. Even when we stopped to refill our water, he didn't say a word. I'd thought we'd moved past this taciturnity, broken down the walls between us, but apparently not.

"Did I do something to upset you?" I asked.

He stood from where he had knelt next to the stream. Turned to me slowly. "Not that I'm aware of. Why?"

I crossed my arms. "You've been sullen and silent all day, and you're ignoring me."

"I apologize if I haven't been paying you the proper amount of attention." There was a dark note in his voice that sent a shiver down my spine. "I've had other things on my mind."

His expression warned me not to ask, but I couldn't help myself. "Such as?"

"Such as all the different ways I want to make your sorcerer pay for what he's done to you. All the ways I'm going to dismember him slowly and make him feel every bit of the pain he's given you. And I was thinking about what I want to do after that, once you're finally free of his curse."

I swallowed. "Oh?"

"Once you're free, Csilla, I want to take you outside and fuck you beneath the stars." He licked his lips, and my breathing went ragged. "Do you want to know why I haven't spoken all day?"

I nodded, unable to move.

"I haven't spoken," he said, stepping closer so I had to look up into his eyes, "because I'm afraid that talking will shatter the fragile hold on myself. I want to find your sorcerer and kill him so he's not lingering in the back of our minds when I finally get you beneath me." He leaned in, and his lips brushed my ear. "And right now, you're testing my resolve."

I let out a shaky breath. "I'm s—"

"If you apologize, I swear I will throw you against that boulder and take you here and now."

A familiar voice came from too close behind Tancred. "I strongly suggest you don't. The sorcerer would be most displeased."

Tancred

I drew my sword as I turned, but there was no one there.

"Show yourself."

The air shimmered in front of me, and a man appeared, pulling his hood down. "You stole my master's firebird. He'd like her back."

Izsák, the servant the sorcerer's note had mentioned. I didn't look away from him as I shifted so Csilla was behind me. I could feel her body trembling. She wasn't afraid of this brute, was she? He was broad-shouldered and short, and a dark beard framed his face. In his right hand he held a long peasant flail. Nothing more than a hired bully. I wouldn't let him touch her.

"Who are you?" I asked, stalling for time.

"Nagy Izsák, second-in-command to the supreme sorcerer Kálmán the Immortal."

Immortal. My body went cold.

"I've come to fetch his firebird for him." He craned his neck, trying to see over my shoulder. I stepped toward him with the promise of death in my eyes. "He's promised me a grand reward for her return."

Csilla put a hand on my arm. Her voice was steady, though I could sense her fear. "Stay out of this, Izsák. This is bigger than you."

"No one asked you, firebird."

"I'd be happy to give the lady over to your care," I said. Csilla sucked in a breath. "But I don't believe she wishes to go." I dared a glance down at her, and my chest tightened at her pallid face.

"Don't make me," she whispered.

Never, I wanted to say. But I couldn't make her that promise. I didn't know what the future would hold. Not if we were facing an immortal sorcerer.

Later. We could worry about the sorcerer later, after I'd dealt with his lackey.

He snorted derisively. "I'll give you one chance to walk away. Leave her with me, and we'll pretend none of this happened."

I knew better than to believe him. I saw the way he gripped his flail with both hands, sizing me up. Before he could attack, I lunged at him.

He was slow and clumsy, but he managed to get the flail up in time to block my blow. The sword bit into the wood and stuck there. I yanked it free and lunged again. He swung his weapon in a wide circle.

I blocked the shaft on his next blow, but the head swung into my arm, leaving a bruise I was sure would last for weeks. I shook it off.

He pressed his advantage. Backing me toward Csilla, he struck again. The heavy wood cracked against my sword incessantly, the force of each blow enough to shaky my bones. He was stockier than me, stronger, and he had a longer reach even without the long flail. I was at a vast disadvantage. And unlike him, I had someone to defend. I had to keep him away from Csilla. He wouldn't care if an errant blow injured her.

Slowly, I maneuvered him away from Csilla, off the path and closer to the uneven ground next to the stream. The change in footing didn't leave him off balance as I'd hoped. He swung the flail at my head. It hit my temple, and the world went dark.

When I came to a few moments later, I was lying on the ground. My sword was gone, and Izsák had backed Csilla against the boulder.

"—doesn't matter what condition you're in, as long as I return you," he was saying. With one hand, he held the shaft of his flail against her neck, and he dragged a knife along her arm with the other. "Maybe I'll take the skin from your pretty little arms and leave it here by your lover's body before I drag you back to Kálmán. That should teach you not to fight me."

Fury roared through my throbbing head at Csilla's wordless whimper. I grabbed for a weapon, and my hand wrapped around an arrow that had fallen from my quiver.

I forced myself to my feet as he sliced into her skin. Swaying, I staggered toward him, spurred onward by Csilla's cries. I grabbed his head and drove the arrow through the side of his neck.

THE SORCERER

CSILLA

Izsák dropped to the ground, clutching the arrow in his neck as blood poured from the wound. Tancred stood over him, his hand stained red. I leaned against the boulder, nauseous and trembling.

"Are you hurt?" Tancred grabbed my arm, rolling up the sleeve. I hissed as the movement sent a stinging sensation through the fresh cut.

"I'm fine."

He released me, and a moment later I felt cold water pouring over my arm.

"I'm fine," I said again, but Tancred ignored my protests. He tore a piece off the bottom of his shirt and wrapped it around my arm. "You're bleeding, too."

He tied off the fabric and released me. His eyes searched my face, his brow knit together in frustration. "Why didn't you tell me he was immortal?"

"I didn't know." I should have realized, though. Why else would he look fifty years younger than he was? How else could he survive cyanide poisoning?

"*Fuck!*" Tancred turned and kicked a stone, then stared off into the distance, rubbing his fingers together. He didn't seem to see me.

After a moment, his eyes refocused. "No," he said, half to himself. "No, this doesn't change anything. It's just a momentary setback. We'll figure it out." He looked around. "Did you see where my sword landed?"

I pointed at the water next to where he'd fallen. He knelt next to the stream and reached in, fishing around until he found the sword, which he dried on his clothes.

I dropped to my knees next to him. "I thought he'd killed you," My hands shook as I took a handkerchief from my bag and wet it in the water. "When that flail cracked into your head and I saw you fall—"

"He didn't," he said. "He didn't kill me, and he didn't take you. He can't hurt you anymore."

I let out a shaky breath, then nodded. As I started dabbing the blood from Tancred's head, I asked, "What do we do now?"

"Are you sure the sorcerer is immortal? That wasn't just some lie made up to distract us?"

"I wish it was, but it explains everything. His age, why I wasn't able to kill him. I should have seen it."

"How did he do it?" He tapped his leg, the cogs in his mind whirring. "A potion, a spell, some sort of a charm? He has to have a weakness."

Did he? Not one that I'd ever seen. "Michal would know. She's been with him longer than me. Maybe she saw or heard something."

"Will she help us?"

I shrugged. "She won't stop us. I don't know if she'll help." She wouldn't do anything that risked her sons. I couldn't ask her to.

He was silent for a moment, thinking. Then he said, "Help me move the body out of sight."

The nausea that had started to fade came back in full force. "What?"

Tancred stood and offered me a hand. "We can't just leave him here in the middle of the road, and we don't have time to bury him. Help me push him out of the way." He bent down to grab the legs.

Izsák wasn't moving anymore. The gurgling of the blood leaving his neck had stopped, I took a step toward him, then doubled over, gagging.

"Nevermind!" He waved me off. "Just turn around. I'll do it myself."

I nodded shakily and turned away, squeezing my eyes shut. I heard shifting sounds and grunting as Tancred moved the body. My stomach turned, but I breathed deep. In through my nose, out through my mouth. Again. Again.

"It's done."

I turned around to see him washing his hands in the stream. The puddle of blood had been mostly covered with dirt, leaving a reddish-brown patch of mud. Tancred dried his hands on his shirt and stood. He slung his bag back over his shoulder, grim determination set on his face.

"You're not going to be sick, are you?"

I shook my head.

"Then let's go," he said. "The sooner we end this, the better."

I wiped my sweating hands on my dress and followed him, a tight knot of fear lodged in my chest.

Tancred

We traveled all day and, once Csilla's transformation was complete, all night as well. She stayed low, hovering over the treetops and flying at a pace I could follow. In the darkness, I watched the curling flames of her body dance in the wind as she led me toward the sorcerer. Toward our salvation or—more likely—our doom.

At dawn, we stopped for a brief rest. We lay curled up together in one bedroll, out of sight of the path in a shady alcove of trees. I held her body tight against mine, letting the soft sound of her breathing lull me to sleep. When we woke a few short hours later, I took her hand and pulled her back onto the road, and we resumed our fevered pace.

It was late afternoon before Csilla pointed ahead. "There it is."

A crenelated stone tower jutted out from the side of a mountain. It was smaller than I'd expected, hardly worthy of a sorcerer who could turn beautiful women into birds made of fire, but if his intention was to remain inconspicuous, he'd achieved it. As long as he didn't give the nearby villagers—I could see a small village not far from the base of the tower—cause to complain, the king would take no notice of him.

I scanned the tower. Plenty of windows, but only one door. Only one way out, unless he could turn himself into a bird and fly away. Which, I reminded myself, he could.

Not that he would. No, I didn't expect the sorcerer to try to flee. Why should he? He was immortal, powerful. He wielded magic, and mine was long gone. There was no reason for him to fear me, even if we managed to figure out his weakness.

I wished once again that I still had my magic. Before we left Laute, I would have been an equal to any sorcerer. I could have played a death tune that stopped his heart or caused his lungs to shrink inside his chest. Now I was reliant on my wits and my strength.

He kept to a strict routine, Csilla had told me. A late supper, followed by a bath in the hot springs beneath the tower. An hour of work by candlelight at the desk in his room. Once he doused the candle, it could take another hour for him to fall asleep.

I could imagine why she knew how long it would take him to fall asleep. How many nights had she been trapped there in his room, a living flame, watching and waiting for him to finally close his eyes? His presence, his very existence was her prison, more than any tower or cage he could lock her in.

Tonight, I would free her.

Or I would die trying.

MICHAL

CSILLA

Michal's family lived on the outskirts of the village, nearest to the tower. As we hurried toward the house, I prayed we weren't spotted. That Kálmán wasn't looking out his window, or his spies in the village weren't watching us approach. Any number of people would be willing to turn me in for a chance to curry favor with the sorcerer.

Despite the summer heat, I'd wrapped a blanket around my head like a scarf to hide my face. I kept it pulled tight as we reached Michal's home and I pounded on the door.

After a minute, she opened it, and her eyes went wide as she took me in.

"Baruch HaShem! You're safe." She grabbed me by the shoulders and kissed both my cheeks before holding me to her chest. "Where have you been? I've been worried sick."

"There were some... delays," I said, stepping aside and gesturing for Tancred to approach.

She looked him up and down, then narrowed her eyes at me. "If you're leaving, you know I don't fault you, but you can't be here. He won't let you go. He's already sent Izsák after you."

My stomach flipped at the reminder, but I pushed the image of Izsák's lifeless body out of my head. "Can we come in, auntie? There's a lot to explain and not a lot of time." Already the sun was crawling toward the horizon.

"Yes, yes, come in. Quickly." She stepped back, scanning the street behind us.

I pressed a kiss to the scroll on the doorpost as I crossed the threshold. Tancred followed me in, removing his hat.

Michal's eyes caught on the silver horns atop his head, shining dully in the afternoon light.

"It's a long story," I said, taking Tancred's hand. "But he's with me. This is Lord Tancred, formerly of Laute."

Her shrewd eyes didn't miss the proximity between us, and I could almost hear her unspoken question. *With you, or* with *you?* I didn't have an answer for her, though. If we survived the night, what came next? He'd promised to fuck me beneath the stars, but was that all there was between us, or would he be willing to explore the feelings we seemed to share?

I gave Michal a subtle shake of my head, and she sniffed in disapproval.

"Well. Come sit down. Have you eaten?"

My stomach was too knotted to eat, but she would see through a lie. "No." I led Tancred to the table, where Shabbat dinner had already been cleared away. "Where is everyone?"

Michal disappeared into the kitchen and returned a moment later with bread, plum jam, and broiled fish. "Áron and Elza went to visit her sister this evening. The boys went with them."

I'd hoped to see the boys, at least, before we went to the tower. Not to say goodbye—I wouldn't resign myself to that. But I'd watched them grow up. No matter how tonight went, things would be different by morning. I wanted to hug them one more time before everything changed.

Michal's eyes met mine and softened. "They should be back before sunset," she said. "Now. Tell me everything."

I launched into the story, relating the details as best as I could. Tancred filled in what I couldn't. As we spoke, I nibbled at the food, anxiously watching the sun sink lower out the window.

"Did you know?" I asked her finally. "That he was immortal."

"There were rumors, even before I started working for him. I assumed they were true. As long as I've known him, he hasn't aged, gotten ill, or been injured."

"Do you know how he did it?" Tancred asked, leaning forward.

She frowned at him. "I don't know where you got the idea that the sorcerer keeps me in his confidence, but no. He hasn't told me how he made himself immortal. Or how to kill him."

I reached across the table and took her hand. "Please, auntie. Maybe there's something you saw or heard that could help us."

"Is it really so bad?" She squeezed my fingers. "Is the risk worth what you'll have to go through if he wins?"

My eyes burned. "I can't. I can't do it anymore, Michal. I'd rather die than go on like this." The past two weeks had taught me what freedom tasted like, and I couldn't go back to my cage.

She sighed. "My mother was young when Kálmán first came here, but she remembered it. She told me about him. He was different then, she said. Powerful, but not like he was now. He was reckless, as likely to use physical violence as magic to get his way. He fought with the local boys. My grandmother was the one he came to when he needed to be patched up. Then one day, he just stopped coming."

"He stopped fighting?" I asked.

"He kept fighting. He stopped getting injured. Stopped aging, too." She pursed her lips, looking between me and Tancred. "If I had to guess, I'd say he managed to create a charm, something he keeps on his person at all times. If you could find the item and destroy it, he'd be mortal again."

Mortal, but still powerful. Still dangerous.

I thought back on all the years I'd spent with Kálmán. Was there any item he always had with him? A totem he kept in his pocket? A piece of clothing or jewelry he always wore?

"The amulet," I breathed. He'd worn it as long as I'd known him. Black, with bronze images painted on it. A talisman, I'd assumed. He rarely took it off, and even when he bathed, it never left his sight. I'd never asked about it. "The one he wears around his neck. Has he always had that?"

She screwed up her face, thinking. "I don't remember. Maybe?"

"That could be it. The source of his immortality." The tiny spark of hope bloomed into an ember in my chest. "He wears it everywhere. If we smash it, that should leave him vulnerable."

"Unless you're wrong," Michal said. "You're going to get yourselves killed."

"I appreciate your optimism, auntie." She was right, of course, but I masked my fears with my dry tone. We had to do this.

The sound of voices heralded the arrival of the boys, and a moment later, they tumbled through the door, dripping with sweat and laughing. They'd obviously raced home.

"Auntie Csilla!" Ádám came running over and threw his arms around my neck. "Where have you been?"

I hugged him back, breathing in the smell of summertime on his skin. "My errand took longer than I expected."

Álmos eyed Tancred warily. "Who's that?"

"Don't be rude, boys," Michal said. "This is Lord Tancred, a friend of Csilla. Lord Tancred, my sons, Ádám and Álmos."

The boys bowed clumsily, and I smiled fondly at them. They were both getting too tall for their own bodies, their limbs long and gangly. Álmos still considered Tancred, his gaze suspicious.

"It's getting late," Michal said. "Go wash up before prayers. Auntie Csilla needs to head back to the tower soon."

I pulled both boys to me and pressed a kiss to each of their heads. I would see them again, I vowed to myself. No matter what happened tonight, I would see all of them tomorrow. "Goodnight, boys."

"Night, auntie!" Álmos ran off without a backward glance, but Ádám gave me a strange look, as though he realized this wasn't a normal goodbye.

"I'll see you tomorrow," I promised, patting his arm.

His frown deepened. He had his mother's eyes, shrewd and piercing. They caught everything. He looked from Tancred to his mother and back to me.

"Ádám," Michal said, a warning note in her voice.

"See you tomorrow, auntie." The words carried a weight, more of an order than a casual comment. With a final glance back, he followed his brother out of the room.

"I'll say a prayer for you." Michal stood. "Be careful, Csilla."

I wrapped her in a hug, letting the touch say what words couldn't. "Thank you. And—" I couldn't finish the request.

She understood me anyway. "You know I will."

Tancred

Outside, the sky was beginning to dim. Csilla kept her head covered as we headed for a copse of trees within sight of the tower, thick enough to hide her transformation, but with a view of the sorcerer's window.

"Michal doesn't like me," I said as we settled in for the next few hours.

She chuckled. "She's protective. You're a stranger."

I could understand that. I didn't trust strangers easily either. "What happened to her husband?" She'd mentioned a brother and his wife, but no husband.

"He died in a hunting accident. I never met him. She started working for Kálmán after he died, just before I arrived." Her expression was drawn. From fear that she wouldn't see her friends again? Or was it the transformation or the impending fight that tightened her face?

"This will be your last night as the firebird," I said.

She sighed, staring up at the clear sky. "God willing."

"You don't seem pleased." She seemed almost wistful, in fact. "I thought you hated being the firebird."

"It's more complicated than that," she said. "The transformation is painful, but there's a freedom in being able to fly. With my wings, I can imagine, if only for a while, that I'm my own master." She shook her head, picking a strand of grass and twisting it around her fingers. "It's stupid, I know."

"It's not." I could understand her need for freedom after everything she'd been through. I longed for freedom, too, in a way. To be free from my responsibilities. To have power without duty, like I had before my father died. "You deserve to be free. But after tonight, you won't need your wings for that."

She looked up at me through her lashes, her olive skin flushing before she glanced away.

"Csilla, if I don't make it tonight..."

He head shot up, brows knitting together. "Why would you say that? You don't think we can do this?"

"We can. We will." No matter what it took, I would end this sorcerer. For Csilla and for my people. "But if one of us doesn't make it—if *I* don't make it, I want you to take the news back to my king and queen." I had no intention of becoming a martyr, but we were facing an immortal sorcerer. The odds were against us. Someone had to survive, but if only one of us could, I'd make sure it was her.

"We'll go back together," she said.

"But if—"

"Together," she insisted, and I knew that arguing would do me no good. I had to trust that if I died, she'd make sure my people weren't killed for my failure.

She let out a quiet groan as her transformation neared.

"It's almost over," I reminded her. I tried to take her hand, but she yanked it back.

"I don't want to hurt you."

"You won't." I brushed a hair out of her face. She was so strong. "One more night," I said, leaning in to kiss her.

Her mouth was hot, skin feverish against mine. I slid my hands along her waist, wishing I could feel her naked body.

Soon, I reminded myself. One more night of this. One way or another, I'd see her sorcerer dead. And if we both survived the night, I'd taste every inch of her glorious body, with the stars and the moon looking down as witness.

When I pulled back, she tilted her head at me in question. I kissed her again, softer this time. "One more night," I said again.

A convulsion wracked her body, and she pushed me off, scrambling back. "Get away!"

I did as she ordered, my chest tightening in sympathy as she squeezed her eyes shut with the pain.

She'd forgotten to take off her dress, and when her transformation was complete, she was trapped inside the fabric. She gave a low cry of distress, struggling beneath the cloth. I pulled it off. The fabric was hot, though it didn't ignite, and I burned two of my fingers as I freed her. I cast the dress aside and stuck my burned fingers in my mouth.

Csilla looked at me and cocked her head, ember eyes holding a question she couldn't voice.

"I'm fine," I said, dropping my hand to my side. I took a seat on the grass and patted the ground next to me. "Get some rest if you can. I'll wake you when it's time."

She bobbed her head, settling herself down a few feet from me. The air had begun to cool in the darkness, but the heat of her body warmed me as she tucked her head beneath her wing.

I set my gaze on the light coming from the sorcerer's tower. A few more hours, and this would all be over. One way or another.

THE TOWER

Csilla

I hadn't expected to sleep, but I jolted awake to Tancred's voice.

"It's time."

He was little more than a shadow on the edge of my vision. I stood and stretched, looking toward him.

"Are you ready?" he asked.

Ready to kill the man who'd taken me prisoner thirteen years ago? To lose my wings and gain the freedom I'd longed for? Not even a little bit, but this was our one chance.

Tancred already had the rope harness fitted around his legs, the ends of the rope trailing on the ground behind him. I took them in my talons and flew up to a branch just above his head.

"All right." He checked the tightness of the knots again. "Let's go."

I lifted into the air, straining as the rope reached its full length. Then we were up, the wind flickering through my flames. I ascended above the trees, then approached the tower. We circled the mountain once, twice. All was dark and quiet. No signs of life.

My heart pounded out a quick, steady rhythm as I landed on the turret above Kálmán's window, bringing Tancred even with the opening. The day had been warm, and as was the sorcerer's custom, he'd left the window open. Unguarded. I breathed out a wordless prayer of thanks and asked HaShem to grant us victory. Down below the village, I knew Michal was praying for the same.

The rope in my talons slackened as Tancred took hold of the stones and heaved himself up onto the ledge. I craned my neck just in time to see him disappear into the tower.

Tancred

Shadows and silence filled the room. Only the sorcerer's breathing, deep and even, broke the stillness.

Sword in one hand and dagger in the other, I slipped through the window, and my shoulders relaxed a fraction of an inch. He was asleep. Vulnerable. Arrogant, to think no one would come through his open window. We might succeed after all.

Leaning out the window, I waved up at Csilla, who swooped down and landed on the sill. Her light illuminated the enormous room, revealing rich furnishings. A large, sturdy table stretched along one wall, covered with potions and ancient, dusty spellbooks. Gold shavings peppered one of the books, the remains of King Rudolf's missing golden apple. Opposite the table was a giant canopy bed, curtains of red velvet hanging open to reveal the sorcerer.

My heart dropped into my stomach. The sorcerer was no feeble academic like I'd pictured. He lay naked on the bed, a blanket draped across his legs. He was well-formed, with glistening blond hair, a strong brow, and firm muscles. An egg-shaped pendant, onyx in color, dangled from his neck on a leather cord.

I crept closer, peering at the pendant. Could this truly be the source of his immortality? It was large, nearly the size of my palm, but simple. On its face were four bronze images: a rabbit, a duck, an island, and a needle.

I looked at Csilla, her eyes dark among the yellow and orange fire. She stared at the sorcerer one long moment before bobbing her head. She was ready.

Hardly daring to breathe, I leaned over him.

The pendant was feather-light as I gingerly used the tip of my dagger to lift it from his chest.

He bolted upright, catching my wrist in an iron grip.

Csilla let out a hawk-like shriek, wings beating a hot gust of wind through the room. I thrust my sword into the sorcerer's stomach, but it slid to the side as though skating off stone.

"Fool," he hissed, rising to his feet. He bent my arm, forcing me to my knees before him. "You thought I would leave myself unguarded? I knew the moment you reached my window."

I should have expected it. Stupid, really, to assume he would have no spells on the window. He twisted my arm until it screamed with pain, but I bit back any protest, clenching my jaw.

He looked at me with disdain. "So you are the reason my firebird was delayed." Csilla stood on the windowsill, head bobbing and wings fluttering back and forth. I wanted to tell her to fly away, but what good would it do? He'd find her again.

His next words were directed at her. "I suppose you were bound to attempt a real escape sooner or later. A pity it didn't work. It will be that much worse for you now."

Her flames dimmed, and she ducked her head, trembling. She was terrified, and with good reason. He had everything in his favor—speed, strength, magic. Once I was dead, nothing was stopping him from doing whatever he wished with her.

But I wasn't dead yet.

He'd left my other hand, the hand holding the sword, free. Why not? It couldn't harm him.

I brought it up point-first and drove it between his legs. It skidded off his skin again, but the action had the desired effect. He turned his attention back to me.

"Haven't you realized?" He leaned closer, bringing his face even with mine. "I can't be killed."

"Not yet." I dropped my sword to the ground and caught the dagger from my immobilized hand. In one quick move, I sliced the leather cord around his neck.

The onyx pendant fell to the ground, and before the sorcerer could react, I smashed it beneath my knee.

He released me, scrambling to pick up the pieces, but it was too late. I rose to my feet, dagger outstretched, as he rounded on me. Rage twisted his face.

He reached out his hand in a claw-like motion, speaking a guttural series of words in a language I didn't know. I kicked his knee, knocking him off his feet, and his words disappeared in a huff of breath as his head hit the floor.

His lip had split in the fall. He stood, wiping away the blood. We were right; the source of his immortality, his invulnerability, had been in the pendant. He was mortal now.

I swiped at his neck, but he jumped back and continued the incantation he'd started. A gleaming black rope shot from its hands, aiming for my neck. I stepped to the side, and it thwacked harmlessly into the wall. Csilla lifted off from the windowsill and circled around us, her wings sending out unbearably hot air.

The dagger wasn't enough to kill him, not when he could attack without contact. I needed the longer reach of my sword, but it was still on the floor near the bed.

I slashed his wrist. The strike glanced off, drawing a superficial amount of blood, but it was enough of a distraction. He snarled and moved closer. I stepped sideways, shepherding him away from my sword. He shot rope after rope at me. Each one I ducked put me closer to my goal.

Finally, I was inches away. All I needed was a lapse in his concentration, just enough that I could reach down to grab it.

Csilla's next frantic pass around the room brought her close enough to singe his hair, and he jerked away from the heat. This was my chance.

My fingers wrapped around the hilt, but as I straightened, the sorcerer tossed the contents of a jar into my face. A dry, gritty powder filled my eyes. I couldn't see, could only strike out wildly with my sword as he began speaking.

My throat closed up, and the air in my lungs vanished.

Both my weapons fell to the floor. I clawed at my neck, tearing the skin in a desperate attempt to breathe. Air. I needed air. Stars danced in the corner of my vision.

Hands grabbed the front of my shirt, lifting me up. The sorcerer laughed, a deep booming sound that seemed to come through a tunnel. "It will take more than that to kill me."

Pained shrieks and smoke filled the room, thickening the trickle of breath I could suck in through my suffocating throat. Was he hurting Csilla? I had to stop him. Had to save my people.

He dropped me. I landed on my knees, then forward. My face smashed into the floor.

I had to save her.

This couldn't be the end.

Then the vise around my throat was gone. I lay still, taking deep, gasping breaths. Somewhere above me, the sorcerer was shouting, his words incomprehensible amidst the sound of crackling flame and rushing wind.

Csilla.

I pushed to my knees, forced my eyes open. Her flames were white and blue, filling the room. Smoke and screams poured from her as she clawed at the sorcerer's face. His naked chest was burned raw, skin blackened in patches. Flakes of ash floated around us, along with the rancid smell of overcooked meat.

He swatted at her with his arms, shooting black sparks from his palms, but everywhere her talons touched, the skin melted away. Blisters covered his body, his perfect hair singed off. He retreated, stepped back, back, back, still blindly aiming bursts of magic at her. She had him against the windowsill.

She let out a final cry, lunging for his neck, and he flinched away.

His body hit the ground below the tower with a sickening thud.

In the next moment, Csilla stood staring out the window, human once more, her naked body trembling in the moonlight.

"Are—" The word came out garbled, and I coughed.

She whirled around. "Tancred!" Running across the room, she sank to her knees at my side. "Are you hurt?"

"I'll live." I groaned as I sat up, pressing a hand to my neck. It came away bloody; I'd gouged pieces of skin out with my nails.

"You're bleeding!" She scrambled to her feet, clumsy in her haste, and began digging through the contents of the sorcerer's table, up-ending potions and sending books crashing to the ground.

"I'm fine," I said, but I didn't resist when she returned a moment later with a clean cloth and a jar of ointment.

Her hands shook as she tried to open the jar, so I took it and set it aside. I wrapped her hands in mine.

"It's over," I whispered. "He's gone." Even if he'd been able to survive the massive burns Csilla had inflicted on his body, the fall was too high. He was dead.

She nodded, eyes fixed blindly on our linked hands. Tears trickled down her face.

"He can't hurt you anymore."

She took a shaky breath. "He's gone," she repeated. With steadier hands, she picked up the jar of ointment and opened it. As she tended to my wounds, heat flared beneath her touch. I let out a hiss of breath at the sting, but by the time she set the cloth back down, the pain was gone.

I stood, reaching out a hand.

She blinked up at me. In the dim moonlight streaming through the window, I could see her still-naked body shiver, though from cold, stress, or exhaustion, I didn't know.

"You need sleep," I said. We'd both pushed hard the past few days. "Show me your room."

She nodded mutely and allowed me to pull her to her feet.

I kept a tight grip on Csilla's hand as we walked through the dark halls of the tower. Keening cries, almost human, came from behind one door; the next emitted an eerie green light. What monstrosities waited in those rooms? I didn't want to find out.

She led me down a narrow staircase into another long hallway. It was cooler here, like this part of the tower had been carved deep into the heart of the mountain. Polished white sculptures and rich tapestries lined the walls, illuminated by a faint glowing fungus that spread along the ceiling like a web. It made my skin crawl, but Csilla didn't seem to notice any of it.

At the end of this hall, a door stood open, revealing a room crammed full of luxuries. A desk held rich jewelry and alabaster jars of beauty treatments. The wardrobe hung open, showing richly colored silk garments. A small bed was tucked into one corner, and opposite it was a golden cage.

Her room. Her cage, where he'd kept her locked up. It was even smaller than I'd imagined, better suited to an exotic parrot or monkey than a human woman. Anger spread through my veins like poisonous sludge. The sorcerer had died too quickly. Justice would have been locking him in the cage and slowly roasting him alive.

Csilla ignored it all. She went straight to the bed and curled up into a ball, not bothering with the blankets. In a moment, she was asleep, her breathing deep. Moonlight shone on her face, peaceful in sleep.

Every bone in my body ached, but I still wanted her. She was a goddess in human form, fire made flesh. Any man would desire her. And for the next few days, at least, she was mine.

I'd promised myself not to get involved with anyone. I had nothing to offer a woman, nothing to offer *her*. But seeing her lying there, knowing she was safe and we were together, some traitorous part of me wished for more. Wanted desperately to beg her to stay with me after we returned to the capital and convinced Rudolf to free my people.

She deserved better than that. I couldn't free her from her captivity and then ask her to willingly bind herself to me. It would have to be enough that we were together for now and that soon, the Pipers would be free.

I pulled the blanket over her motionless body and pressed a kiss to her forehead. My body screamed for me to lie down and rest as well, but there were things I needed to do first.

INTENTIONS

TANCRED

The sorcerer's body lay crumpled at the base of the tower, maimed by fire and the fall. With the proximity to the mountain, the ground here would be too rocky to bury him. I shook out a sheet I'd taken from his bedroom and wrapped him up in it. We wouldn't be here for long; as long as he remained undiscovered until we left, I could leave the body to rot in one of his rooms.

He was heavy in death. I lugged the body inside and deposited it on a long wooden table in the dining room.

"It's done, then?"

The sharp-eyed woman, Michal, stood in the doorway, examining the scene.

"He's dead," I confirmed. I slipped past her into the kitchen and looked around for a meat cleaver.

She seemed to know what I needed. She pulled one from a bottom shelf and passed it to me handle-first. "And Csilla?"

"Healthy, human, and asleep."

"Baruch HaShem," she murmured, looking upward. "Thank you for protecting her, Lord Tancred."

"I didn't." She'd protected me, not the other way around. "I need to deal with the body. You may want to step outside."

She snorted. "I've butchered enough animals in my life not to be squeamish. Do what you need to."

I uncovered the body, and she let out a low whistle at the sight of the burns mutilating his skin. "Csilla did this?"

"Yes." Clenching my jaw, I pulled back the cleaver and brought it down onto the sorcerer's neck. It gave me a sick sense of satisfaction watching the muscles and tendons split beneath my blade. I hadn't killed him, but at least by desecrating his corpse, I could prevent him from finding peace in death. With just two blows, I'd severed the head from his body. Picking it up by his once-perfect hair, I looked into his lifeless eyes. Disgusting.

"I'll bring you something to hold it in," Michal said. She stepped into the kitchen, returning with a deep wooden bowl and a large jar. She set the bowl down and held up the jar. "Honey will help the head keep until you get it back to the king."

"Thanks." I dropped the head into the bowl, then emptied the honey on top of it.

"How does she feel, now that it's over?"

I covered the body with the sheet again, hiding the puddle of blood on the table. "We haven't spoken about it. She fell asleep." Despite the fact that this monster had tormented her for thirteen years, I could imagine Csilla had mixed feelings about being the one to kill him. She was far from fragile, but she'd never had to kill a man.

"Have you spoken about what happens next?"

I looked sideways at the woman. "What do you mean?" We'd told her what happened next; we would take the head back to Rudolf and free my people from the threat of extermination that they faced.

She crossed her arms. "You know full well what I mean. Once your people are safe, what are your intentions? Are you going to run off and leave her?"

"You make it sound as though I have an obligation." Like I was responsible for Csilla now that her master was dead. How was that any better than the captivity she'd already suffered?

"Don't be dense." She raised her chin at me. "Any fool could see there's something between you two. Csilla's family, and she doesn't have anyone else. Are you going to treat her right?"

I walked out into the kitchen, the implications of her question rattling around in my head. Did Csilla want me? More than the physical attraction that was obvious. We had a shared attraction, but was there something deeper? Something like the love my parents had shared?

The thought was ridiculous. I'd only seen a love like that twice, first between my parents and then between the king and queen. How arrogant was I to assume I could find something so rare?

Michal followed me as I found a pitcher of water and a bar of soap to wash my hands. "Maybe you don't know what you want from each other yet," she said, "but I have to say my part. She's been through hell since Kálmán took her. Don't hurt her."

"I have no intention of hurting her." The best way to keep from hurting her would be to leave her alone entirely, but I couldn't do that. Not yet, at least.

"Good." Michal turned to the door. "I'll be back in the morning to check on her. Keep her safe tonight."

I nodded, unsure what to make of this woman. She didn't seem to disapprove of me, but she didn't seem to approve of me, either. I had the distinct impression that if I harmed her loved ones, she could be more dangerous than any sorcerer or king.

Once I was alone, adrenaline still lingered in my veins. I kept my dagger close at hand as I climbed the stairs back up to the sorcerer's bedroom. Nothing approached me, but the colors and sounds coming from the rooms I passed made the hairs on the back of my neck stand up.

The room smelled like roasted meat and burnt hair. Potions and powders had spilled all over the worktable, and the sorcerer's amulet still lay in broken pieces on the floor. I went to the table and gathered the remains of the golden apple into a small empty vial. Our evidence against him would be airtight; even Rudolf wouldn't be able to deny it.

Spellbooks covered every inch of the table that wasn't already filled with jars and vials. I picked up one and flipped through it. The contents made little sense to me, but they wouldn't have to. Something in one of these books could be the key to restoring our magic. Even if I couldn't understand it, my king and queen would find someone who could.

As I piled the books together, I knocked a bag loose. It fell to the ground with the clanking of coins.

Stooping down to pick it up, I noticed the seal, now broken. It was gold, and the mark on it was illegible, but I thought it looked somewhat like a letter. B, maybe, or R.

Some instinct urged me to take it back with me, so I added it to the top of the stack of spellbooks. If nothing else, King Loic would find some use for the money.

I didn't recognize any of the various powders and potions on the table, so I left those alone. We'd have to leave soon, and the more things we had to carry, the slower our progress would be.

Our departure could wait a little while longer, though. I'd made a promise to both myself and to Csilla, and another day's delay wouldn't make a difference to my people's fate.

NEW BEGINNINGS

CSILLA

I woke in darkness.

At first, I thought I was still asleep. The only time I got to experience complete darkness was in my dreams. It took a moment of blinking for me to notice the glow of the fungus along the hall ceiling outside my room before the events of earlier that night came rushing back to me.

I'd killed Kálmán.

The scene flashed through my mind. Tancred struggling on the floor, clawing at his neck. Kálmán standing over him. Rage filling me, growing hotter and hotter. Leaping at the sorcerer with outstretched talons. His screams as I burned him. The thump of his body on the grass below the tower.

My stomach turned over, and I scrambled out of bed, toward the open window. I needed air.

The night was cool against my sweaty skin. I drank it in greedily, letting it soothe my roiling gut. Where was Tancred? I couldn't have been asleep for more than a couple hours. Had he already left to go back to his king? Left me here? Tears burned in the back of my throat at the thought.

No, he hadn't done that to me. He wouldn't. I leaned against the windowsill, pressing my head to the cool stone. Maybe he'd gone to find another bed to sleep in, or went down to the kitchen to find something to eat. He wouldn't leave me alone in this tower.

Unless he decided he didn't need me.

I stared at the ground far below me. I couldn't see Kálmán's body, but I knew it was down there somewhere. Mutilated by my claws and flames. I could smell the smoke, feel the skin sloughing off beneath my touch. I wrapped my arms around me, and my shoulders shook with the force of suppressing my tears.

"What's wrong?"

I spun around at the sound of Tancred's voice. I could hardly see him in the darkness, but I breathed a sigh of relief at his silhouette, dark against the gray-white glow from the hall. "You're still here."

"Of course I am." He sounded offended by the implication. "I had some things to deal with. I thought you'd still be asleep."

Now that I was awake, I knew I wouldn't be able to fall asleep again. "I can't. Not with—not with those images in my mind."

"Then allow me to replace them." He took my hand, sending a spark up my arm. "Come with me."

I was suddenly hyper-aware of my nudity. Tancred was bare-chested, but he still wore the pants he'd been wearing before I fell asleep. His eyes seemed to roam over my body, though I couldn't imagine he could see me in the darkness.

I grabbed a silk robe from the footpost of my bed and wrapped it around me. He led me through the halls and upstairs, toward Kálmán's room. I stiffened as we approached it. He was dead. My captor, my tormentor, my master was dead. I'd killed him.

A whimper of breath escaped me, and Tancred looked at me over his shoulder. "Eyes on me," he said. He led me past the sorcerer's room, up to an old wooden door that led out onto a balcony.

His expression was inscrutable, half-obscured by darkness, as he twisted the handle and pushed the door open.

In the middle of the roof, a few pillows and quilts had been laid out, and above us...

Above us were a million stars.

I'd never seen the sky so bright. Even in my memories, it wasn't like this. Had I really forgotten such beauty?

"It's incredible," I breathed, stepping out of the doorway to look around. There were so many colors, blues and purples I'd never noticed before. Above the peak of the mountain, a ribbon of white haze threaded through the stars. My eyes couldn't settle as I tried to look at everything at once.

Tancred wound his arms around me and pulled my back tight against his chest. I leaned into him with a sigh. "Thank you."

"Don't thank me yet." He nipped at my neck, sending a flutter of desire through me. "This was just the beginning." He spun me in his grasp and claimed my mouth. His beard rasped against my skin. I met his energy with a kiss just as fierce. His hand found my backside, bunching up the fabric, and he pushed me backward until I hit the wall of the balcony.

"I'd forgotten there were so many stars," I murmured when he pulled back to look into my eyes.

"Save your breath." He knelt before me, and my breathing hitched. "You'll need it."

I braced myself on the wall as he lifted the hem of my robe to my waist. His horns glinted in the starlight, the silver a stark contrast to his black curls. When I ran my finger along the ribbed curve of one of them, he looked up at me, slitted pupils blown out.

"Hold this here," he said, pressing my robe into my hand. "And don't let go."

I could only whimper in response as he spread my legs and buried his face between them. The first swipe of his tongue had me arching my back. The stars surrounded me. I could see nothing else as he kissed and licked and touched. He pinned me in place, grip bruising as he explored each fold. When he finally reached my clit, he sucked, tearing a cry from my throat.

Without his hands holding me to the earth, I would have floated off into the night sky. His mouth drove me higher, until I begged for mercy with wordless moans. Finally, my whole body erupted in tremors, my vision dimming as I threw my head back and cried out his name.

When my mind returned to my body, he stood and pulled me close. The stars lit up his grin. "Breathtaking." His hand grasped my breast, thumbing my nipple, before making a path down between my legs.

"You're so wet for me," he said, dragging a finger through my center. "Do it again." He plunged one large finger into me, and with his thumb, he traced circles around my clit.

"It's too much." I grabbed his shoulders, the pleasure bordering on painful.

"You can take it." He kissed me, fingers unceasing in their movement. "Just like that. I can feel you tightening. Come for me."

This time was less explosive, but it left my knees weak. I clung to Tancred, who guided me over to the blankets and laid me down. My robe fell open, and he took in the sight.

Even though he'd just had his fingers and mouth between my legs, the sweep of his eyes over my body felt different, almost too intimate. I moved my hands to cover myself, but he pushed them up above my head. "Don't hide yourself from me," he said, his voice husky with desire.

A familiar command, but where the words had come from Kálmán's desire to control me, to keep me as his toy, I could see in Tancred's eyes that he only wanted to see me. That he *did* see me. More than just my body, he saw straight down to my soul, and what he saw there didn't drive him away.

"I'm sorry," I murmured, twining my fingers together.

He narrowed his eyes. "I warned you before about apologizing, didn't I?"

Just two days ago, he'd threatened to throw me down and take me if I apologized. Something I'd wanted him to do for days now.

Longer.

I reached out and cupped the back of his head. Pulling him down so our lips were inches apart, I traced his horns again. "Sorry," I whispered.

He made a sound low in his throat, and before I could blink, he was bare, his erection pressing at my entrance. "I warned you," he murmured, and sheathed himself.

The sudden fullness tore a gasp from my lips. I wrapped my legs around him as he drove me deeper into the blankets. The muscles in his arms and neck rippled as he held himself above me. I ran my fingers along his bristly chin, staring into his eyes, and for once, he didn't look away. My liberator. I tangled my hands into his coarse hair as he pumped in and out of me.

I was already sensitive from my previous climaxes, and when he hit a deep spot inside me, tears squeezed from my eyes as I reached that peak again.

"Csilla," he groaned. "I'm close. Where should I...?"

"In me." I wrapped my legs around his back, holding him inside me. "Please. I need it." I needed him to wash away the memories, to replace Kálmán's poisonous touch with his own healing one.

He nodded, seeming to understand what I was asking. His movements grew urgent. He ducked his head to kiss me, and as our lips met, he reached his own climax.

Tancred

I eased myself off of her, and we laid there together staring up at the stars, both breathing hard. Csilla rolled over and rested her head on my chest, her breath tickling my skin. I inhaled her delicious scent, smokey and sweet and musky. If I'd doubted what this was between us, my doubts were gone now. She was everything I'd never dared to hope for. She'd ruined me with every touch, every sound she'd made beneath me. I could never let her go.

I felt a sudden wetness on my chest, and I looked down at Csilla. Tears streamed down her face, dampening my skin.

"What's wrong?" I asked, alarmed. I sat up and gathered her onto my lap. Had I hurt her? Pushed her too hard? Maybe it hadn't meant the same for her that it had for me, and she was afraid to tell me. "What happened?"

"It—I never—" She couldn't seem to make the words come together, but my fears diminished.

"Never climaxed before?" If that was the case, I'd spend every day of the rest of my life making up for it. She deserved to be worshiped.

She shook her head again, mouth opening and closing without a sound.

"Never more than once?" I could imagine that she had few opportunities for self-pleasure under the sorcerer's captivity, and it was clear that he'd treated her as little more than a toy.

She nodded, still crying.

"Did you want it?" I needed to be sure. I should have asked first, made my intentions more clear. She'd wanted me, but the timing could have been wrong. She'd just been through a devastating ordeal, escaped thirteen years of captivity. It wasn't fair of me to push her like that.

She nodded again, and the tightness in my chest loosened.

"And you're not hurt?"

"No." It seemed to be the most she was capable of saying. She was wrung out, as much from the pleasure as from the stress of the past couple weeks. I hadn't meant to overtax her, but I hadn't realized how intoxicating the feeling over her clenching around me would be. She needed a warm bath and rest to recover her senses.

I lifted her into the air. "I thought I saw a set of baths below the tower. Right?" I asked her. "Just nod or shake your head."

She nodded, slumping against my chest.

A natural-looking cave beneath the tower held heated pools. Steam filled the room. Setting Csilla on the edge of one pool, I peeled off her robe. She stared off into the distance, barely cognizant of my movements.

I stepped into the water, which came up to my waist, and picked her up again. She stirred, wrapping her arms around my neck. Were the pools a natural phenomenon, or some magic of the sorcerer's? I wondered, but she wasn't in a state to sate my curiosity.

"I'm so proud of you," I whispered as I sank down into the water, dousing both of us up to our necks. "You've been so strong."

Bars of beeswax soap, scented with dried flowers, sat next to the pool, and a stone shelf held towels. I used the soap to wash her slowly and thoroughly, murmuring words of encouragement as I did. Whenever I reached a particularly sensitive spot on her body, she let out a long, shuddering breath, but intoxicating as it was, I didn't linger. She needed rest more than pleasure right now.

Her hair was long and soft in my hands. I worked the soap through it, massaging her scalp. When I finished, I gathered her back onto my lap, and her eyes finally focused on my face.

"Thank you." Tears rimmed her eyes, but she didn't seem upset.

"You need sleep," I said, setting her on the edge of the pool once more and wrapping her in a towel. "We have a long journey to make."

Her gaze grew distant again. Was she worried about facing the king? Unsure what would happen when it was all over? I didn't want to admit it, but so was I.

I kissed her, putting everything I couldn't say into the touch. She looped her arms around my neck, clinging to me like I was her lifeline.

I pulled away too soon. "It's late." It had to be two, maybe three in the morning, and I didn't want to linger here long. We'd already taken far longer for this journey than I'd planned. I just hoped my king had managed to forestall Rudolf's aims against the Pipers.

GOLDEN CAGE

TANCRED

I slept with my arms tight around Csilla's waist, and when I woke late the next morning, she was still sound asleep. I slid out of bed, careful not to wake her. We could leave that afternoon, taking the shorter route and traveling overnight. It would take us a day and a half, maybe two days at most. We wouldn't have to worry about being spotted by any unfriendly eyes now. Csilla would remain human after sunset, and there was no sorcerer searching for us.

As I stretched, I looked around the room. It was a study in opulence, filled with the most expensive luxuries money could buy. And in the midst of it all stood the cage, golden and garish. The sight made my blood boil. For too long, the sorcerer had used it against her, threatening her, taming her fire. It was a grim reminder of what she'd faced since coming here.

I grabbed one cold bar and pulled, testing the metal. It gave a little. Not iron, then. Made of pure gold, or perhaps gilded silver.

Quietly, I picked up the cage and carried it out the door. I hadn't been able to free Csilla—she'd freed herself—but I could still gift her the destruction of her cage.

I found a hammer in the sorcerer's room, amidst the jars on the table. The cage door was first. I swung the hammer at the hinges, breaking each one off in a single blow. The door clattered to the ground.

One step closer to ensuring she was never caged again.

I struck the cage over and over, smashing the bars loose and letting them fall to the floor. Each piece had witnessed her humiliation. Each piece had contained her, fettered her.

I destroyed them all.

We'd both been trapped. Csilla had been locked in this tower, in this cage. My bonds were less obvious, but with the loss of my magic, of my home, I'd become bound to the needs and desires of others. First to my mother and brothers, then to my king, and now to the capricious whims of King Rudolf. I didn't know if I'd be able to find my own freedom again, but at least one of us could.

I poured all the strength of my rage into every blow until the cage lay in bits all over the floor. Sweat covered my brow, my bare chest rising and falling with the aftermath of exertion. Sinking to the ground, I gathered the scattered remains and tossed them into a nearby basket, piling it full.

It was done. She'd killed her sorcerer, and I'd destroyed her cage. Now all that mattered was to free my people.

Csilla

My body was pleasantly sore when I woke to find Tancred gone once more. I lay there with my eyes closed and relished the feeling. The sun streamed in through the window, warming my skin, and I burrowed into the blankets. My bed smelled of beeswax soap and Tancred—his own unique smell, something like pine and leather.

But I couldn't lie in bed forever. I sat up and stretched. The room felt larger, more open than it ever had before. I looked around, and my heart gave a stutter.

My cage was missing.

It had been here last night. The only person who could have taken it, would have taken it, was Tancred. But where? Why?

My instinct was to panic, to assume he'd moved it so he could use it on me. I could feel the press of the bars on my skin. My breath came short, and I held the blankets up to my neck. I couldn't go back into that cage.

He wouldn't do that, I told myself

But I'd only known him a couple weeks. How well did I really know him?

Well enough. What about last night? He wouldn't treat me like that if he didn't care. He'd given me pleasure unlike any I'd experienced before, had been exquisitely gentle as he bathed me and carried me to bed. He cared for me.

Was that true, though? Or was he luring me into complacency so he could trade me to King Rudolf for his people's freedom? He'd been clear about his intentions from the beginning. His people, his king, came before everything else.

How stupid was I? I'd spent thirteen years under Kálmán's hand, and the instant a handsome stranger promised me freedom, I lost my mind. I'd killed Kálmán for him; when we faced the sorcerer, I hadn't done a thing in my own defense, but when I saw Tancred on the ground, suffocated by a band of magic, I'd finally attacked. I'd killed Kálmán not to save myself, but to save him. For him, I'd done what I hadn't been able to do for my own sake.

I hadn't changed. For the past thirteen years, I'd convinced myself that what I had with Kálmán was anything but slavery. That I enjoyed his touch, even felt something for him. And now I was doing the same thing with Tancred. He didn't need to cage me. He'd managed to ensnare me without a cage.

I hugged my knees to my chest, thinking back on his every move since we met. I hadn't misinterpreted his motivations, had I? Something roiled low in my gut at the thought of going back to the capital with him, of letting him sell me to the Aranite king.

There was no use sitting here wondering about his plans. If he wanted to become my new captor, I could at least face him with dignity. I rose and put on my nicest dress, then sat down before the mirror and brushed and braided my hair.

Armed with nothing more than my beauty, I began searching the tower for my missing—whatever he was.

He wasn't in the kitchen, but I did find a used cleaver on the table, blood congealed on the blade. The door to the dining room across from the kitchen was closed. Maybe he'd gone hunting while I was asleep and was using the dining room to clean his kill. But then why was my cage missing?

I pressed my ear to the door. No sound, but I smelled something odd, like copper and rotting meat. Hesitatingly, I twisted the handle and pushed it open.

The sight I saw doubled me over in disgust. The sheet on top of the headless body did little to hide its presence. Blood colored the white fabric. Flies buzzed around the body, and the smell of decay was so strong I could taste it.

Kálmán. This was Kálmán's body. I did this to him. The room spun around me, and I clung to the door frame for support. I was a monster. He'd taken me in, cared for me. Yes, he'd killed my parents and forced me to be his whore, but did he really deserve the death I'd given him? He gave me gifts and luxuries. He taught me about art and history. He hadn't *wanted* to punish me when I acted out. He—

"Csilla?" Tancred's voice came from a long distance away.

I killed him. I turned his skin to flakes of ash and pushed him out a window. He was my benefactor, my caretaker, and I *killed him.*

"Breathe." His arms wrapped around me. Kálmán's? No. Tancred's. My eyesight was blurred, foggy, but I forced myself to look up at him.

My cage." My tongue felt wooden, but I forced the words out. "It's gone."

"It's gone," he repeated. "He's gone. He can't hurt you again."

Gone. Gone gone gone. All my fault. My face was cold. Wet.

"Are you going to cage me, too?" I whispered, clinging to him.

"Listen to me." He grabbed me by the shoulders. *"Listen to me, Csilla. You will never be caged again. Do you understand? Not by the sorcerer, not by the king, and certainly not by me. Your cage is in pieces, and the pieces are yours to do with as you wish. You're free."*

Free. "What do I do with freedom?" I blinked away my tears. "I don't know what to do with myself."

"Come with me."

"Yes, I'll help you save your people, but after—"

"No. Come with me."

Tancred

Why did I say that?

I'd been deliberately not addressing the issue of what would happen after we dealt with Rudolf. Now wasn't the time. We still had things to focus on. So why, with Csilla clinging desperately to the front of my shirt and tears streaking her face, would I ask her to come with me?

Her silence spoke volumes. She didn't want me. Not like that. I tried to gather up the frayed ends of the conversation and tie them together. "Not with me specifically. With us. The Pipers. You said you want to travel. We're traveling. You can see the world with us, and once you're more comfortable on your own, you can figure it out from there.

"I—" She shook her head.

No. She was saying no. A knot formed low in my stomach, but I let her go. Stepping back, I said, "I understand."

"Am I interrupting something?"

I'd been so focused on Csilla that I hadn't heard Michal arrive. She took in the distance between us and Csilla's tears, and her eyes narrowed.

Csilla fell into her arms. "He's dead," she whispered. "I killed him."

Michal stroked her hair. "I know."

"Am I horrible?"

"Of course not. You did what you had to."

I stood there with my hands hanging uselessly at my side as Michal guided her out of the dining room. She felt guilty about killing that monster? After everything he'd put her through?

"Maybe this isn't the best place for you right now," Michal said. "Have you eaten this morning?" When Csilla shook her head, she tsked. "I didn't think so. Come home with me. We'll get you something to eat, and you can let your nerves settle."

Csilla looked to me as if for confirmation. "We can spare a couple hours," I said. Truthfully, we needed to get back to the capital, but I couldn't deny her this brief bit of comfort.

LIGHT

TANCRED

Twenty minutes later, Csilla was settled in a corner at Michal's house, a shawl around her shoulders despite the warm day. A short, heavily pregnant woman—Michal's sister-in-law, Elza—brought her a bowl of soup, and she and Michal took a seat on either side of her.

"You can stay here as long as you like," Elza said. "There's no need to go back there."

There? The tower, or the capital? Either way, I cleared my throat. "Actually, we'll have to leave this afternoon. We're expected."

A minute narrowing of the eyes was all the reaction she showed, but Michal was less reticent. "You have your proof," she said. "You can take it to the king without burdening Csilla further. She's been through enough."

"No." Csilla pulled the shawl tighter around her shoulders. "I promised."

"If I come back with just the sorcerer's head, there's no reason for the king to believe me," I explained. "I need a witness."

Michal glared at me. "And now that the sorcerer is dead, what is the king going to do? He'll want someone to punish."

"Someone has been punished. If King Rudolf wants to make an example of him, he can hang Kálmán's head on a spike above the gates of the castle." Csilla flinched at that, and I wished I could take back the callous words. He deserved all that and more, but she didn't need to hear the details.

"Or he could throw Csilla in a cell as an accomplice."

"I'll protect her." I wouldn't let that happen. I'd die before seeing her caged again. Even if she didn't want me.

"And if you can't?" She took Csilla's hands and looked earnestly into her eyes. "I have a bad feeling about this. If you go, I'm afraid you won't come back."

Csilla worried her lip, looking between Michal and Elza. "He needs me," she said, her voice small.

I did, but not for the reasons she thought. King Loic would find a way to convince Rudolf of my story, even if I didn't bring back a witness. But selfishly, I wanted to keep her with me for a little longer. No matter what she chose to do after this was ove.

"*We* need you," Michal insisted. "The boys and I do. I'm telling you, Csilla, this is a bad idea. You should stay here, where you belong."

Where she belonged? She'd been brought here by force to serve an abusive master. She didn't belong here more than anywhere else. I opened my mouth to say so, but Csilla spoke first.

"Can I talk to Tancred alone for a minute?"

Michal gave me a suspicious look, but she patted Csilla's knee. "We'll be in the kitchen if you need us."

Csilla looked out the window as they left the room. Michal's sons were playing at sword-fighting with two long sticks. The older one, Ádám, was Michal's clone, with his mother's shrewd eyes and dark hair. His brother had him on the defensive, his long, gangly arms giving him the advantage. Álmos looked little like his mother, his dark eyes laughing and his nose long and proud. His hair was lighter than his brother's, almost golden in the sunlight. We watched them play as Csilla gathered her thoughts.

"What if Michal's right?" she said at last.

I frowned, waiting for her to explain.

"She said she had a bad feeling about this. What if we go to the capital and it all goes wrong?

It wouldn't. It couldn't. My people had suffered enough. "That won't happen."

She set the bowl of soup on the table, untouched. "I trust her instincts. She's never led me wrong."

"She let that man abuse you for thirteen years." As far as I was concerned, Michal was almost as bad as the sorcerer. "She wants to keep you trapped here. You don't belong in this town, any more than you belong in that cage."

"Don't talk about her like that." Csilla stood, shawl falling onto the chair. "You have no idea what she's done for me."

"If she cared for you, she'd tell you to go. You said you want to see the world, didn't you? How will you do that if you're stuck here in the shadow of that tower?"

"Michal needs me here. I told her I'd help her take care of the boys." Her glance flicked toward the window and away.

"Fine." I curled my hands into fists. "Once we've finished with King Rudolf, I don't care what you do. Come back to your tower and hide away for the rest of your life." If she didn't want to chase her dreams, I wasn't going to force her. I wouldn't make her stay with me.

"And what if I can't? You heard Michal. If I go with you, I'm not coming back."

"Is she a sorceress like your master?" I taunted. "Does she know the future?"

"Michal would never," she snapped. "You don't know anything about her. You don't know anything about me."

I took a step toward her, eyes locked on hers. "I know all I need to know about you. I know the way you bite back a scream when you're in pain." Venom crept into the edges of my voice. "I know the sounds you make when you climax around my fingers and my tongue. I know that even before Kálmán took you, you wanted to see the world. I know you pretend you're a good little pet for whoever's pulling your strings, but deep down inside, you long to be free."

She held my gaze, fire blazing there. "Don't act like a brute, Tancred. It doesn't suit you."

"Maybe I am a brute." Every word was a brick in the wall between us, blocking off my heart. This was why I'd never let myself look for what my parents had. The pain that came when things inevitably fell apart. The arrow to your heart when they left you. The misery when they died and left you to raise your children alone.

"You're not."

"You claim I don't know you, but in the same breath you pretend you know everything about me." I'd let her see too much. I couldn't let her keep this grip on me. "What if I've been lying to you?"

"I know enough about you," she said. "I know you wouldn't hurt me."

"That doesn't mean anything. I wouldn't hurt most people." Lie, lie, lie. In such a short time, she already meant more to me than anything—and I couldn't let her know. Couldn't let her use that against me.

She pressed her hands to her head. "Would you just listen to me, Tancred? I don't think we should go back to the capital. *I* can't go back. I have to stay here."

"Why are you so desperate not to see this through?" Did she think I'd let Rudolf hold her culpable for the sorcerer's sins? Did she really think so little of me? I never should have opened myself up to her. "Is Michal holding something over your head?"

"That's not it," she insisted, but her eyes flicked toward the window again.

I followed the look, and the younger boy, the one who looked nothing like Michal—

"He's your son."

The blood rushed from her face. "What?"

"The boy. Álmos. He's your son. Isn't he?" I considered the boy. His hair was lighter than hers, but his nose had the same arch to it. He held his shoulders back with the same confident attitude Csilla affected, and when he smiled, the corner of his mouth dimpled like hers. "Don't lie to me."

She didn't look at me. "He doesn't know."

"Why is Michal raising your son as her own?" He couldn't have been much older than twelve. He'd have been conceived not long after

Csilla was taken, so not only was she held captive by the man who abused her, but she'd also been forced to carry his child.

Shame colored her cheeks as she sank back into the chair. "He was born a few months after I came here. Kálmán didn't want a child. He was going to kill him, but I—I couldn't let him kill my baby. When I found out I was pregnant, that's when I tried to..."

"That's when you poisoned the sorcerer."

She nodded. "It didn't work, obviously. He agreed to let Michal raise Álmos if I would stop fighting him." She stared at her hands. "My reward for good behavior was time with my son. A son who didn't even know who I was."

I knelt next to her, my heart twisting in my chest. "I'm sorry, Csilla." I took her hand and pressed a kiss to it. "I shouldn't have said those things."

She blinked away her tears. "You didn't know. You couldn't have."

I hadn't known about her son, but that didn't excuse the hateful words I'd thrown at her. "I'll bring you back to your son," I vowed. "But my people need you. Please. Come back to the capital with me, help me convince King Rudolf of my people's innocence in all this, and I'll make sure you make it back here."

"What if Michal is right, though? What if I can't come back?" She twisted the ends of her shawl as she watched the boys play. "She's got an instinct for things like this. Rudolf might not believe us. He could kill me, imprison me."

"I won't let that happen." I hadn't killed her sorcerer, but I wouldn't let anything else happen to her. She wouldn't be caged again. Not by sorcerers or kings or anyone else.

"I know you won't."

My heart swelled at the certainty of her words. She trusted me to protect her, to bring her back safely to her son.

We were silent for a moment. Then she said, "Before, you asked me to come with you."

"I shouldn't have asked you that," I said quickly. "I don't expect you to leave your family behind."

"But you want me to. Don't you? To come with you wherever the Pipers go next."

I couldn't say the words. Throat tight, I nodded. I wanted her with me, selfish as it was. I wanted her at my side for the rest of my life. It was insane. We hardly knew each other. An hour ago, I hadn't even known she had a child.

Mother had told me about this. That when you found the person you were meant to be with, things felt right, no matter how long you'd known them. I couldn't tell Csilla how I felt, not unless I wanted to drive her away, but there was only one word for the way I was feeling.

"Maybe—maybe it would be okay if I don't make it back," Csilla said.

I kept my voice low, hardly daring to hope. "What are you saying?"

"Álmos is safe and loved here. I'd miss seeing him grow up, but he'll have a better life than I can give him. I don't think I could raise a child. I couldn't take him away from his home, his brother. And I—" She broke off, looking down at the ground.

"And you?" I prompted.

"I want to see the world with you, Tancred."

My heart swelled so much I couldn't breathe. "You'll come with me? With the Pipers?"

"Will you have me?"

As if I could say no. "Of course."

She gave me a shy, tentative smile, like she didn't know quite how to process her emotions. I took her head in both my hands and brought her in for a kiss.

Long before we were breathless with each other, footsteps sounded behind me. We broke apart, Csilla wiping her face and blushing madly.

"Csilla, I—" Michal started, then cut herself off with a shake of her head. Csilla stood, reaching out to her with both hands.

"I have to go," she whispered. "I don't belong here. Not really."

Tears brimmed in Michal's eyes. "You do. You're family."

"You're like a sister to us, Csilla," Elza said.

"And I'll try to come back to visit. But Kálmán brought me here against my will. I'm grateful for the love I found here, but I wasn't meant to be here. Not permanently."

"You were made to fly," Michal whispered.

She was. The sorcerer had made her the firebird, but he didn't control her identity. That was who she was at heart. Fiery and independent, untamed and untamable. Even without her flames, she was and always would be the firebird.

"You could come with me." Tears filled Csilla's eyes as well, and for once, she didn't fight them. "All of you."

Michal gave her a sad smile. "I can't leave Bandi's grave. We can't uproot the boys like that. This is our home."

"I know." Csilla sniffed, laughing halfheartedly. "I had to ask anyway."

When Michal released her, she hugged Elza, then leaned down to press a kiss to the other woman's swollen stomach. "Write and tell me all about this little one," she said. "I'm sorry I'll miss the birth."

"I won't forget a single detail," Elza promised.

Michal was digging in a chest in the corner of the room. After a moment, she pulled out a small cloth-wrapped bundle.

"We had this made months ago," she said. "We were waiting for the right time to give it to you."

Csilla took the bundle, holding it gingerly, as if it were going to explode. She peeled back the cloth. Inside was a small silver candelabra with space to hold nine candles. A menorah. Carved into the base was a firebird, its wings spread wide in triumph. She pressed a hand to her mouth.

"You'll carry our light with you wherever you go," Michal said.

Csilla threw her arms around Michal's neck, the menorah still clutched tight in her hand. "Thank you, auntie."

"We packed some provisions for your trip." Elza nodded to a second bundle over on the table. "In case you decided to go."

"Plenty of halva," Michal said with a small laugh.

"I'll go tell the boys to come say goodbye." Elza kissed Csilla's cheek and headed for the door.

Csilla set the menorah on the table next to the bundle of food. "I don't want to leave him." She wrung her hands together, eyes darting toward the window. "I know I have to—I know it's best for both of us—but..."

I put a hand on her shoulder, offering silent encouragement. I felt like an outsider here, a voyeur watching an intimate family moment, but she gave me a watery smile.

Michal took her hand. "You'll see him again someday. You'll see all of us again."

"I know." She took a deep breath in and held it. Then she let out the breath, long and slow. "I'm ready."

As if they'd been summoned, the door burst open, and we were beset by the two boys.

"Auntie!" Ádám, the older, frowned at her, the effect somewhat marred by the dirt spattering his face. "You're leaving?"

"Is it Kálmán?" Álmos, Csilla's son, asked. "Is he sending you somewhere again?"

"It's not him, no." She ruffled Álmos's hair, throat bobbing with emotion she didn't want to show. "I'm—I'm free now. It's time that I move on."

Ádám narrowed his eyes, the expression like his mother Michal's. "Move on from us?"

"Of course not." She slung an arm around his shoulders, affecting nonchalance. "I'll come back to visit, but I've been working for Kálmán for so long. I have some things I need to do before I can settle down."

"How long will you be gone?" Álmos asked. He seemed more carefree than his brother, less serious, but his eyes watched Csilla with an intelligent depth behind them.

"I don't know. It may be a few years, but I'll write whenever I can."

"Maybe when you're older, you can visit her," Michal chimed in.

Csilla smiled. "I'd like that. And I'll send you things from my travels."

Álmos brightened. "Like a fairy's wings?"

"Fairies aren't real, idiot," the older boy said.

"Firebirds and magic are real, but fairies aren't?" Álmos shoved his brother, face flaming like Csilla's did when she was embarrassed.

"I'll find trinkets for you. I promise." Csilla pulled them both to her, laughing. "Oh! That reminds me." She pulled the rock she'd found in the stream from her pocket. "I found this for you."

He held it up to the light, examining the orange streaks through it. "It's perfect. Thank you."

"I know you said you're too old for trinkets, but I brought you one anyway." She took another stone from her pocket and handed it to Ádám.

"I'll treasure it always," he said solemnly.

She pressed a kiss to each of their foreheads. "I'll miss you both."

"Miss you, too," Álmos said.

"Zei gezunt, auntie." Ádám kissed her cheek and stepped back.

I offered both boys a handshake. "Take care of her," the older one said, and I got the sense that his shrewd eyes saw more than he let on.

"I will," I promise. Michal, standing behind her sons, watched the exchange, and her expression softened slightly.

Csilla hugged them both once more, kissed Michal's and Elza's cheeks, and turned away with tears in her eyes.

I gathered her things from the table. As we stepped out the door, I murmured, "You'll see them again."

I hoped I was telling the truth.

JOURNEY BACK

CSILLA

Tancred seemed to sense that I wasn't in the mood for conversation, but he kept a hand on my arm as we walked silently back to the tower. His warm presence gave me comfort. I was saying goodbye to my son, but not forever. Álmos would be happy with Michal, with his family. And I was gaining something precious as well. Freedom. The chance to control my own destiny.

Tancred's things were already packed, but he didn't rush me as I went from room to room, gathering whatever I thought I might want. Kálmán wouldn't need any of it. There were enough riches here to keep me comfortable for the rest of my life, but I didn't want to be greedy. Beyond the necessities, I packed a single sack of gold. In Kálmán's workshop, I dug through the jars and bottles searching for one specific container of red-black powder, which I slipped into the pocket of my dress.

As I turned to go, my gaze snagged on a basket full of golden bars. My cage. My eyes burned, and I sank to the ground next to the basket. Tancred had destroyed it for me. He'd made sure I could never be caged again. *The pieces are yours to do with as you wish,* he'd said.

It didn't feel right, taking the cage with me. Kálmán had used these bars to imprison me, but I'd used the flames he gave me to kill him. I knew it was wrong to feel indebted to him after everything he'd done to me, but I couldn't help it. He'd twisted me, transformed me into a creature of his will.

But someone could still benefit from my cage. Grabbing a quill and paper from the desk, I wrote a short note to Michal urging her to use the metal to care for the boys. I couldn't parent my son, but I could still provide for him and his brother. My cage would be the means for his freedom.

I hefted my overstuffed pack onto my shoulder and carried the basket downstairs, where I set it along with the note in a conspicuous place on the table in the kitchen.

Tancred sat on a stool in the kitchen, waiting. He watched me set the basket down. "You don't want to keep it?"

"I can't give my son much," I said. "At least I can give him this."

He walked over to me and pulled me to his chest. "You've given him a home and a family that loves him."

"And now an inheritance," I agreed. I wiped away the tears I wouldn't let fall. "Are you ready?"

He nodded at his own bags, stuffed as full as mine. On top of one was a lumpy leather sack whose contents I didn't want to think about. The reason for our journey.

I pulled the jar of powder from my pocket. "I thought you might want this. It was made from the flowers from the mountains."

His eyes darted from the jar to my face and back, widening. "The ones you showed me? The musical ones?"

"I don't know if they can be of any help in restoring your people's magic, but—"

His lips swallowed up the rest of my words. "Thank you," he said when he released me. "Thank you, Csilla."

I flushed. "It's nothing. I don't even know if it will work."

"I took his spellbooks." He gestured toward his bags. "King Loic will find someone who can use them. We'll figure it out."

My heart swelled. Maybe his people could be healed. His magic, the thing that he valued so much, more than anything else in the world, could be restored.

A strange energy seemed to overtake us as we set out, and we traveled all through that afternoon and deep into the night. By midnight, we both should have been exhausted, but I was wide awake. I was finally seeing the night sky clearly. I watched the moon and stars trace a path across the blue velvet expanse, too full of adrenaline to suggest we take a break.

We finally stopped several hours past midnight, and once Tancred had pitched our tent, he pulled me into it and made love to me with a fierce urgency that left me sore but satisfied. Neither of us spoke; there was no need. We slept tangled up in each other's arms until the sun rose.

The next day was much the same. We traveled in silence, our pace hurried. Late that afternoon, we reached the collection of houses that marked the river crossing.

The bridge hadn't been rebuilt yet, but the water had gone down from the flooding, and a boatman had set up to ferry people across.

"Where are you headed?" the brown-bearded man asked as he helped us into the boat.

"The capital," I answered as Tancred settled me onto the bench next to him. We kept our packs on our laps to keep them out of the puddle that had formed on the bottom of the boat.

"Better watch your backs while you're there." He used the oars to push off from the shore. "I hear there's some strange folks visiting the king. Horns and yellow eyes and the like."

Tancred shifted in his seat, fidgeting like he wanted to adjust his hat. I took his hand and squeezed it, even as my chest tightened with nerves. "Thank you for the warning. We'll be careful," I said.

He looked at Tancred as he rowed us across. "You're not Aranite. Where you from?"

"Konstantiniyye," Tancred said, at the same time that I said, "Istanbul."

"A Turk, huh?" He seemed more curious than wary.

"He defected." I leaned into Tancred, clinging to his arm like a lovestruck new bride. "We're going to the capital so he can offer his services to the king."

The suspicion on the man's face dissipated. "We could use all the help we can get, between the strangers, the Turks, and Hungary. You can fight?"

"If I need to."

The ferry came to a stop with a jolt. We'd reached the other side of the river. Some of the tension in my chest eased as Tancred paid the man and helped me onto the shore. I couldn't help worrying about what the man had said about the Pipers, though. What would we find when we reached Tancred's people? Had the situation grown worse since we set out? Looking at the wrinkle of worry on Tancred's forehead, I could tell his thoughts reflected my own.

"We'll be there by tonight," I reminded him. "Just a few more hours."

"As long as we're not too late."

Tancred

The sun was nearing the horizon when I finally caught sight of the tents in the distance. I scanned them as we approached, looking for any signs of distress, but everything seemed the same as when I left. I noted familiar faces walking through the camp, and while a general air of anxiety hung about the camp, it was no stronger than it had been for the past year since our magic disappeared.

I wanted to go directly to my own tent and see my mother and brothers, but the king would be waiting. With a heavy sigh, I hefted my bags onto my shoulder and led Csilla through the camp toward the king's tent.

"You're limping." Lady Teta appeared in front of us as if from nowhere. She looked me over and wrinkled her nose. "And filthy. What took you so long?"

"Weather. A sprained ankle. The sorcerer was expecting us."

She raised a brow. "Sounds like you've had quite the journey. Loic and Annika are up at the castle right now. I take it you managed to find what we needed?"

"It's here." I raised the sack containing Kálmán's head.

"I'd say you need a bath before meeting with the kings, but I don't think there's time. Rudolf's getting impatient."

"We're not too late, though, are we?" Csilla shifted nervously on her feet.

"Sorry?" Lady Teta turned her attention to Csilla, watching her lips. "I didn't catch that."

"Are we late?" Csilla asked.

"No, Rudolf hasn't done anything but talk. Yet. I'll take you to the castle myself." She looked us over again. "They might not let you in otherwise. You look like vagrants."

"Nice to see you, too," I muttered, low enough that she wouldn't realize I'd spoken. Lady Teta always looked well-groomed, even after weeks on the road or days at sea. Right now, her hair was braided in tight coils around her horns, and kohl lined her eyes. Even with Rudolf threatening to destroy us all, she found time to primp herself.

Csilla and I dropped our bags just inside King Loic's tent. I tucked the pouch of apple peels into my pocket and grabbed the sorcerer's head. As we left the camp, Teta let Csilla go ahead of us.

"It's almost sunset," she signed, glancing at Csilla. "Should we be expecting trouble, taking her into the castle?"

"No. She won't transform again." I gestured with the head, using my free hand to answer her. "His spell ended when he did."

"Good. The last thing we need is Rudolf getting curious about her magic."

Even without her ability to transform, there was always the possibility that Rudolf would want to keep her anyway. Michal's words haunted the back of my mind. *If you go, you won't come back.* What if she was right? What if her words had been more than just a need to keep Csilla safe? Mothers, I'd learned, had a natural instinct for danger when it came to their families. She could know about what awaited us up ahead.

Eyes watched us from every angle as we passed through the city. Several people made signs against evil at me and Lady Teta. Her usually cheerful face grew bleaker as we neared the castle. Public opinion regarding us, which had never been overwhelmingly positive, was turning toward open hostility, and I doubted that convincing Rudolf of our innocence would mend our reputation among his people.

We didn't have to convince his people, though. Just him. Just long enough that he would let us leave his kingdom without a challenge.

"Lady Teta." The guard at the castle gate sneered at her. He'd been with me in the orchard the night I met Csilla. His gaze passed over me as if I was nothing but a piece of garbage. "Bringing more beggars to the king?"

She looked down her nose at him. "Lord Tancred has been traveling. He comes with news for both our kings."

He looked at me again. "Ah, Lord Tancred. Your absence has been noted. I hope your news is good. King Rudolf won't listen to your excuses much longer."

"Are you going to keep talking all night, or do you plan on actually letting us in?" Teta snapped.

"Follow me."

The throne room was full of Aranite courtiers. Rudolf sat on his throne, absently drumming his fingers on his knee. King Loic and Queen Annika sat next to him, my queen interpreting for the two men.

Conversation died down as we entered. Bernat led us to the front and bowed to his king. "Lord Tancred and Lady Teta have arrived, your majesty." He gestured to us, his sneer still plastered on his face.

Queen Annika crossed herself, looking up at the heavens in obvious relief. King Loic's face remained blank, and Rudolf scowled at us. Rudolf's wife was nowhere to be seen—perhaps his queen wasn't permitted to be involved in matters of state.

"Your prodigal lord has returned, Loic," Rudolf said, looking down at us. "And looking somewhat worse for the wear after all his travels. Come forward, Lord Tancred. I trust you've brought me my thief?"

I stopped before the dais and dumped the sack out. The sorcerer's head, gruesome and sticky, landed on the ground with a thunk. From the corner of my eye, I could see Lady Teta signing rapidly with the king and queen.

"What is this?" Rudolf demanded. "Loic?"

"Your thief, as requested, your majesty." I bowed. "I killed him for you and brought you his head."

His eyes narrowed. "You bring me a dead stranger's head and expect me to believe this is the thief. Do you have any proof?"

"I hope you're not implying my man is a liar, Rudolf," King Loic said.

"I hope you don't expect me to take his word for it, Loic," he shot back.

"I have proof, your majesties." I took the vial of apple peels from my pocket. "The remains of the apple, and a witness." I waved Csilla forward, to stand next to me.

Csilla bowed, waiting for Rudolf to speak before she lifted her head. He considered her, letting the silence drag on until she was squirming.

Be patient, I willed her silently. He was trying to throw us off guard. Discomfort was a tool to catch her in a lie. I didn't dare to give any indication of outward support. Rudolf's beady eyes caught everything. Diplomacy wasn't my strong suit, but I wouldn't give him any reason to suspect us. For all he knew, Csilla was nothing but an innocent bystander who knew Kálmán had taken the apple. I intended to keep it that way.

"You may rise," he said at last. "What is your name?"

"Novakné Csilla, your majesty."

Good. She was doing well. No need to embellish or ramble on. Answer the questions exactly as he asked.

"And you saw this sorcerer take the apple from my orchard?"

My pulse hitched, but Csilla was prepared for the question. "I saw a golden apple in his possession."

"You were well-acquainted with him?"

"I was his servant."

Servant. An innocuous word for the way he had possessed her, body and soul. I glared daggers at the head, wishing I could bring him back and kill him again.

Rudolf's lips formed a line. He was obviously displeased with her terse answers. "And in the course of your servitude, you became aware of his theft. How did you discover it?"

"He told me where it came from."

"He told a servant girl about stealing a magic golden apple from his king," he said dryly.

The hairs on my neck prickled. *Careful,* I willed her. One wrong word could implicate her in the crime.

"Kálmán was arrogant," she said, her voice even. "He bragged liberally about his crimes. He killed my parents in front of me and showed no remorse. Why would he hesitate to tell me about this?"

Another bout of silence as Rudolf weighed her words. "This sorcerer sounds like he was a danger to my kingdom. You should both be rewarded for bringing him to me."

A weight lifted from my chest, and I could breathe normally. I made a formal bow. "No thanks are necessary, your majesty. I wish only to be of service to my king and his friends."

"Nonsense." Rudolf gave me one of his patronizing smiles. "You brought me my thief. You deserve your reward." He clapped his hands, and Bernát stepped forward. "Bernát was with you in the orchard that morning, Lord Tancred. The morning you left, I mean. I'm sure you remember him."

I dipped my head in recognition, wary. He'd been asleep when Csilla arrived. He couldn't know anything.

"Come, Bernát," the king said. "Tell our guests what you saw that morning."

The guard cleared his throat. "I saw a bird made of fire try to steal one of the apples."

SACRIFICIAL LAMB
TANCRED

A murmur ran through the room as my blood turned to ice.

"And what happened when the bird tried to steal the apple?" Rudolf prompted.

"I shot it. Or I tried to," he said. "Lord Tancred shouted, warning the bird, and it flew off. He rode off after it."

Liar. I opened my mouth to say so, but King Loic caught my eye. "Don't," he signed. "You'll make things worse."

He was right. I wouldn't be believed no matter what I said, but was I expected to just listen to these lies?

Bernát went on. "I followed them. It landed in a grove not far from the city and transformed into a human woman. *That* human woman." He pointed an accusing finger at Csilla, who looked wide-eyed and open-mouthed at me.

I didn't know what to say, what to do. He'd followed us? Seen Csilla in the grove? I couldn't stop the lies and half-truths from pouring out of his mouth.

"Lord Tancred met the woman there. He embraced her, and then he took her back to his camp."

"You saw Lord Tancred and the woman—the firebird—enter the Piper camp together?" Rudolf asked. He wasn't watching us or his guard. He was watching King Loic, whose face remained impassive as Queen Annika, white-faced, translated the words for him.

"I did, your majesty."

"Thank you, Bernát. That will be all."

The guard bowed, a look of smug satisfaction in his eyes. When he walked past me, his shoulder bumped mine, too hard to be anything but intentional. I ignored him, eyes locked on my king. *Tell me what to do*, I begged him silently. *Fix this.*

The silence around us was deafening. King Loic watched me, but he didn't speak, whether aloud or in signs. Queen Annika's face held open horror, and her fingers flew as she and Lady Teta signed rapidly to one another.

This was a disaster. Whether he knew it was a lie or not, Rudolf was going to set me and Csilla up as the means to destroy my people. He was making an excuse to turn against the Pipers. He'd kill us all, king and queen and council, and force the rest of the Pipers to serve him in a land that openly despised us.

There was only one thing to do. I couldn't allow my king and queen to bear the responsibility for my actions. Even though I'd been following their orders when I took Csilla to find the sorcerer, even though I knew King Loic would lay down his life for his people, his death or abdication would do nothing for us.

"Well, Loic." Rudolf turned to my king. "It seems you've been lying to me."

"I acted alone," I blurted out.

All eyes turned to me. Rudolf's gaze was thunderous. "What did you say?"

"My king and queen had no knowledge of the firebird," I said, locking my knees to prevent them from shaking. "I acted alone."

Queen Annika opened her mouth to refute it, but her husband put a hand on her knee. "Don't," he signed.

Bernát snorted derisively at my claim. "He's lying, your majesty. I saw him take her into their camp."

"Csilla was enslaved by the sorcerer. He was forcing her to do his bidding. When I realized that, I knew I could make her lead me back to him, but we needed supplies. I took her to my own tent so I could pack for the journey." *Whatever god might be listening, let him believe me.* Our hopes of making an alliance with Arany were long since gone, but I could still stop Rudolf from destroying my people.

He turned his scowling gaze back to my king. "Is this true, Loic? You deny involvement in your man's schemes?"

King Loic stood. "I regret having allowed such a treacherous snake a place of honor in my court. Believe me, Rudolf. Had I known of his deceit, he would never have been allowed to get this far." He stepped down from the dais, watching me. "I hereby strip you of all rank and rights within my court."

I let out a shuddering breath of relief that I hoped would be interpreted as shock by everyone watching. Rudolf could say nothing. He had his scapegoat, and I would go to the altar gladly if it meant my mother and brothers, my people, were safe.

"Fine." Rudolf nodded to his guards. "Arrest him."

I didn't dare to look at Csilla as they grabbed my wrists and forced them behind my back. I'd claimed I forced her to go with me, to fight her sorcerer. She had to go along with it. I looked back at my king. *Protect her,* I begged him with my eyes. *Don't let him punish her, too.* She'd been through enough.

Rudolf's mouth twisted as he looked down at me. "Stealing from the king's orchard is high treason. As you have confessed to the crime, we'll dispense with the formality of a trial. I sentence you to be beheaded at dawn."

A vise tightened around my heart. It was no worse than I'd expected—I knew that confessing would lead to my death—but I didn't relish the thought of being beheaded.

"As for you," Rudolf continued, shifting his gaze to Csilla. I couldn't breathe. "I believe we can dispense with a trial in your case, as well. Two witnesses have placed you in the orchard that night. Do you deny stealing from me?"

"I think it's been made clear that the woman wasn't there of her own volition," Loic said.

"Regardless of her reasoning, she stole from me." Rudolf scowled at my king. "Unless you're claiming responsibility for her?"

"Of course not," my king said smoothly. "As my former councilman said, he acted alone in taking her prisoner. I merely wish to see justice done."

"If you wish to see justice done, let the woman speak for herself."

I tried not to look, but I couldn't keep my eyes from being drawn to Csilla. She was pale, trembling. She watched the two kings.

"Well?" Rudolf barked. "Speak! Did you steal from me?"

"I did." Her answer was barely audible among the murmurs of the crowd around us.

"And did anyone force you to?" King Loic asked, ignoring the glare Rudolf shot at him.

She swallowed hard, eyes darting toward the sorcerer's head on the ground. "Kálmán did. The sorcerer."

Rudolf gritted his teeth together. "It matters not. You stole from me. The penalty is the same, no matter the reason."

No. No, he couldn't. I'd promised her this wouldn't happen. I was supposed to protect her. I struggled against the guards who held me, but they tightened their grip on my arms.

"I'll be merciful," Rudolf went on. "Since you seem to believe you had no choice but to steal from me, rather than executing you as well, I will allow you an alternative. You stole from me in servitude to another. You can work off your debt by serving me."

Her knees, already shaking, collapsed from under her. After what she'd been through, captivity was worse than death. She wasn't making a sound, but her sobs echoed in my ears, a deafening roar.

Rage billowed through me, and I tore free. I had no more weapons, but I placed myself between Csilla and the guards, fists up. I'd fight everyone in this room with my bare hands if it meant I could save her.

"She goes free," I snarled.

"You seem to be laboring under a misapprehension." Rudolf's voice was cold. I didn't dare to turn to look at him. "Her fate is no longer your concern. In a matter of hours, you will be dead and unable to protect her."

A roar of fury tore from me, and I charged at the nearest guard. The crowd of nobles scattered as I tackled him into the wall.

My vision tunneled until all I could see was his face. Bernát, the guard who'd lied to them all. My fists hit flesh and bone, his stomach, face, ears, throat. Whatever I could reach. I flailed against him, hardly feeling the blows he returned. He struck my eye, and a shooting pain sent half the world into darkness.

Someone grabbed my collar and jerked me backward. I whirled on the new assailant, but before I could do more than strike out blindly, Rudolf's voice tore through the room.

"Enough."

His words weren't what stopped me. It was the whimper—Csilla's whimper—that came after that sent a cold shock of fear through me. The guard who held me turned me toward the king, and all the breath rushed from my lungs when I saw the gold-hilted dagger held against her throat.

"One more move, and she dies," the Aranite king said. He pressed the blade into her skin, and she stiffened as a thin line of blood formed.

All the fight went out of me. I slumped in the guard's hold.

"Are you finished?" Rudolf asked. When I ducked my head in agreement, he lowered his weapon, though he kept his hand fisted in Csilla's hair. "Take him away," he told the guard.

CAPTORS

CSILLA

Twin flames of rage and grief burned in my chest as I watched them lead Tancred from the hall. After all we'd done, after all he'd done, his king was allowing this? It wasn't right. It wasn't *fair*.

"As for you." King Rudolf tugged my head up to look at his face. "I assume you'll go quietly?"

"Yes," I whispered. There was nothing I could do. We were outnumbered, without allies. Michal was right. I never should have left. I should have begged Tancred to stay with me, to let his people fend for themselves. Then none of this would be happening.

He would never have agreed to it, though. I knew that. Protecting others was in his nature, and he'd done what he could. He'd saved his people, ensured Rudolf wouldn't kill the Piper rulers. He'd tried to protect me, too, no matter how foolhardy his attempt had been.

"Good." The king released my hair. He waved over a young man in servant's livery. "See that she gets a bath and fresh clothes. Then take her to my receiving room so we can discuss her new position."

There was nothing improper in his look or what he said, but the words still made me shiver. Was I to be a bedslave again? This time without even the respite of night, when my flames had left me untouchable.

Lady Teta held my gaze as the man took my arm and guided me toward the door. *Don't give up hope,* her eyes seemed to say. *We'll figure this out.* I wanted to believe the determination on her face, but how could I? I didn't belong with the Pipers. There was nothing they could do for me. Even though I'd never met King Rudolf, he was my king. His dominion over me was almost as absolute as Kálmán's.

The manservant took me down a back staircase to the servants' quarters, where two maids helped me bathe and put on a plain blue linen dress topped with a maid's apron. I went through the motions in a fog, not bothering to fight. Why should I? There was no hope.

At last I was led on wooden legs to the king's chambers. The maids left me alone, locking the door behind me. If I was going to escape, now would be the time, but why bother? The only way out of the room was the giant glass window, and I was several stories up. The sun was down now, but my wings were still absent. Despite the pain they'd caused, despite the horrors I'd faced while wearing that flaming body, I missed it. It had been the source of my captivity, but also the source of my freedom. Now I couldn't fly away, couldn't burn the men who laid hands on me. I was trapped more securely than I ever had been before.

I hardly noticed the sumptuous furnishings and tapestries hanging on the walls. A table held writing supplies, paper and gold sealing wax, as well as a bowl of gleaming golden apples. My stomach did flips. Those were the things that had started this whole mess. If he hadn't grown them, if Kálmán hadn't craved them, if I hadn't stolen one, none of this would be happening. I'd still be trapped in the tower with my tormentor and my cage, but Tancred would be safe. He wouldn't be sentenced to die in the morning.

The lock rattled behind me, and the door opened. I whirled around, nausea rising in my throat as I saw the king. He was alone. What would he want from me?

"So." He strode into the room, eyes raking over me. "You're the firebird Kálmán has been hiding in that tower of his."

I blinked at him, trying to parse out the meaning in his words. He spoke like he'd known Kálmán. Like he'd known who I was even before I entered his castle.

"I assume your transformations have stopped, though, now that he's dead?" He walked around me, scanning me like a piece of property, an exotic pet or a new horse. "Otherwise you would have transformed at sunset. A shame. Still, perhaps his tower will reveal the secret of his power, and we can remedy that."

I shuddered as he reached out and took my chin in his hand. "Yes," he said, "you'll make a fine adornment to my halls, even if you don't still have those lovely living flames."

"You can't do this." My voice trembled, but I forced myself to go on. "You can't keep me here. You can't kill Tancred."

He looked at me with mild surprise, like he hadn't realized I would dare to speak to him now that we were alone. "You stole from me. Of course I can."

"I was forced to." I lifted my chin. "And Tancred and the Pipers had nothing to do with it." I might not be able to defend myself, but I wouldn't let him kill Tancred. Not after all he'd been through—him and all his people. "If you have to punish someone, it should be me." I didn't want to die, but it would be better than knowing Tancred died for me.

The thought sent me spiraling, and I bit my tongue against a fresh wave of nausea. A sickly smile spread across King Rudolf's face. "He didn't tell you anything, did he? He said he didn't, but I never trusted him to tell me the truth."

Who? I couldn't bring myself to voice the question, but I didn't need to. The king was still speaking.

"Of course I know the Pipers had nothing to do with the theft. But I couldn't let them just wander through my lands unchecked."

"You planned it all." How hadn't I seen it before? The message Kálmán had received just before he sent me to take the first apple, his sudden caginess around his private correspondence. He'd been in contact with Rudolf all along.

"It was Kálmán's idea, actually. With a race of magic-wielders—no matter how powerless rumors said they now were—coming to my capital, I needed advice from a sorcerer, and conveniently, I had one hiding out only a few days' ride away.

"Kálmán, of course, knew the stories of the Pipers, their powers. Everyone did. They were even more feared than Suleiman's army. But they were rich, too, and their numbers could boost my own. If I could take control of them, we might stand a chance against Hungary and the Turks. Your sorcerer proposed we work together. He wanted a few of my golden apples, and I wanted an excuse to absorb the Pipers into my kingdom."

"You framed them." My skin prickled with shock and fear. "You knew I was coming." He planned to take down King Loic and put a puppet in his place.

His grin widened. "One of my precious apples went missing within a week of their arrival. Who else was I to blame? And when another one went missing, the trap would be complete." Then his gaze narrowed on me. "Only you fucked it up. You were supposed to take the second apple, but instead you let that Piper catch you. You let him kill your master, and you didn't even have the decency to contradict his lie about acting alone."

My ears sounded with a distant ringing. This had all been planned for weeks, months. He'd been working to take the Pipers down even before I took the first apple. What could I do against this? What could any of us do?

"You could fix this." He reached out and stroked my cheek. "Be a good subject for your king and country. I saw how you looked at the Piper lord. You obviously have feelings for him. If you do as I ask, perhaps you can even save his life."

I could still save Tancred. "How?" The word came out as a gasp.

"Tell the truth, naturally. Stand up before my court and tell them the Piper lord was working under direct orders from his king. That Lord Tancred used you to help him steal the apples for his king and forced you to lie about the sorcerer."

And if I did, King Rudolf would have the right to arrest King Loic. Possibly even kill him. But... "You'd let Tancred go?"

That smug smile again. "If he cooperates, why not?"

I shouldn't trust him. I knew that. He'd promised friendship to Tancred's people while plotting to destroy them. He could easily be doing the same to me, but his offer tempted me. Tancred's life for that of his people. I could do it. "Why? Why does this matter to you so much?" Was it just greed that motivated him? He was already rich, if I could believe what Kálmán had told me about the world outside of our little village. Richer than the surrounding kingdoms, thanks to his golden apples.

"Because all the money in the world won't save my throne if the Turks invade." He rested his hand on the ornamental sword at his side and looked out the small window. "I need all the men I can get, and I don't trust soldiers with divided loyalties. For years now, I've been slowly siphoning soldiers away from my ispans, drawing them to me. I will have the full allegiance of those who serve me, or I will have none at all."

"You'd rather destroy any chance at earning their love than make an alliance with them?"

He turned back to me, a wrinkle on his brow. "Fear has merit. Love has none."

He was wrong. I'd feared Kálmán for thirteen years, but it didn't earn him my loyalty. It earned him death beneath my talons. In contrast, I'd only loved Tancred for a short time—

My mind stuttered. Love. It was too soon, too impossible. But I'd killed for him, almost died for him. How could I deny that I loved him? How could I do anything but save him?

"Enough of this conversation," the king said. "Choose. Will you speak before my court? I warn you that denying me will cause you to meet the same fate as Lord Tancred."

There was only one choice, only one thing I could do.

"No."

His eyes widened in surprise. "No?"

Tancred would never forgive me if I caused the captivity of his people and the downfall of his king. He'd sacrificed himself for them; I couldn't negate his sacrifice. "I won't lie for you."

Anger twisted his face, but his words were calm, even. "Not a lie. A truth. Your man acted on the orders of his king."

"But not to rob you. To help you."

"It matters not. His lie threatens to unravel everything I've been working for. You have a choice. Support him and die, or support me and save you both."

"Him." To my dying breath, no matter how soon it would come. I would go to the scaffold with Tancred to keep his people safe, because that's what he wanted. I couldn't condemn Lady Teta, Queen Annika and her sons, Tancred's mother and brothers...even King Loic, imposing as he was. I couldn't force them under Rudolf's thumb to save myself.

The rage on his face took over. He grabbed my arm, fingers digging into the muscle as he dragged me toward the door.

"Take her to a cell," he told the guard that waited outside. "She's in league with the Piper and will face the same fate." As the guard took my arm, he added, "Oh. And make sure they're kept far apart. I don't want them plotting through the night."

The embers in the bottom of my stomach burned, hopelessness and rage dragging me down as the guard led me away.

DUNGEON

TANCRED

Rudolf's dungeon was dark and damp. Without windows, I couldn't tell what time it was, but it had to be after sunset. I wondered where Csilla was, if she was safe. Hated myself for not being able to protect her. She'd protected herself for so long, and now she was alone again.

I'd had no choice. If I didn't take responsibility, Rudolf would have attacked my people. Possibly even killed my king. If it came down to my life or theirs, there was no contest.

But I still wished I could explain myself to Csilla.

The door to my cell banged open. "You have visitors," the guard said, stepping aside to reveal my mother in the light of the torch he held. Lady Teta stood behind her, grim-faced.

"Tancred!" Mother fell to her knees next to me and threw her arms around my neck.

"No touching," the guard growled. "You have five minutes." He turned on his heel and slammed the door, locking Mother and Lady Teta in the dark cell with me.

"Are you hurt?" Mother asked. She ignored his instruction about physical contact as she ran her hands over my arms, searching for injuries. "Have they hurt you?"

Typical of my mother to worry about my physical well-being when I was going to die in a matter of hours. "I'm fine, Mother." A lie, but a necessary one. In the darkness, she wouldn't be able to see that one eye was swollen shut, or the bruises that peppered every inch of my body. She wouldn't see that my right hand was almost certainly broken from pummeling the guard Bernát.

"No, you're not. They said you stole from King Rudolf. That you killed one of his guards. King Loic said he can't—won't—do anything." She was angry, her tone unmoderated. With every word, her voice grew louder. "After everything you've sacrificed. *We've* sacrificed. And he's going to give you up to them for these lies?"

"Shh! Keep your voice down." I pulled her face down to my shoulder, wincing when the movement pulled at a bruised or fractured rib. "I chose this. King Loic doesn't have any other options."

"He could do *something,*" Mother wailed.

My right hand was unusable from the break, but I used the left to sign with Lady Teta behind Mother's back. "I killed the guard?"

Her mouth tightened. "You must have hit his throat when you attacked him. His airway collapsed. I saw his body myself."

I swallowed. After his efforts to condemn my people, he deserved death, but that hadn't been my goal in attacking him. I hadn't *had* a goal. I'd just moved, desperate to save Csilla from the fate she was undoubtedly suffering at this moment.

I couldn't think about her right now. I focused back on Mother, lifting her head so I could look at her and sign my words for Teta at the same time. "Listen. There's not much time." I had too much to say and no time to say it. "Lady Teta will take care of you. So will the king and queen. Trust them. Once you're out of Arany—" I lowered my voice, making sure the guards couldn't hear me. "—talk to them about what to do with the boys. They can make sure Luc and Theo get a proper education. But if things turn against the Pipers, go back to Laute. Find Grandma and Grandpa and hide yourselves as humans." My father's parents had stayed in Laute, claiming they were too old to move. They could find someone to remove the boys' horns and surgically round off the tips of their ears, so at least my brothers could find some safety among the humans. Even if it meant they had to lose a part of themselves, at least they would be safe.

"We're not leaving without you," she started, but I grabbed her by the shoulders and shook her.

"You have to. For Luc and Theo." Rage billowed through my veins. My family had already lost so much. Why did they have to lose me, too? The boys wouldn't understand. First their father, then a magic they'd never had the chance to wield, and now me. And Mother... No parent should have to bury their child, but tomorrow, she would have to.

Tears shook her frame. I held her close, silently comforting her, but I couldn't surrender to despair yet. This was probably my last chance to speak to any of my people. I signed quickly to Lady Teta, painfully aware of the pass of every second. "I found something in the sorcerer's tower. A bag of coins sealed with a golden seal. I don't know if it means anything, but I brought it back. It's in my bag in King Loic's tent."

Her jaw set. "If Rudolf was working with the sorcerer…"

"You have to get our people out."

"We will." Teta was practical. She'd been Loic's right hand for years before he became king. I knew she'd see our people to safety, as surely as I knew that Queen Annika would be back in our tent, raging at her husband for denouncing me before Rudolf's court. My queen hadn't been raised to handle the difficult decisions of ruling.

"About Csilla," I added. My chest condensed at the mention of her name, but I pushed past it. "If there's anything you can do to free her…" I trailed off. There was no way they would be able to release her from her service to Rudolf. Not unless she became a Piper, and it wasn't as though my displaced people had a method to accept new citizens.

"We'll do whatever we can," she assured me.

"And tell her I'm sorry. Tell her—" *I love her.* I couldn't make my fingers form the words. Not now. Not when they wouldn't mean anything, not when I'd be dead in a few hours. "Nevermind."

Mother was still crying into my chest. My shirt was soaked through, but I held her tighter, pressing a kiss between her horns.

The guard banged the door open. "Time's up."

Lady Teta put a hand on Mother's shoulder, but she clung to me, fingers digging into the bruises the guards had left. "I won't leave you, my melody."

"I'm sorry, Mother." I pried her arms from around my neck. "I love you."

"I'll never forgive him for this!" she vowed, and I knew she didn't mean Rudolf.

I didn't need her to forgive our king. Just to trust him. "Don't come tomorrow," I told her. She didn't need to see me die. "Stay with the boys."

"Don't make me do this," she whispered, body shaking with the force of her emotion as Lady Teta pulled her to her feet.

I couldn't say anything else past the boulder lodged in my throat. Teta dragged her toward the door, and I turned toward the wall, unable to stomach the heartbreak on her face. When the door closed behind them, Mother let out a cry that raised the hairs on my neck, so full of grief and pain that it seemed to shake the walls around us.

"I'm sorry," I whispered again as tears began to pour down my cheeks. "I'm sorry."

Csilla

An inhuman wail of agony echoed through the dungeons, sending a bolt of sympathetic pain through me. Were the guards torturing someone? Was it Tancred? Rudolf was still hoping for someone to turn against the Pipers, I knew. Since I had refused him, I didn't know how far he would go to implicate King Loic in the theft. If Tancred withstood torture, would he come for me again, to force my cooperation by pain since logic hadn't worked?

I curled up in the corner of my cell. It was cold, a kind of cold I hadn't felt in years. Were nights always this cold? I hadn't noticed it while with Tancred—we'd been curled up too close to each other the past couple nights for me to feel anything but warm.

The cold didn't matter. In a few hours, I'd never be cold again.

EXECUTION

Tancred

The early morning air was chilled when two stone-faced guards bound my hands together with ropes. My legs were stiff, my whole body numb as they led me from the dungeon and out to the courtyard where a scaffold had been erected.

King Loic was there, but he was alone. I hadn't expected him to bring the queen to the gruesome display, and he wouldn't leave our people unprotected. Lady Teta and Lord Dominik would be guarding the camp in case things with Rudolf turned worse.

Clouds above us threatened rain. The scaffold stood silent and foreboding in the center of the courtyard, a grim reminder of my final destination. And standing at the base of the scaffold, eyes bloodshot and empty, stood my mother.

I should have known better than to expect her to stay away. She'd left the boys with Lady Teta, I assumed. That, at least, had been a good decision. They didn't need to see this. The loss would leave them damaged enough already. Teta and Prince Falk would keep them distracted while I—

While I died.

The guards marched me up onto the scaffold, next to the black-hooded executioner. He didn't speak or even look at me. The ax hung at his side, impossible to ignore.

A herald announced the king's arrival as he entered the courtyard, surrounded by his entourage. And next to him, wrists tied together, walked Csilla.

I'd promised her no more captivity.

I'd promised my mother and the boys I would protect them.

I'd promised King Loic I would find the thief.

I'd failed them all.

Csilla

Tears blurred the sight of Tancred standing at the scaffold, a hooded executioner next to him. I couldn't watch this. All it would take was one word to Rudolf, and I could save us both. Save us and doom his people.

King Rudolf nodded at the executioner, who turned to Tancred. "You have been charged with crimes against the kingdom of Arany." His voice rang out over the crowd, punctuated by the sobs of Tancred's mother who stood at his feet. Tancred didn't seem to hear any of it. He wasn't looking at me, nor at his mother. His chin was clenched, eyes locked on his king. It wouldn't be long before I was in his place. Would I face my death with the same dignity and resolve?

I doubted it. My blood boiled inside me, seeking a release. If I could, I would explode, raining fire down on Rudolf and all who supported him.

Tancred

"For conspiracy against the king, for theft and treason, you are sentenced to death by beheading." The executioner's voice echoed in my head as he listed the charges. My heart felt like an ax-head in my throat. I couldn't look at my mother, whose gasping sobs were growing louder with each word. I couldn't look at Csilla, either. Not after I'd let her down so completely.

"If you have any final words, you may say them now."

The whole yard seemed to hold its breath awaiting the wisdom I would bequeath them, but when I opened my mouth to speak, no words came out. I closed my eyes and bowed my head. *Whatever god might be listening, protect them where I could not.*

I felt no calmer than I had before the prayer, but I raised my chin. "I am ready."

As someone fitted a hood over my head, my eyes sought one last glimpse of Csilla.

Csilla

The executioner placed a black hood on Tancred's head and pushed him down to kneel before the block. My heart was pounding out of my chest. My whole body burned with rage. *Stop them!* I wanted to scream. *Stop them stop them stopthemstopthemstopthemstopthem.*

The executioner raised his ax, and I erupted.

Tancred

I waited for the whoosh of steel through the air and the slice of the ax through my neck. It never came. Instead I heard screams. The shriek of a bird—a terrifyingly familiar shriek—pierced the hood.

I couldn't see anything. I tried to reach the fabric covering my face, but my hands were still bound behind me. I could still sense the executioner, death looming just inches away.

Another shriek rang out.

I struggled against my bonds. "Csilla!" They were hurting her, torturing her. I had to stop it.

Csilla

I was the firebird once more. The bonds that had held me fell to the ground. King Rudolf scrambled back, screaming for his men. "Stop her!"

I let out a shriek, turning on him. Much like I'd done with Kálmán, I clawed at his face with talons of ember. I was a flame made flesh, a fire of vengeance. His screams filled my ears, but I kept clawing.

Tancred screamed my name, and my heart flickered. As guards converged on me, swords drawn, I lifted up into the air, turning my attention toward him.

He was still on the scaffold, kneeling before the chopping block. The black hood covered his face, and the executioner stood behind him, ax forgotten but still half-raised. He struggled against his bindings, fighting to get free.

I dove between him and the executioner, who stumbled backward and fell off the scaffold. King Loic charged toward us, taking the stairs two at a time. As he passed Tancred's mother, he shouted, "Go! I'll get him out!"

The king pulled a dagger from his side and used it to cut the rope around Tancred's wrists.

Tancred

The hood over my face lifted, letting in bright light. King Loic stood before me, dagger in hand, eyes scanning the courtyard for threats. Heat beamed down from above us, and when I looked up, I saw Csilla. My firebird. She swooped down and landed on the chopping block, cocking her head at me.

"I'm okay." I rubbed the back of my neck. I could almost feel the ax, cold against my skin. "I'm fine." And her? There wasn't time to ask.

King Loic jerked his head at the gate. "We need to go."

I grabbed his arm with one hand, holding the other up and using it to tap my chin with my thumb. "My mother?"

"I got her out. Let's go." He took off toward the castle gate.

The courtyard around us was in chaos. A crowd swarmed around the spot where King Rudolf had been standing. Through the mass of bodies, I could see him lying on the ground. Dead? There wasn't time to ask. I glanced at Csilla to make sure she was coming. She plunged past us, a trail of sparks leading us toward the castle gate.

The guards there had determined something was wrong. As we approached, they trained their crossbows on us. The gate was lowering, the planks dropping to lock us in.

"Faster!" Loic roared. Arrows bounced off the ground, barely missing us. We both dove under the gate, missing it by inches. Csilla was too high; she wasn't going to make it—but she pulled her wings in tight and swept through the bars.

We were out.

The bells were ringing now, warning the citizens of danger. Before long, the whole city guard would be after us. We'd never reach the city gate before they closed it. Every inch of my body hurt as we ran through the city. My broken rib felt like it was stabbing my lung, but I kept pushing on, praying to whatever gods might be listening that we'd make it back to camp. All of us.

REGROUPING

CSILLA

By some miracle, the city gate was still wide open as we tore through it, and the guards didn't pursue us outside of the city. I stayed high over Tancred and his king, watching for signs of danger.

As we reached the camp, I descended, and outside the king's tent, I shifted back into my human form as easily as breathing. The transformation hadn't been painful this time—not like when Kálmán had forced it on me every single night. It was like my being and the firebird's were fused, like she was a part of me in a way she hadn't been before. She'd been created by Kálmán, and while he was alive, she'd belonged to him. Now, she'd saved us all. She was mine.

Queen Annika was pacing outside her husband's tent, carrying on a frantic signed conversation with Lord Dominik and Lady Teta with one hand while she used the other to jostle the baby prince on her hip. Tancred's mother sat on a stool next to her, eyes swollen with tears. When she saw Tancred, she gasped and threw her arms around him.

"My melody!" She rocked back and forth, holding him tight. "You're alive. You're alive."

Someone wrapped a cloak over my shoulders. I glanced back to see Lady Teta. "I can get you a dress," she started, but Cordula had noticed me.

Tancred's mother grabbed my hand without releasing him. "You saved my son." She squeezed my fingers, almost to the point of pain. "Thank you."

Tancred

Mother's grip was bruising, and the pain from exertion on my injured body had me seeing spots. I couldn't pull away, though, even if I had the strength. I didn't dare to look at Csilla, just inches away from me and holding Mother's hand. I'd failed her, and she'd had to save me again. And we still weren't free. King Loic could send both of us back to the Aranites if he determined it was what was best for the Pipers. I wouldn't fight him for myself. I'd go back if that's what was required. But I wouldn't send Csilla back there.

The king looped an arm around his wife. "If Rudolf's men can regroup, they'll head straight for us. Have we started preparing to leave? Have defenses been activated?"

"Silvia is going through camp as we speak, telling everyone to be ready to leave at a moment's notice," the queen said.

Dominik linked his hands behind his back, adopting a soldier's stance. "As soon as Cordula returned, I started organizing the patrols. They're going out now." The men of fighting age would guard the camp as everyone else began packing up. The Pipers could be on the road in a matter of hours.

I pulled back from Mother's embrace. "You need to find the boys. Get ready to go. I'll be there as soon as I can." *If I can,* I didn't say.

Her bottom lip trembled, but she patted my cheek, looking at my face as if memorizing my features. Reluctantly, she dragged her eyes away and left to find Luc and Theo.

"Let's get inside," the king said. "I want to be gone by nightfall."

We filed into the tent. Hand pressed tight against my throbbing rib, I almost collapsed into a chair, uncaring of the social dictates or etiquette that demanded I wait to sit until my king and queen had. Neither of them even noticed. Everyone else filled in the seats around the table. Csilla wore nothing but a long cloak, and she kept her head down as she sat next to me.

King Loic took Prince David from his wife's arms. The baby tugged at his father's good horn, babbling contentedly. He, at least, was unaware of the danger we were all in. "I don't think Rudolf survived," the king said. "But whether he did or not, the Aranites will be looking for his attacker."

"I didn't mean to put you in this situation." Csilla looked up at my queen, who signed the words for her husband. "I wasn't thinking when I changed. I didn't even know I could. I just—"

"You saved Lord Tancred," Queen Annika interrupted her. "You helped my husband come home safely. No one will say any word in objection."

"If you need to turn me in to buy time, I won't fight," I said. The welfare of our people came before my own, and I wouldn't let Csilla be punished for saving me.

Teta leaned forward. "This whole thing was a plot for Rudolf to take control of our people. He planned it all. He admitted as much to Csilla, and we have evidence in the form of his seal on a bag of gold given to the sorcerer."

"We won't give up any of our people," the king said. "With luck, Rudolf is dead, and in the chaos caused by his death, it will take hours, even days before they can send men after us. Dominik, I want you to go into the city. Find out what's happening and report back here as soon as you can."

Dominik was gone almost before the king finished speaking. Under the table, Csilla squeezed my knee, but I didn't dare to breathe easy yet.

"You said you wouldn't give up any of our people. What about Csilla?" She wasn't a Piper, and as the one who may have struck the killing blow against the Aranite king, she would be the first person the Aranites would come after.

The king shifted his son in his arms. "We do not have a legal claim over King Rudolf's subjects."

I clenched my jaw. "I won't abandon her. If you leave her, I stay, too." Csilla's grip on my knee tightened, but I didn't look at her.

"We do not have a claim over her," the king went on, ignoring my objection, "but I'm not inclined to leave an innocent woman to an undeserved fate. You saved one of my people, Csilla, and I'm grateful for that. Nonetheless, I don't wish to be followed across the world for stealing another king's subject. You may stay—*if* you become our subject."

"We can't offer you much," Queen Annika said softly. "We have no home, no army, no magic. But we would protect you with our lives."

"What would I have to do?" Csilla asked.

"Marry a Piper."

Csilla

The words hung there like a death sentence. I removed my hand from Tancred's leg, not daring to look at him. He'd told me he would never marry. He'd told me why. He wanted love, real love, something he didn't believe existed for him. He'd faced the executioner's ax to save me, but would he marry me? I didn't want anyone else. Wouldn't marry anyone else.

"We have to leave tonight," the queen said, signing as she spoke. "I hate to rush you, but we'll need your answer this afternoon."

A reasonable expectation. They needed to be out of Arany before Rudolf's council organized enough to send someone after them. But what if Tancred refused to marry me? What if he still wanted to hold out for a wife he loved, a wife who could give him children?

"Thank you, your majesties." I stood and bowed, holding the cloak closed with one hand. "I'll—umm, I'll let you know my answer soon."

Tears ached in the back of my throat as I pushed the tent flap aside and stepped out into the morning. Voices followed me outside, but I didn't catch the words. It had started raining; I walked blindly through the rain, unsure where I was going. I belonged nowhere. My cage was destroyed. I'd killed both my master and my king. I had my wings, but I had no place to land.

All around me, Pipers were preparing the camp to leave. I passed women, children, and old men breaking down tents and packing belongings into wagons. No one even stopped to look twice at me.

"Csilla!" A rough hand grabbed me by the shoulder and spun me around. Tancred. I blinked droplets from my eyes as I looked into his face. He was breathing hard, clutching his side like it pained him. "What the fuck?"

I wiped my face with the damp fabric of the cloak. "Sorry. I didn't hear you calling."

"Don't you think we should talk?"

"You've made your position on marriage clear," I said. "I don't expect you to change that just to keep me from facing the consequences of my actions." I had killed my king. I'd done it to save Tancred, but that didn't absolve me of guilt. If I couldn't be with him, I'd go back and submit to whatever execution awaited king-killers.

"Are you saying you won't marry me?" His good eye narrowed, the slitted pupil going wide. "You'd rather be executed for saving me than stay with me?"

My mouth had gone suddenly dry. I licked my lips. "Of course not."

"Did I say or do something that implied that I wouldn't go to the ends of the earth to save you?"

Anger flashed up, as hot as my wings. "I'm not a charity case."

"No, you're not." He stalked closer, forcing me to take a step back. His silver horns, inhuman eyes, and bruised face should have been terrifying, but I couldn't be afraid of him. I could see the pain tightening the corner of his eye, the way he picked every step carefully so he didn't jostle his injured body. "But I promised I'd take you to see the world. I didn't almost *die* just to have you run back to the people who want you caged."

"What about your dream? You said you wouldn't settle for less than your parents had."

"Who said I was settling?"

I could hardly breathe. "What are you saying?"

"I'm saying nothing about this makes sense. I shouldn't be willing to give up my life for a woman I met less than a month ago, much less think I'm in love with her. But I'm going to save your life, no matter what it takes. You'll marry me, Csilla. Today."

Love. My thoughts snagged on the word, and I searched his face. "You love me?"

He didn't answer the question. Wouldn't even look into my eyes. "If you don't want to be my wife, you can leave as soon as we make it out of Arany. Just let me get you out of here first."

I cupped his cheek, mindful of his bruises. "Do you love me?"

Neither of us was breathing. He met my eyes, his pupils blown out until they were almost circles. "I do. But I don't expect anything from you."

"I already told you I want to see the world with you." My words were barely more than a whisper. "I want to be your wife, Tancred. I don't care if it's too soon. I love you, too."

A slow smile spread across his face, tugging the mottled bruises upward. "You love me?"

"I do."

He pulled me close, exquisitely gentle. "I think we need to go talk to my king, then."

I gestured to the cloak I wore. "It might be best if I get dressed first." I had no intention of getting married in a borrowed cloak, no matter how spontaneous the wedding.

"I agree." He kissed me, soft and slow. "I'm the only one who gets to see you like this from now on."

BOUND

TANCRED

I'd been to plenty of weddings in my life. Mine was unlike any of them.

When King Loic and Queen Annika married, we'd been preparing to leave Laute. A priest the queen had befriended made the brief journey from Augsburg to the palace, where he'd performed a traditional Catholic wedding. Or as traditional as it could be, considering it wasn't in a church, and the groom had been labeled a king of demons by the pope.

In traditional Piper weddings, the only requirement to solemnize a marriage was the ability to wield magic. The bride and groom would take hands and state their vows to one another, and while they spoke, the officiant would play a tune, growing a plant—usually a vine of some sort, although floral plants were popular, as well—to wrap around their hands. Once the vows were finished, someone would cut the plant at its base, and the couple would carefully extricate themselves, leaving the binding whole to display over the door of their new marital home.

Neither Csilla nor I were Catholic, and without the Pied Piper's magic, a binding ceremony wouldn't be possible. Instead, we stood in my tent. Mother had dug out Father's finest suit from the bottom of her trunk for me and helped me clean the worst of the dirt and blood from my face before I dressed. Csilla had put on her nicest dress, red and white with tiny crocuses and other white and yellow flowers I didn't recognize dotting the apron. Her hair had been brushed to gleaming, left long over her shoulders like it had been on the day we met, a few short weeks ago.

Mother, Luc, and Theo stood behind us, next to Lady Teta and Prince Falk, who held his baby brother. For once in his life, Theo didn't have a book. He and Luc looked as baffled and overwhelmed as I felt. This morning, I'd been kneeling over a wooden block, an ax hovering above my neck, and now I was about to marry the most beautiful woman I'd ever met. And unlike the rest of the world, who'd always looked at my people as demons, there was nothing but love and admiration shining in her eyes.

I rubbed my knuckle against the palm of my hand. What did I have to offer her? No home, no safety, not even the protection of my magic. By marrying me, she would become a fugitive from not just her own country, but of every Christian nation on the earth. Meeting me had brought her nothing but trouble. The broken bone in my hand cried out at the movement, but I kept rubbing. What was the point of all this? She'd be safer away from me. Happier away from me.

She caught my hands between her own, stopping my movement. *I love you,* she mouthed.

She loved me. And by marrying her, I could save her from the most pressing danger. She'd saved me twice already. I could do this much for her. Whatever happened next, we would face it together. I drew her hands to my mouth and kissed the knuckles.

Finally, Dominik appeared in the entrance to the tent. "Update?" the king asked him.

"Rudolf is dead." He'd been in the city, seeking out information on the events of this morning. "One of the ispans took the castle and declared himself regent. Queen Sarolt has taken her son and fled south. The new regent sent most of the castle guard after them."

Csilla squeezed my fingers. The movement sent a shock of pain through my broken bone, but I squeezed back. This was good. If the Aranites were busy hunting down the Aranite heir and his mother, they wouldn't be focused on us as we moved north, out of the country.

"Good," the king said. "Are we prepared to leave?"

"We will be by sunset," Dominik replied.

The king gestured to me and Csilla. "We're short on time, so I'll make this quick. Join opposite hands."

We did as he bade, crossing our wrists as Mother stepped forward with a long vine. Tears streamed down her face, but unlike this morning, they weren't tears of fear or despair. She took the vine and began weaving it around our joined hands.

The king continued speaking. "As this vine binds you together, so do your two melodies become one harmony. In sadness and joy, in peril and security, in good times and bad, may this harmony be with you. May it give strength when you are weak and comfort when you mourn.

Should new melodies spring forth from it, may you find patience and wisdom, and when dark notes creep in, may you find beauty in the darkness, knowing the darkness will not last forever."

The traditional blessing was bittersweet. The same words had been spoken at my parents' wedding before I was born, and at countless weddings through all of Piper history. My people were irrevocably changed now, and the words held a different meaning than they had in the past. But looking at the tears Csilla refused to let fall, I knew we had made the right choice. We could face whatever happened next together.

As King Loic finished the blessing, Mother tucked in the last bit of the vine and stepped back, wiping the tears from her cheeks.

"The harmony has begun," the king said, "and no one now living can come between you."

At that, I leaned forward, brushing a chaste kiss to Csilla's lips. Carefully, we pulled our hands from the vine, leaving the shape Mother had woven complete. We had no doorpost to hang it on, but for now, it would hang in my wagon to dry. When we found a home, a place to settle, I would hang the dried wreath above the door.

Mother took the wreath from me and wrapped her arms around my neck. "I'm so proud of you, my melody," she murmured. Her tears wetted my shoulder as I hugged her back. After a moment, she released me and drew Csilla into a hug. "And you, my daughter."

Csilla made a choking sound. Was she displeased at the term? She'd lost her own mother so long ago. I knew Mother meant well, but—

"Thank you, Mother," Csilla said, squeezing her tight. "I'm honored."

I hardly noticed the rest of the congratulations as everyone came forward to wish us well. I was too busy watching my new wife smile and embrace our guests.

Finally, they left, and Csilla and I were alone.

She looked around the tent, which was almost empty. Most of our belongings had been moved into the wagon in preparation for our upcoming departure. We'd spend the first few weeks, maybe even months of our marriage on the road.

"No second thoughts?" I asked.

She looked up, eyes wide. "No! No, of course not."

There was silence between us for a moment. Then she asked, "Where will we go?"

"North." If we couldn't find a land that would take us, we'd claim our own. "King Loic says there's land beyond Muscovy. A boyar of a small island of swan shifters invited us to settle the land near his and offered us assistance in settling. It won't be easy, though." The swan shifters were at war, and the land so far north was inhospitable. "Cold and crawling with predators. We'll have to build our houses from the ground up. We'll have to hunt for our food. We might go hungry. We—"

She stepped forward and slapped her hand over my mouth. A determined look furrowed her face as she looked into my eyes.

"I wasn't asking you to convince me to leave. I just wanted to know what will happen next." She moved her hand from my mouth, resting it on my chest. "If you're going somewhere cold, you'll be glad to have a firebird with you."

"I'd be glad of you anywhere," I said, grabbing her by the waist and pulling her tight against me.

"Then take me to see the world."

EPILOGUE

My dear family,

It's a relief to hear that everything was resolved peacefully after the death of King Rudolf. Allowing Queen Sarolt to act as her son's regent will be best for everyone. I'm even more glad that the Pipers—myself included, now—were able to leave Arany before the succession conflict was resolved. We are now safely settled with the Lebedi in this land. Although it is the middle of the afternoon, I'm writing this letter by candlelight. A few pale hours of daylight peek over the horizon around noon, but most of our days are spent in darkness. It's a beautiful land, though. Until this war with the Medvedi is resolved, we're living on an island with the Lebedi. You should see the sky. Rainbows dance across it, lighting up the ocean around us. I've made friends with the youngest princess, and she tells me that in the summer, the sun never sets. I'll be glad to see it.

Maazel tov to Áron and Elza! I wish I could meet your new son. I'm so glad everyone is healthy and handling the new changes well.

Álmos, I hope you are busy preparing for your bar mitzvah. While I'm disappointed to miss it, I am honored to know the man you're becoming. I know you'll make me and your whole family proud. Ádám, I'm proud of you as well, and—

I swatted Tancred's hand as it crept up my stomach. "I'm writing a letter."

"That can wait." He pulled me to him, my back against his chest, and nuzzled my neck. "I have a better idea."

My skin tingled at the feel of his beard on my skin, but I turned and scowled at him. "Don't you have a meeting soon?"

"That's not for hours. And I—" He picked me up and dropped me unceremoniously on the bed before crawling on top of me. "—intend to take advantage of the free time."

How could I resist him? My letter could wait. I twined my arms around his neck, pulling him down for a kiss. Our tongues tangled with one another as he snaked his hand under my dress and traced my inner thigh.

"How long do you think it'll take before I have you screaming?" he murmured against my lips, sliding a finger through my wetness.

"I don't *scream.*" Usually.

I felt him grin as he pushed a finger inside me. "Liar."

"I don't—" He slid his finger out and back in again, making me groan. "—lie, either."

"Then prove it." Adding a second finger to the first, he curled them, hitting a spot that left me panting. "Try to keep quiet."

Our conversation evaporated after that, as he played my body with expert touches designed to drive me wild. His thumb circled my clit, and his fingers drove in and out until my body finally snapped, releasing my climax in a spiral of bliss.

I'd barely caught my breath before Tancred was stripping off his clothes next to the bed. "Take your dress off," he commanded, his voice so tight it was almost a growl. His weeping cock jutted up toward his stomach.

I tossed my dress into a corner, drinking in the sight of him. I still couldn't believe he was mine.

"How do you want me?" he asked, pumping himself slowly with his hand.

"I—what?" My mouth was dry, and I couldn't tear my gaze away from his body.

"Do you want me to fuck you against the wall, or do you want to ride me?"

I swallowed. "Ride. Definitely ride."

He gave me a crooked grin and laid down on his back. "Take what you want, then."

I straddled him but didn't let him enter me. Not yet. I rocked against him, teasing us both. I loved testing our limits, seeing who would give in first. It was almost always Tancred.

It didn't take long before he grabbed me by the hips and he thrust into me. We both groaned.

"I thought you told me to take what I want," I said, sliding up and down on him.

"You were taking too long." One hand roamed my body, caressing my breasts and stomach and waist as the other hand slipped between us to massage my clit. "Now come for me. I want the whole castle—the whole fucking island to hear you scream for me."

I didn't scream, but I did gasp out his name a few minutes later, crashing into him as we climaxed together.

"Close," he said, breathing hard. He flipped me over and nipped at my breast. "But not quite."

"What are you doing?" I asked, scooting back against the pillows and considering him warily.

He grabbed my legs and spread them apart. Dragging his fingers through our combined wetness, he looked up at me with a grin. "Proving that you're a liar. Now hold onto my horns." He bent his head down and buried his tongue in my center.

"I can't," I said, clinging to his horns. "It's too much." My whole body buzzed with the orgasms I'd already had, and the sensations were becoming overwhelming. Every flick of his tongue had me whimpering. Not that it would matter to him. He delighted in pushing me past my physical limitations, in showing me what pleasure could be. If I really wanted him to stop, he would—but my objections were half-hearted at best. I loved when he tormented me like this.

As expected, he redoubled his efforts, pinning my legs down and feasting like a starved man. And when I came, I did scream out his name.

When he finally let me up, my legs were boneless. I slumped against the pillows, grateful for the chill coming from the stone castle walls. The blood pulsing through my skin left me heated, but here, further north than even the Muscovites or the Golden Horde would dare to lay claim, the air was cold even in the dead of summer, let alone now with the approaching winter.

Tancred's grin was incorrigible as he climbed back up my body to kiss me. "Yes, just like that," he teased.

I glared at him, but my mouth wouldn't form words. "Ass," I signed. Lady Teta had been teaching me the silent language King Loic and his council shared. Starting with the profanity, which seemed to be her favorite method of communication. It wasn't much use when communicating with the king, but I'd found it profoundly helpful in dealing with my new husband, who seemed to delight in vexing me.

He'd gained a new light in his eyes since we reached the Lebedi territory. The land was inhospitable, the politics deadly, but Tancred seemed to be at peace here. For once in their history, his people had been accepted without question. Nomadic tribes of Selkup and Nenets lived throughout this region, along with the Lebedi and their enemies, the Medvedi, and in certain areas, magic still dwelled deep within the land. As he settled against my chest, I stroked his bristled cheek with my finger. Of all the places I'd expected to find a home, this land of endless night was the last.

I must have dozed off, because a knock woke me a while later. Tancred groaned and rolled over with the blanket, so I reluctantly dragged myself from the bed, wrapped a robe around my naked body, and went to the door.

"I hope I didn't wake you, Lady Csilla." The boyar's youngest daughter, Marya, stood in the hall. She had long black hair that almost brushed her bare feet, worn loose. Her skin was pale, her round face smiling. She was in her early twenties, unmarried, and as free-spirited as her appearance seemed to suggest

"I'm still not entirely used to the darkness," I said by way of explanation. "What can I do for you?"

"I know Lord Tancred is supposed to be meeting with the boyar and King Loic—"

A muffled thump and a curse behind me interrupted her. She hid her smile behind her hand as Tancred scrambled behind the divider screen to get dressed.

"—and I thought you might be up for a flight," she finished. "If you're not otherwise occupied."

"If the boyar allows it, I'd be happy to." My wings were no longer a punishment, and the transformation was as natural as breathing. Since we'd left Arany, I took every opportunity to stretch my wings.

Her face lit up. "Papa won't mind," she said quickly. "I'll meet you out by the gate in ten minutes?"

"I'll be there." As she took off down the hall, I closed the door and turned back to Tancred. He'd managed to find his clothes, and now he was sitting on the bed pulling on a thick pair of wool stockings.

"I shouldn't have fallen asleep," he grumbled, shoving a newly stocking foot into one of his boots.

"You can't blame me." I traded my robe for a loose Lebedi-style dress, with ties at the shoulders for easy removal. "I warned you before you pounced on me that you had a meeting this afternoon."

"That was hours ago. It's this damn light. I can't keep track of—"

I cut him off with a swift kiss. "I'm sure they'll understand." Boyar Stribog and King Loic had set their wisest scholars to studying Kálmán's spellbooks, testing various remedies for the matter of the Pipers' magic. None had worked yet, but they were hopeful. In the meantime, the Pipers were helping formulate a new battle strategy against the Medvedi, the Lebedi's oldest enemies. It was a mutually beneficial alliance, and the Pipers were thriving here.

When we reached the gate, Marya was waiting for me, her clothes already piled in one of the boxes left there for that purpose. She had shifted before we arrived, and she was swimming impatiently in circles near the shore.

Tancred let go of my arm, leaning in to kiss my cheek. "Enjoy your flight, wife."

The word sent a thrill through me. I didn't think I'd ever grow tired of hearing him call me "wife." I tugged the ribbons of my dress loose, letting it pool at my feet. "Enjoy your meeting, husband."

His eyes darkened as he looked over the expanse of skin I'd revealed. "On second thought, maybe we should go back upstairs."

I grinned at him. "Later, Lord Tancred. You have obligations."

He groaned. "Fine." Snatching me by the waist, he kissed me thoroughly. "Later."

Stepping out of his reach, I let the flames engulf me. A shriek burst from my chest as I rose into the sky, followed a moment later by the Lebedi princess, whose honk of joy answered my own call. As we circled the castle, Tancred waved, and I swooped over him, cascading a shower of sparks high above him. Then I flew higher, up toward the ribbons of green and blue and pink that were beginning to form in the sky. After so many years, so many trials, I was finally free.

Acknowledgements

Wings of Living Flame was a labor of love, and that labor would not have been possible without massive amounts of support from all corners. First and foremost, to the One who created and sustains me, it is all for Your glory.

My family, of course, is both the reason I write and the reason I need to escape into fiction. Thank you for supporting me, even when you drive me insane. Andrew, your critique and encouragement on the final pass through the book was invaluable, especially in shaping Tancred's unique personality. I love you.

My beloved alpha and beta readers, who helped me turn this pile of ashes into the beautiful phoenix it became: Zara J. Black, Kelly Keith, T. M. Mayfield, and K. L. Mielke. Elizabeth Myrva, without every Friday night date and body doubling session, it would never have gotten done, and I'm so grateful you were there to push me. Courtney Taylor, I can't thank you enough for being my geopolitical advisor, my worldbuilding guide, and my voice of reason (and sometimes spite) when I wanted to throw in the towel.

I would be remiss not to thank Dr. Jocelyn Mory for graciously taking time from your schedule to advise me on the history of the mbira. I can't count how much time I spent poring over your dissertation and the notes from our call. Thank you for your work and education on this beautiful instrument.

Finally, as always, to my wonderful readers. Without you, there would be no story. And yes, I promise Teta's story is coming.

Eventually.